A FATHER'S FURY

The newspaperman lived and worked in a one-room log cabin at the south end of the gold camp's one and only street. It was barely big enough for his Washington hand press, a cot, and a small kneehole desk. But that didn't matter to Harley. The place suited him. He had never been overly concerned with creature comforts or material things. The only thing that he really cared about was his work. And usually he did the lion's share of that at night.

The knock on the door startled him. Rarely did he have any visitors, especially at such an hour. Curious, he went to the door and opened it.

A tall, wide-shouldered man in buckskins stood there. He had sandy hair and beard, and piercing blue eyes. They were the most haunted eyes Harley could remember ever having seen. A rifle in a fringed and beaded doeskin sheath was cradled in the man's left arm. This man was clearly no gold hunter.

"Can I help you?" asked Harley.

"My name is Gordon Hawkes," said the man, "and I've come for my boy."

Stunned, Harley took a step back. "My God," he gasped. Staring at the face of the man before him, he experienced a profound dread that chilled him to the bone. He thought, *I am literally looking into the face of Death*

D1622637

MOUNTAIN VENGEANCE

Jason Manning

A SIGNET BOOK

Man

SIGNET
Published by New American Library, a division of
Penguin Putnam Inc., 375 Hudson Street,
New York, New York 10014, U.S.A.
Penguin Books Ltd, 27 Wrights Lane,
London W8 5TZ, England
Penguin Books Australia Ltd, Ringwood,
Victoria, Australia
Penguin Books Canada Ltd, 10 Alcorn Avenue,
Toronto, Ontario, Canada M4V 3B2
Penguin Books (N.Z.) Ltd, 182–190 Wairau Road,
Auckland 10, New Zealand

Penguin Books Ltd, Registered Offices:
Harmondsworth, Middlesex, England

First published by Signet, an imprint of New American Library,
a division of Penguin Putnam Inc.

First Printing, April 2001
10 9 8 7 6 5 4 3 2 1

Chapter One

When they realize that they are going to die, some men whimper. They feel sorry for themselves and bemoan their fate. Other men quietly resign themselves to the inevitable. They won't put up a fight, sensing its uselessness, but rather passively await the end. Still others resist, even though they know that resistance is futile. They will rail against Death and go down kicking and biting.

George Jackson's nature led him down the latter path. He cursed—cursed for hours on end, cursed everything and anything: himself, God, the Devil, the mountains, the snow that entrapped him, the overcast sky that sealed his doom by dispensing even more snow to block the mountain passes, even the gold that had lured him into this death trap. Jackson was genuinely angry, and the anger was like a hot flame in his belly. When he had time to reflect on it he thought that maybe the heat of that anger kept him going beyond the point where most men would have given up and lay down to die.

He wasn't lost. That wasn't the problem. George Jackson knew exactly where he was. He had that sure sense of direction enjoyed by all born wanderers. He knew that salvation—in the distinctly unattractive form of the town of Denver, in the Kansas Territory—was a mere thirty miles away, as the crow flies. But Jackson was not a crow, and only by sprouting wings was he going to be able to leave the valley that a sudden snowstorm had transformed into an icy prison from which there was, apparently, no escape.

Denver didn't amount to much in the winter of 1859. It was just a town with two dozen cabins located at the foot of the Rocky Mountains. But it was the base of operations Jackson had selected when he decided to do a little prospecting in the high country. Denver saw many a lone prospector venture dauntlessly into the mountains to seek his fortune, and quite a few of them never came out again. Jackson was aware that no one would miss him, or even think twice about his prolonged absence if he failed to return from the high country. There would be no rescue undertaken, no search parties organized and dispatched. He was, absolutely, on his own. Ever since leaving Missouri to participate in the California gold rush ten years earlier, he had been a loner. He preferred it that way.

Now, though, for the first time in his life, Jackson longed for a little human company.

"Least I'd have somebody to talk to," he told his two dogs as he huddled with those canine companions in a shelter made of snow-laden spruce boughs, trying to thaw frozen fingers over a small fire. "It's funny how a person has an urge to talk about his life when it's about to end. And at least with a partner I'd have someone I could kill and eat when I get to the point where I'm starving enough to do something like that. As it is, I'll have to have you boys

2

for dinner, and I'll have one hell of a time deciding which one of you'll go first." He grinned at the solemnly quizzical expression one of the dogs gave him. The hound tilted its head slightly and whined, as though asking its master how he could repay years of unquestioning canine devotion in such a despicable manner. "Don't worry," said Jackson. "I wouldn't do that to you. Even though, I have to say, you let me down these past few days. Nary a snowshoe hare or tree squirrel has either one of you managed to scare up." Jackson gazed forlornly along the snow-covered mountain slope on which he found himself. Towering over him above the timberline were cloud-draped peaks. Below was a steep and rock-strewn draw that led to a valley also blanketed with several feet of newly fallen snow. The gold seeker had begun to think that maybe he and his dogs were the only living things left in the mountains.

Ordinarily Jackson preferred living alone. He just didn't get along with other people very well. That was why the vocation of prospector suited him so. The gold fields of California had become too crowded for him, though. Seemed to him as though half the population of the world had descended with a fury on California after gold was discovered near Sutter's Mill on the American River. Nearly four hundred thousand gold seekers had flooded California, and before long most of the placer gold—the stuff that was located near the surface, relatively easy to find—had been harvested. That left the veins hidden, usually, in the bowels of the earth, and only the big mining companies had the wherewithal to get at those. Risking life and limb for low pay in a mine

3

just so investors back East could get rich had not suited George Jackson at all. So he had put California behind him and come to the mountains to seek his fortune anew. After all, as any prospector would tell you, gold was where you found it.

Jackson had dug deep into a deadfall to find wood dry enough to burn, and he had very little of it left, so he resisted the urge to add some now to his meager little fire and saved the handful of sticks that remained for the morning—on the assumption that he might still be alive in the morning. The day was darkening. He hadn't seen the sun in three days but he could tell it was close to sundown. He lay on his blankets, drawing his knees up and hugging himself and trying to ignore the terrible gnawing emptiness in his belly. The dogs curled up against him. Together they watched the snow fall. Would it ever stop? Jackson wondered what the dogs were thinking. For his part he was wondering if he dared go to sleep. If he slept, would he awaken in the morning? If he did die, would the dogs that he refused to eat be forced by their own hunger to eat him? Or would he be too frozen by then? His legs were numb below the knees, and he was afraid that this numbness would spread during the night, creeping up his thighs, into his belly, then his chest, stopping his heart. George Jackson started cussing all over again. Damn it, he wasn't ready to die. Not just yet. Not before he found the mother lode. It was here, somewhere close by. He just knew it.

When he came to, Jackson was groggy. Regaining consciousness took more of an effort than he really wanted to exert. Belatedly he realized that something was wrong. He wasn't sure what it was, at first. Then it came to him—*he wasn't alone.*

A man was sitting on his heels about six feet away. He wore a white capote, or blanket coat, over fringed buckskins. There were beaded moccasins on his feet and a broad-brimmed beaver hat on his head A Hawken Plains rifle was laid across his legs—a .58-caliber full-stock percussion long gun. The man seemed content to just squat there and watch Jackson with piercing blue eyes. Jackson figured he was in his middle years due to the liberal dusting of gray in his sandy beard.

Jackson snapped out of his fog and sat up quickly, instinct making him reach for his own rifle.

"No call for that," said the man. "If I'd meant to do you harm you'd already know about it."

Jackson noticed that his dogs sat flanking the man, their tails flicking back and forth across the snow. This perplexed the prospector. His dogs did not generally cotton to strangers. They should have barked up a storm at this man's approach. Instead, they appeared quite taken with him.

The stranger seemed to read Jackson's mind. "Good dogs. Don't fault them for not making a ruckus. For some reason animals like me." He smiled. "I get along better with animals than I do with people, to tell you the truth."

"Same with me." Jackson started to relax. "My name is George Jackson. I'm from Missouri by way of California."

"Gordon Hawkes. Though most know me as Henry Gordon."

"Two names. Usually means you've had a spot of trouble somewhere along the line."

"I've had my share," said Hawkes, but instead of elaborating he changed the subject. "What are you doing out here?"

"Looking for gold."

"I see." It was obvious that Hawkes didn't approve. "Find any?"

"Not yet. But I will. Well, assuming I get out of this valley alive, that is."

Hawkes took a long, slow look around. "This isn't a good place to be when the blizzards come. The first good snow blocks both ends of the valley. Only way out is a high pass to the west and it's right hard to find unless you know exactly where to look."

"Can you take me out of here, Hawkes? I'd be obliged."

"I reckon I could do that, yes."

Jackson stood up—and promptly fell back down. "Damn it all to hell. I can't feel a thing from the knees down," he confessed anxiously.

"I better have a look."

Hawkes pulled off one of Jackson's boots, pushed up the leg of the prospector's stroud trousers and the longjohns he wore underneath. Jackson's skin looked grayish blue and was hard and cold to the touch.

"Bad case of frostbite," diagnosed Hawkes. "We don't take care of that, you could get gangrene and lost both legs."

Jackson grimaced. "Don't bother cutting off my legs, Hawkes. Just cut my throat. I would not want to live a sit-down cripple the rest of my life."

"Well, let's hope it doesn't come to that."

"If I can't walk, how the hell do I get out of here?"

"There's a way," said Hawkes.

Inside of an hour he had constructed a sturdy travois, using a hatchet to cut down and trim saplings, and a length of rope from his possibles to lash the poles together.

"Did you come all this way on foot?" Hawkes asked the gold seeker.

"Nope. I had a mule. Critter slipped its tether my first night in this valley." Jackson was embarrassed. "I have a tendency to misplace things, I'm afraid."

Hawkes nodded. He secured the travois to his own horse, strapping it to his saddle. Jackson noted that his benefactor's horse looked pretty wild and shaggy, a dun-colored mountain mustang with a mean disposition.

"He's surefooted," said Hawkes, again demonstrating what seemed to Jackson to be an uncanny ability to know his thoughts. "But I'd advise you don't get too close to him if you don't have to. I'm just about the only person he will tolerate."

"Don't worry. I have no desire to try and befriend that horse."

Once Jackson was laid out on the travois, covered with blankets and tied down, Hawkes got on his way, leading the mountain mustang. Jackson's dogs fell in alongside. Occasionally one or the other would stray, but never too far. It was as though the hounds realized, as Jackson did, that Hawkes was their salvation and they needed to stick close to him.

The ascent to the high pass took most of the day. It was a steep and arduous climb and Jackson was impressed by the stamina of both Hawkes and his

7

horse. They made the pass, a rocky narrow chute well above the timberline between two looming peaks, and were on their way down into the next valley over by sundown. Hawkes pressed on, negotiating the treacherous trail in the darkness, and a time or two Jackson feared that the travois to which he was bound would go over the edge, sending him to his death in the icy abyss.

Late that night they entered a box canyon where several warm springs were located. Hawkes made Jackson strip down and get into the steaming water. Submersion in the springs was a very painful treatment, but Jackson didn't question or complain about it. While the prospector soaked in the warm waters, Hawkes dug a hole in the frost-hardened ground, built a small hot fire in the hole, and after letting the fire burn to embers, covered it with dirt. He then bade Jackson to sit cross-legged over the covered firehole and draped a blanket over him.

"You'll have to sleep sitting up," Hawkes told him. "The warmth of the fire will rise up through the dirt and keep you from freezing those legs and feet again. That would be very bad, now that we've got you thawed out. You would lose your limbs for sure."

"Thank you," said Jackson. "I cannot repay you for your kindness now. But when I've found gold up here in these mountains, and I know I will, I will make you a rich man."

"Gold doesn't make you rich."

"You're telling me you wouldn't accept it? You would turn down a fortune in gold if one was offered you?"

"I'd have no use for a fortune in gold."

"Well, for one thing, you could get out of these godforsaken mountains. Live anywhere your heart desired. Build yourself a big fancy house. Have servants to wait on you hand and foot."

"I don't hanker after any of those things. And I sure don't want to leave the high country."

Jackson mulled this over. "The last thing you want is for me to find gold up here, isn't it?"

Hawkes nodded. "I've heard about what happened in California. I would hate to see that happen here."

"You a trapper, Hawkes?"

"Not really. I've done a little trapping, and came out here with the Rocky Mountain Fur Company."

"Looking for 'brown gold'—beaver. Well, me, I'm just looking for another kind of gold, so we're not so different."

"I never trapped for profit. Only for enough plews to trade for the supplies I needed."

"Then what did you come to the mountains for, if not to trap?" asked Jackson. He thought he already knew the answer, but he wanted to see how candid the mountain man would be with him.

"I was wanted by the law back East for something I didn't do. It was either hang or run. So I ran."

"The lesser of two evils. How long have you lived in these parts?"

"Going on twenty-five years now."

Jackson let out a low whistle. "That's a long time to spend all by your lonesome."

"I'm not alone. I have a wife and two children."

"Indian wife?"

"No, she's white."

The prospector looked about him. With the day's

end had come, at long last, a clearing of the skies, so that now moonlight poured through a patchwork of clouds to bathe the snowy peaks in a luminous pale blue glow. He had never been one to appreciate the natural beauty of the world around him. When he saw a mountain he thought only of the gold or silver that it might contain.

Of course he had heard stories about men like Gordon Hawkes. Mountain men who relished the isolation of the high country, who had turned their backs on civilization and happily lived like savages. Someone in Denver had warned him to be on the lookout for such resilient and self-reliant men. "They're as wild as the beasts, and would just as soon kill you as look at you," the Denver resident had told him. "They think the mountains belong just to them. You go up yonder and you're the trespasser in their book."

So Jackson had to wonder why, if this was so, Gordon Hawkes had saved his life. *He could easier have left me to die in that valley*, mused the prospector.

Jackson found that he could sleep quite well sitting up, and when he awoke the following morning he was as warm in his cocoon of blankets as he had been in weeks. Better yet, his legs felt much better. Hawkes nodded with satisfaction after examining the gold hunter's feet.

"Might be some scarring, but you'll keep your legs," said the mountain man.

"I'm obliged. I don't know how to repay you."

Hawkes gave him a long look. "I won't ask you to do what I know you won't do."

"There's gold here. I know it. I can feel it in my bones."

Hawkes made no comment other than to assure Jackson that he would be back. Tying up the prospector's dogs, he racked the Plains rifle on his shoulder and left the camp on foot. Since he had left his horse behind, Jackson was confident that Hawkes would return.

Return he did, an hour and a half later, carrying a mountain sheep draped over his shoulders. Hawkes strung the kill up from a tree limb and butchered it out. The dogs let go with a frenzied baying, lunging at the rope that held them, and Jackson quieted them with some offal. Hawkes cut out a couple of thick steaks which they cooked over a hot fire, and before long Jackson's belly was full.

"My God," he said, completely sated. "I do believe I'm going to live after all!"

"There's plenty of game in this valley," said Hawkes. "The steam from those warm springs melts the snow and uncovers plenty of graze for the deer and mountain sheep, even in the hardest of winters."

"You're telling me this, I take it, because you're about to leave me here."

"I'll take you back to Denver if you want to go."

"No," said Jackson firmly, and without hesitation. "I can't leave just now. Sorry."

"I didn't think you would. If you change your mind, go south, a half day by foot, through a low pass. You'll then come to a river. Follow that east out of the mountains and you'll be a day's walk south of Denver."

Jackson nodded. "You live nearby, Hawkes?"

The mountain man was impassive. "Near enough."

The prospector sensed the futility of asking for more details on that score.

A short while later Hawkes was ready to take his leave. He wished Jackson luck.

Jackson smiled. "Thanks. Though I know you don't mean that."

"I meant luck in staying alive. You're right, though— I hope you don't find any gold."

"If there is anything I can ever do for you, Hawkes . . ."

"There isn't a thing," said the mountain man flatly, and left the camp astride his wild-eyed mustang.

Jackson remained in camp all that day, gorging himself on mountain sheep and recuperating. He figured he might do the same thing the next day, too. But when the sun rose, he found himself getting restless. It was a familiar unease, spawned by the overpowering desire that had driven him for so many years now—the desire to find that mother lode. There was gold in these mountains just waiting for someone to find it, and Jackson had to be the one to do that before someone else did. There was no way to know how many other gold seekers were roaming this country; he knew from talk in a Denver tent saloon that others of his kind had preceded him, though the speculation was that Indians or grizzlies—or mountain men—had probably finished most of them off. Still, if only one other gold seeker prowled these mountains . . . well, Jackson just could not take the chance. He had been too late getting to California to strike it rich; all the best sites had been claimed long before. He was determined to see that that didn't happen to him again.

So he roused himself and, stumbling along on his still weakened legs, followed a frozen creek for several miles, keeping his eyes peeled for a gravel bar or sand spit. Late in the day he finally found what he was looking for. Locating some dry wood, he built a fire on the gravel bar in order to melt the covering sheet of ice. Then he hacked away at the sand, scooped some up and put it in a tin cup, then broke thin ice at the edge of the bar to get to the creek, filling the cup with water. He moved the cup in a gentle circular motion, tilting it slightly, letting the water lift the sand from the bottom and carry it over the rim. This he did until all the sand was gone.

His heart skipped a beat when he saw the yellow flakes of gold in the bottom of the cup.

Trembling with excitement, Jackson panned a few more cups of sand. By dark he had about an ounce of gold dust, which he placed in a small tin canister stoppered with a cork. Then he stood up and danced a clumsy jig. The cold and his weakened conditioned abbreviated his celebration; pretty soon he had to sit down. He sat there on the gravel bar, gripping the canister tightly in his hand and laughed—and laughed some more. Lying nearby, his dogs watched him with good-natured bafflement.

"By God, I'm going to be rich!" he shouted gleefully. "I've finally done it! I knew it was here and by God I found it!"

Eventually, his elation spent for the moment, Jackson left the gravel bar. But he didn't stray far. Though his camp several miles away lured him with the promise of more mountain sheep steaks, he could not bring himself to range so far afield from his find. As irrational as the fear was, he could not help thinking that if he left the vicinity of the gravel bar he would return to find it appropriated by another gold seeker. Jackson knew he would have to leave sooner or later; he had to go back to Denver to get supplies and to replace the tools his errant mule had made off with—the tools he needed to exploit the claim he would stake here. But on that first night he simply could not leave the site. He had found on that day what he had been searching for these past dozen years—a virgin strike—and he could not simply walk away.

So George Jackson spent a cold night on the banks of the mountain stream, guarding the gravel bar, watching over his gold. He did not sleep much, but when he did, he had a vivid dream of a huge white mansion and a fancy carriage pulled by a matching team of Arabian horses, of dining at a cherrywood table as long as a keelboat and polished to a high sheen, eating off of china plates and using solid gold knives and forks, engaged in highbrow conversation with the cream of polite society. It was only a dream—but when he awoke, the early sunlight in his eyes, he was confident that the dream was soon to become reality.

He spent most of that day at the gravel bar. Then he blazed a tree and reluctantly returned to his camp. That evening he ate his fill, cooked a few more pounds of meat for the long trail, and tried to get some sleep. The next morning, he followed the instructions given to him by Gordon Hawkes, and made his way back to Denver.

It was not necessary for him to tell the people of Denver that he had made a strike. They could take one look at him and tell. George Jackson was a changed man from the one who had headed into the high country a few weeks earlier. He was not the same, and never would be again.

And neither he nor the people of Denver knew it yet—but the mountains would never be the same, either.

Chapter Two

George Jackson would have preferred keeping his discovery a secret. But he was pragmatic enough to understand how impossible that would be. To work his claim he would have to stay in the mountains for a long spell, and for that he needed plenty of supplies. He also needed tools. He would need to build a rocker or Long Tom to facilitate separating the gold dust from the sand. He would need at least two sturdy mules as pack animals. And he could not acquire all of these necessities without arousing suspicion.

More than that, he could not get everything he needed because he lacked sufficient funds. There was really no alternative left open to him—he had to have partners. Much as he hated to, he had to share his gold strike with others; a few good men who could help him pay for the tools and the provisions, who could help him harvest the gold, and who could assist him in protecting his claim from other prospectors. And there would be other prospectors—and soon—of that Jackson was sure. Once news of his find leaked out, the mountains would be crawling with hundreds of gold seekers. Because somewhere upstream from that gold-rich gravel bar was the mother lode. It had been exposed to the elements and broken down into nuggets and then flakes and then "flour." Jackson had found the latter, the powdery particles of gold. Somewhere nearby there would be nuggets, and not too far from the nuggets lay the big veins of gold. Jackson and men like him would risk anything, sacrifice everything, to find that mother lode. They would lie, steal, cheat, even kill to find it. Such was the power gold had over men's minds. It could corrupt even the best of men.

Destined to winter over in Denver, Jackson took his sweet time and carefully selected two men to partner up with him. Both were experienced prospectors and both had a grubstake to contribute. Both men had come to Kansas Territory in response to the rumor of a gold strike on the South Platte, in the Pike's Peak country, the previous summer. Some gold had indeed been found, but not enough to justify the rush that ensued. Tens of thousands of gold hunters had poured across the prairie, many in wagons with "Pike's Peak or Bust" painted on the sides. Newspapers foolishly trumpeted this modest gold strike as a bonanza to rival what had occurred in California, and called those who headed for Pike's Peak "the Fifty-Niners." Some died on the way, and those who made it were doomed to disappointment In a matter of months the human tide had reversed course, and the Fifty-Niners were being called "the Go Backers," as tens of thousands admitted failure and headed for home.

Jackson's new partners had opted to linger awhile in the Kansas Territory, and they were more than happy to throw in with him. What did they have to lose except their money and their lives? A small price to pay for the chance to strike it rich!

The mountain passages cleared by mid-April, and Jackson and his companions returned to his find. Six weeks later one of the partners showed up back in Denver and went to Doyle's General Store to buy supplies. He had a sack bulging with gold dust. Ignoring George Jackson's admonition to keep his mouth shut tighter than a number 4 trap, the man boasted that he was taking more than two thousand dollars' worth of dust out of the creek every week. That was all it took.

The rush was on.

A man who had made his living as a gambler, Charles Devanor had become an excellent judge of character, and when he first laid eyes on the Doone brothers he knew with unshakable certainty that the three men were pure, unadulterated trouble.

They were big brawny characters, all of them—Chandler, Harvey and Mitchell—tall and broad in the chest and shoulders, with muscled legs and arms, thick necks, and square jaws. Chandler and Harvey were twins, and while they weren't identical, there could be no question in anyone's mind that they were kin. Both had curly red hair and chilly blue eyes, small and set close together. A deep crevice across the bridge of a fleshy nose connected bushy eyebrows in both instances. Their lips were thin and wide and cruel, and both men were clean-shaven.

Mitchell Doone was distinguishable from his brothers in several significant ways. His hair was the yellow of ripe wheat. He had a bad leg, stiffened by a past wound or affliction. The youngest of the brothers, he was also the meanest. Here was an angry and bitter man who had a chip on both shoulders. Where his brothers were boisterous and profane; Mitchell was quiet, watchful. Chandler and Harvey were violent; Mitchell was vicious. There was something distinctly sinister about him, thought Devanor. Riding with him in the mud wagon that ran between Denver and the new boomtown of Gilder Gulch was akin to traveling with a diamondback rattler. Charles Devanor had nerves of steel, but still, Mitchell Doone made him edgy as hell.

There were two other passengers in the wagon: a heavy-jowled man of middle age clad in a seedy, rumpled suit, and a young woman wearing a brown serge traveling dress. The former had introduced himself right off as Luther Harley, a journalist by profession. The woman had not deigned to provide her name to her fellow travelers. Devanor and Harley were too polite to inquire after it without having just cause, while the Doone brothers had no interest in her handle.

That was not to say that the Doones weren't interested in her. Though it was obvious that she had no desire to fraternize—indeed, she acted as though the five men sharing the mud wagon with her did not even exist—the Doones would not be put off. She was quite pretty, decided Devanor, with ringlets of chestnut brown hair framing an oval face, big brown eyes, an aquiline nose and beguiling lips, her upper half gracefully curved, the lower full and wide. Her skin was the hue of pure honey, and without blemish. She was of medium height and slender—Devanor predicted that her body would prove to be as perfect as her facial features. But what piqued the gambler's interest most of all was the mysterious young woman's aura of profound sadness. He intuitively knew that she had a tragic past. It was apparent in the way she carried herself, aloof and with a kind of forlorn dignity. Her composure did not run as deep as she would have liked; she was emotionally fragile. She had no illusions about life. She was womanly wise and yet still very much like a little girl lost. Harm had been done to her, grave harm, and Devanor's instinct was to protect her from any more hurtful things. This, even though he had only met her a few hours earlier and didn't even know her name. The way Chandler and Harvey Doone openly leered at her nettled him. But what worried him more than that was the way Mitchell Doone's hooded eyes were fastened on her. He looked at her the way a starving man looks at a meal he is about to devour.

The mud wagon had a hard, narrow wooden bench running along either side. The Doones sat together on one side while Devanor, Harley and the young woman occupied the bench opposite, with the newspaperman in the middle. The conveyance had a canvas roof stretched loosely on a frame, with flaps on either side which had been unfurled and tied down to keep at least some of the dust kicked up by the wheels away from the passengers. The road was really nothing more than two ruts cutting across the sagebrush foothills at the base of the mountains. The wagon would carry them as far as Horsehead Pass, a spine-jarring, teeth-rattling journey of six hours' duration. At a station near the pass they would transfer to mules or horses for the ascent to Gilder Gulch. That leg of the journey would be made tomorrow, and it would take the better part of the day. They would spend the night at the station.

The total cost of transportation from Denver to Gilder Gulch was ten dollars. Four for the mud wagon, two for the room and board at the station, and four for tomorrow's excursion into the high country. Devanor thought the cost was exorbitant, but he had paid it without hesitation. He anticipated an excellent return on the dollar once he reached the gold camp. In California he had learned that many prospectors were eager to risk their riches on the turn of a pasteboard. They would sweat and bleed to dig the gold out of the ground or pan it out of the creeks, and he would take it from them effortlessly.

"You're a cardsharp, aren't you?" Harley asked him at one point. "Does it not prick your conscience to rob men of their gold?"

"Rob?" Devanor smiled. He was a tall, slender man with angular features and jet black hair and eyes as gray as gunmetal. "I don't force them to sit down at my table."

"Sure you do," said the newspaperman. "By your very presence, you do. You are a temptation that they cannot resist, sir. These men, these gold hunters, cannot help but take chances. That's what they live for. Caution is a foreign concept to them. Even though they know the deck is stacked against them, they have to test their luck. They are like moths drawn to a fatal flame."

"I run an honest game," said Devanor.

"You do not mark your cards? You do not use

21

some clever device to put the odds in your favor? Most gamblers use some tool or trick of the trade. A card trimmer, a dice shaver, a holdout. That's the game for them—to cheat and not get caught. Like the gold hunter, the gambler lives to take chances."

"The game for me," replied Devanor coolly, "is to match my card skills against those of my opponents. I don't need an edge. I'm simply a better poker player than anyone else."

Harley chuckled. "No false modesty for you, I see. It is so unbecoming, don't you agree?"

"And you," said Devanor. "You're a crusader, aren't you? Don't tell me—let me guess. You intend to start a newspaper in Gilder Gulch. You will use the pulpit of your editorial to warn the gold hunters to beware of people like me. To turn a wide open gold camp into a respectable community—that is your noble cause. And one, I might add, that you know is hopelessly out of reach. You tilt against windmills because you secretly want to fail. You crucify yourself on the cross of civilization because it gives you a sense of worth. Makes you feel superior to others."

Luther Harley gaped at the gambler. "By God, you're no ordinary tinhorn," he said in amazement.

"Gilder Gulch," predicted Devanor, "will die as quickly and probably as violently as it was born."

He noticed that his comment elicited some response from the woman—she looked at him sharply, as though surprised and a little perturbed by his prediction. Devanor smiled at her and touched the brim of his hat. She looked quickly away. He was, nonetheless, grateful for small favors; it was the first time she had even acknowledged his existence.

"Least we know what you two are all about," said Chandler Doone, glancing dismissively at Devanor and Harley. Then his eyes slid back to the woman and very slowly took her in from head to toe, lingering at her breasts, which were tightly encased in the serge traveling suit. He was undressing her with his eyes and wasn't trying to hide the fact and that bothered Devanor, even though he himself had tried to imagine what she would be like in the nude. "What about you, lady?" asked Chandler. "Why are you going to Gilder Gulch?"

She didn't even look at him, didn't appear to have heard him.

Annoyed, Chandler pursed his lips. He didn't like being ignored. "Maybe you're one of those that the newspaperman here will be warning the miners about." He leered.

"I don't think I like what you're implying," said Devanor coldly.

Chandler just grinned at him. "This is a gold camp we're going to, mister, not some prairie revival meeting. She ain't no seamstress or schoolmarm, that's for sure. So this purty little lady is bound to be a calico queen, and I just want her to know that she doesn't have to wait until she gets to Gilder Gulch to drum up some business." He leered at her again. Then he reached out and put his big blunt-fingered hand on her knee.

"I want you to do two things," said Devanor, very quietly. "First, take your hand off her. Second, I want you to apologize."

"Go to hell, gambler," said Chandler Doone, showing his contempt for Devanor by not even looking at him.

Mitchell Doone did look—and saw the over-and-under derringer in Devanor's hand. The pocket pistol was aimed at Chandler.

"He's got a gun, Chand," said Mitchell, as matter-of-factly as if he was announcing that the sun was out.

Now Chandler looked at Devanor—as did everyone else in the mud wagon.

"What the hell are you doing?" rasped Chandler, his grin frozen into a snarl.

"I'm trying to teach you some manners," replied Devanor coolly. "It's a lesson you've obviously never learned."

Like his brothers, Chandler was armed. He carried a Remington Army revolver stuck in his belt, and Devanor could read in his eyes that he contemplated going for the gun. But there was something about the gambler—perhaps it was his icy calm—that dissuaded Chandler from such rash action. There was no doubt in anyone's mind that Devanor was not in the least cowed by the three-to-one odds stacked against him. No doubt at all that he would squeeze the trigger if Chandler didn't do as he had been told.

Scowling, Chandler removed his hand from the young woman's leg.

"And now the apology," said Devanor with a cold smile.

Pride turned the words bitter on Chandler Doone's tongue. "I'm sorry," he muttered, glaring at the gambler.

"No, tell her, not me," said Devanor.

Lips thinning to a knife slit, Chandler looked at the woman and said, "I'm sorry."

She was watching him, but abruptly looked away. Chandler turned his attention back to Devanor, and his expression spoke volumes about how he was not one to forgive or forget. The gambler put away the pocket pistol.

A few minutes later, Luther Harley glanced sidelong at Devanor and said wryly, "Well, you'll have to tell me someday about this death wish of yours."

Devanor just smiled at the newspaperman.

An hour later the mud wagon's driver hauled on the leathers to rein in the four-horse hitch in front of an adobe structure. The Doone brothers clambered out of the wagon, in a hurry to stretch cramped legs. Devanor climbed down, held the canvas aside for Harley, and then offered a hand to the woman. She took it, looked him straight in the eye, and said, "You didn't have to do that."

"Yes, I believe I did."

"You're from the South, aren't you? Bred to play the cavalier."

"I suppose. I was born to a well-to-do Georgian family. Though I was the black sheep, they still tried to make a gentleman out of me. I'm not sure they succeeded—depends on who you talk to."

"Apparently they did succeed," she said, as she stepped down from the mud wagon.

"Thank you. Though I could be more consistent in that regard." He smiled, but her attention had been captured by something else—the snowcapped peaks looming majestically above them. She gazed at them in wonder.

"That's where you'll be going tomorrow," said the driver as he came around to the back of the wagon. He was a grizzled old-timer with a tobacco-stained beard wearing suspenders and a cap cocked at a jaunty angle. "You'll ride right up through that pass yonder." He pointed a crooked finger at the saddle between the pair of peaks that had so captivated the woman. "It's a long hard ride, so I'd advise you folks to get some rest tonight."

The Horseshoe Pass station was run by a man named Parker and his wife. They were a dour and rough-hewn couple, as serious and unsentimental as the New England bedrock which had produced them. Mrs. Parker fed them a bland, spare meal of hard biscuits and favorless stew in the station's common room. Their beds were hard narrow wooden bunks in another room, with thin corn-husk mattresses and a couple of blankets each. What to do with a female traveler presented the Parkers with an unexpected dilemma—it just wasn't proper to put her in with the men. It was decided that she would sleep in the Parkers' bedroom, taking the place of Mr. Parker, who would bunk with the male travelers.

While the others made ready for bed, Charles Devanor stepped outside to smoke a cheroot; he favored the pungent Mexican twists. Savoring the thin cigar, he gazed at the moonlight on the high snowfields. It gave the mountains an ephemeral quality, as though they were half-remembered elements of a dream that would vanish in the cold light of day. Devanor looked on them as a gate through which, on the morrow, he would pass into a new life; he could not shake the feeling that in the mountains he would finally find what he had been looking for—a purpose for living.

"So you want to tell me why you are so eager to meet your Maker, Mr. Devanor?"

The gambler turned as Luther Harley emerged from the adobe station, firing up an old briar pipe.

"Mind if I join you?" asked the newspaperman.

Devanor knew that Harley was just being polite—he had no intention of leaving whether his company was wanted or not.

"Be my guest."

"Those Doone boys, they're hell on the hoof. You made that one fellow back down and he won't rest until you've paid for that sin."

"I've paid my whole life, for one sin or another."

Harley barked a laugh. "Haven't we all, sir! Haven't we all."

"You would have done the same thing I did. I just beat you to it."

Harley chuckled, shook his head. "Oh, no. You're wrong about that. I am merely an observer. I do not get involved. I watch and record the trials and tribulations of the human race, the occasional triumphs, the all-too-common failures. I try not to interfere."

"I live by a few hard and fast rules," said Devanor. "One of those is that I will not see a woman wronged or taken advantage of."

"Oh, well—I think you have a fondness for Miss whatever-her-name-is. The two of you are kindred spirits, you know."

"What makes you think so?"

"You both have deep dark secrets, crosses to bear that burden your hearts and make your steps heavy. There is a certain fatalism." Smoldering pipe clenched between his teeth, Harley reached into a coat pocket and produced a silver whiskey flask. "Care for a shot of nerve medicine, Mr. Devanor?"

"No, thank you. I don't often indulge."

"A cardsharp who doesn't drink like a fish? Well, you are a strange one, my friend. Tell me, how do you drown your sorrows, then?"

Devanor smiled tolerantly. "My mother used to say that only weak men relied on strong spirits."

"I have many glaring weaknesses," said Harley indifferently, and took a healthy swig from the flask. "Ah," he gasped, and smacked his lips. "The nectar of the Gods, truly." He peered at Devanor. "I'm curious, what other words of wisdom did your dear mother impart to you?"

Looking again at the mountains bathed in the ghostly blue light of the moon, Devanor said, "That every person is put on this earth for a reason."

"I see." Harley puffed contemplatively on his cigar. "I suppose I was put on this earth to tilt against windmills. Chandler Doone was put here to remind us that we are not that far removed from lower forms of life. And you—I would hazard a guess that you were put here to make cautious men out of reckless fools by emptying their pockets at the poker table."

Devanor laughed softly. "I never knew I was a benefit to society. But permit me to at least entertain the hope that there is something more to life."

"Go right ahead and hope all you want," said Harley with a regal wave of the hand.

The gambler dropped his spent cheroot and ground it beneath a boot heel. "I'll say good night now."

"You haven't answered my original question yet, you know. Why you don't care if you live or die."

"Maybe later," said Devanor.

As he made his way through the darkened room to his bunk, he heard Mr. Parker snoring, and then Chandler Doone said, his voice a rumbling menace, "Better sleep with one eye open, gambler."

"I always do," replied Devanor, and stretched out on the bunk, one hand behind his head, the other grasping the bone-handled derringer resting on his chest.

They left at the crack of dawn, traveling by horseback and towing a pack mule that carried their baggage. There wasn't much of that—Devanor, Harley and the woman each had one valise, while the Doone brothers contributed one warbag and a couple of bedrolls. Devanor wondered what they intended to do for a living in Gilder Gulch. Clearly they were not prospectors. He surmised that they would frequent dark alleys and relieve miners of their gold in a manner far more violent than the one he employed.

Mr. Parker accompanied them as far as the summit of Horseshoe Pass. There he pointed to the river that curled like a blue snake through the green valley below.

"You folks follow that river until you come to a creek that flows into it from the north. Then go up that creek. You'll pass through a canyon, past some rapids, then the trail will take you up over a saddle. From the top you'll be able to see Gilder Gulch. I reckon you'll be there before dark unless you tarry or lose your way."

They neither tarried nor lost their way, and the only interesting part of the trek as far as Devanor was concerned was the passage through the canyon by means of a narrow trail that clung precariously to the steep rocky edge, with the creek below roaring and foaming and swirling as it crashed downslope. The sun was setting behind the high reaches to the west when they gained the crest of the saddle and looked beyond to see the gold camp for the first time. For a moment no one spoke. Then Harley said, "It's even uglier than I imagined it would be."

"It looks like money to me," said Chandler. "Come on, boys. I need a drink or three."

The Doones moved eagerly on. Harley followed. Devanor smiled at the woman and gestured for her to precede him down the trail.

To his surprise she smiled back at him, and said tentatively, "My name is Alice, by the way," and then urged her horse forward.

"Thank you," said Devanor, pleased, and fell in behind her.

Chapter Three

Gordon Hawkes watched the canker that was Gilder Gulch appear and grow on the mountains he called home, and felt the dismay that comes to one who knows he is powerless to prevent his world from falling apart.

For years he and his family had lived on the north slopes of the Uinta Range, within a day's ride of the Green River, site of a mountain man rendezvous that had marked the zenith of a fur trade that had now dwindled to almost nothing. But then thousands of forty-niners had poured through South Pass and Bridger Pass on their way to California, enduring countless hardships in the hopes that they might realize their dreams of riches. With his help, the Mormons, led by Brigham Young in their flight from persecution in Illinois, had followed the same route to reach the promised land they called Deseret, near the great salt lake located due west of the Uintas— this, even before the onslaught of the gold seekers. These two events had gone a long way toward convincing Hawkes that the Uinta Range was no longer a good place to call home. And then the growing Sioux menace of recent years proved to be the last straw. Having been a captive of the warlike Sioux, Hawkes was sure that full-scale war was destined to come. And if he stayed in the Uintas, it would literally happen on his doorstep.

So he had taken his family and their meager possessions to the south, into the remote mountainous regions of western Kansas Territory, far removed from the vicinity of Fort Laramie and Fort Bridger and Salt Lake City, and far from the problems arising between Sioux warrior and blue-coated soldier, and between Mormon "saint" and emigrant "gentile." He thought he had found a new sanctuary, perhaps better than the one before. But Gilder Gulch plucked the scales from his eyes; now he knew he'd only been fooling himself. There was no place to hide. No matter where he ran, the world would find him.

Hawkes had good reason to feel apprehensive about this turn of events. The civilized world had treated him with a striking lack of civility. Born in Ireland to Scottish stock, he had seen his father's hopes of prosperity first drained by fruitless labor on the barren soil of a potato farm, and then extinguished entirely by ship fever during a sea passage to America, where Tom Hawkes had dreamed of making a new beginning. Abandoned by his opium-addicted mother, a young Gordon Hawkes had fallen in with a rakish Scots adventurer, only to find himself accused of a murder he had not committed. This state of affairs drove him westward in the company of a band of stalwart trappers who pledged allegiance to the now-defunct Rocky Mountain Fur Company. In the Shining Mountains Hawkes had found a home that seemed, twenty-five years ago, to be as remote from the civilized world as the face of the moon. He had also found happiness in the arms of a missionary's pale-haired daughter. He and Eliza Hancock had married and produced two healthy children, Cameron and Grace.

Circumstances had thrice forced Hawkes to come down out of his mountain sanctuary, and all three times he had paid a heavy price. The first time he had been falsely accused of yet another murder, only to fall in with the Mormons and all the troubles that surrounded them. The second time he had felt obliged to do his part in securing government annuities guaranteed by treaty to his friends, the Absaroke Crows—only to become a prisoner of the Dakota Sioux for so long that his wife had nearly succumbed to the fear that he lived no more. And then his code of honor and sense of fair play had embroiled him in the Mormon War, very nearly costing him his life.

After that, Eliza had been more than willing to pull up stakes and retreat with her husband deeper into the wild mountains. So it was that he and Eliza and Cameron, now a young man, and Grace and Pretty Shield, the Sioux woman whose love for Hawkes he could not requite, had made a new home. But only months after Hawkes had gazed with satisfaction at the new cabin in a secluded valley previously untouched by the hand of man, he was gazing with deep concern at the town of Denver, which seemed to spring up overnight on the other side of the mountain range from his new home. And now, even closer, was Gilder Gulch, only a day's walk from his cabin.

"Reckon I knew this would happen when I found out that man Jackson was a prospector," he told Eliza.

"You're not to blame. How could you know that he would find gold here? And if he hadn't found it, someone else would have, sooner or later."

"Yes, probably later, and maybe *much* later," said Hawkes ruefully.

"What were you supposed to do? Just let him die?"

"No, I guess I couldn't have done that."

"Of course not. This is God's will, Gordon. We must make the best of whatever comes our way."

Sometimes Hawkes envied Eliza the ability that her faith gave her to blithely accept the unexpected twists and turns of life. Sometimes he even resented it a little. But he couldn't argue that her faith had been the key element in her forgiving him for his relationship with Pretty Shield. The Sioux woman had saved his life, and during his long captivity among the Dakota he had grown weak; despairing of ever seeing his wife again, he had slept with Pretty. He recognized that act now for what it was—one of the biggest mistakes of his life, and though Eliza had forgiven him, he had never been able to forgive himself.

And how could he, when he saw Pretty Shield every day? She was a constant reminder of his weakness. How Eliza tolerated the arrangement Hawkes still could not fathom. True, when he had escaped the Sioux he'd been obliged to bring Pretty out with him. Otherwise she would most certainly have been killed. Then, to complicate matters, Cameron had fallen in love with her, even though at first Cam had hated her as the instrument of temptation that had demonstrated his father's fallibility and caused his mother so much anguish. Sometimes Hawkes wondered if it was for Cam that Eliza allowed Pretty to stay. Or was it Eliza's way of daily testing the strength of her own dedication to Christian principles? He was wise enough—or perhaps too cowardly, he couldn't decide which—never to bring the subject up for discussion. Whatever Eliza's motives, Hawkes had occasion to wish she had not been quite so tolerant, so forgiving. Because the worst aspect of it all was the fact that Pretty Shield's presence had driven a wedge between him and his son.

Not that Hawkes blamed her, or anyone but himself. Pretty had forsaken her own people for him, and though he had not meant to, he had by his actions encouraged her to do so. Now she was with Cameron, not because she loved him, but because it was as close as she could get to the true object of her affection. And Cam was nobody's fool; he knew what was going on around him. He knew that the woman he loved was in love with another—his own father! And try as all three of them might to make the best of a bizarre and uncomfortable situation, Cameron couldn't help but resent his rival. To Pretty Shield's credit, she went out of her way to make Cam happy, and never tried to do anything that might ignite his simmering jealousy. But then, she didn't really have to *do* anything. The damage had already been done.

"I've lost him," Hawkes told Eliza on one of those rare occasions when he let his guard down and aired his truest feelings and innermost fears. "Things will never be the same between us, I'm afraid."

Eliza was not one to give voice to recriminations. She could have said that it was a problem of his own making—after all, it was because of him that Pretty Shield was here, and Pretty was the wellspring of all the difficulties that had arisen between father and son. But that would have been pointless; it would have been telling Hawkes something that he already knew. So all Eliza could do was provide him with reassurances.

"Nonsense," she said. "Cameron loves you. You are his father."

"Yes, he loves me, as I do him. That's what makes this even harder for the two of us."

"Well," said Eliza softly, "you know I always thought you should have sent her away. But I understand why you could not bring yourself to do that. And now it's too late, of course. Cam would be lost without her. It's so unfair to him, that she cares for you the way she does. But we cannot dictate to our own hearts."

At such times Hawkes marveled at his rare good fortune in having someone like Eliza, and he put his arms around her and held her close. "And I care for you, more than I can ever put into words."

She smiled. Hawkes was not the sort of man to whom expressing such sentiments came easy. He did not often show that side of himself, and when he did she was gratified.

"Don't worry, Gordon," she told him. "The Lord has some purpose in mind for putting us all through this. In time, His reasons will be made clear to us."

In the weeks to come Gordon Hawkes would have good cause to reflect on her words.

And so he spent a great deal of time watching the gold camp grow—watching from high up on the slopes above the valley, using a mariner's spyglass he had obtained some years ago from his old friend Jim Bridger. When they had lived in the Uinta Range, he had gone to Old Gabe's post every year to trade plews for the few necessities he and his family required—coffee, sugar, tobacco for his pipe, shot and gunpowder so that he could make his own cartridges for the Plains rifle he carried. And, too, he had gone to Fort Bridger to give Eliza and his children an opportunity to visit with people, an antidote to the isolations his family endured as a consequence of his past. Eliza did not mind the isolation nearly as much as Cameron and Grace did. Hawkes was particularly concerned about Cam. His son was by nature a very sociable person; he liked being around people, meeting strangers, experiencing new things. He wasn't fearful of the world beyond the mountains. As far Hawks was concerned it was because he just didn't know any better. What worried Hawkes most of all about Gilder Gulch was the allure it held for his son.

"I have a strong hankering to go down there and see what all the fuss is about," Cameron told his father after a fortnight of watching the gold camp's hustle and bustle from afar.

"That would be a fool thing to do," replied Hawkes, resisting the urge to forbid Cam outright from visiting Gilder Gulch. Though his son had seen nearly twenty winters, and had risked his life to lead a band of mountain men deep into Sioux country to free Hawkes from his Dakota captors, Hawkes still caught himself thinking of Cameron as a wet-behind-the-ears kid.

Cameron took offense. "Seems like to you every thing I do is a foolish thing," he retorted.

"I'm just saying you would betray our presence to those people down there. And no good could possibly come of that."

"I wouldn't have to tell them anything. I just want to see what's going on. You know, I've never even seen an honest-to-goodness town before. Closest thing to it was Fort Laramie for me."

"Well, you're not missing anything. And a gold camp is a hard place. A dangerous place. People there are only interested in one thing: getting gold—whether it means taking it out of the ground or out of someone else's pocket."

"Stealing isn't right, but what's wrong with wanting gold?" persisted Cameron. "If you ask me, we should stake our own claim while we've still got the chance. We have as much right to the gold in this valley as anybody else has."

Hawkes sighed. There hardly seemed to be any point in trying to reason with his son. According to Eliza, Cameron was every bit as stubborn as his father. And Cam's mission in life of late—or so it seemed—was to argue every point with his father, no matter how minor, and to find fault with everything that Hawkes said.

"We have no need for gold. It brings nothing but trouble."

"If that were true, there wouldn't be so many people willing to risk everything to get their hands on some."

"And what would you do, Cam, if you did find some gold?"

"Why, I'd buy things, naturally. I'd buy me a new rifle, for one thing. And I'd buy Pretty a new dress. But one for Ma and Grace, too, while I was at it."

"I'd be surprised if Pretty even wants a store-bought dress," remarked Hawkes.

Cameron's expression darkened. "That would be between her and me."

Hawkes grimaced. He never could say the right thing anymore when he was talking to his son.

"Your father is right, Cam," said Eliza, having been content until now to eavesdrop on the conversation. "Beware the deceitfulness of riches. Remember what the Good Book says—that a camel will sooner pass through the eye of a needle than a rich man will pass through the gates of heaven."

Cameron knew better than to argue with his mother, especially when she started quoting from the Bible, which she knew by heart, cover to cover. But though he dropped the subject, Cam wasn't convinced; Hawkes could look at his son's face and see that Cam was still aching to pay the gold camp a visit.

Every week more people came into the valley. Every day seemed to dawn on a new structure hastily erected in Gilder Gulch. The ringing of axes and the crashing of felled trees on the forested slopes above the camp were a constant and, to Hawkes, deeply disturbing din. The once pristine creek that ran through the gold camp became sullied with the effluvium of Gilder Gulch's exploding population. The search for the mother lode, the source of the nuggets and the gold dust harvested from claims stretching up and down the creek at least a mile from the camp, spurred prospectors farther and farther up the valley—and that brought them inexorably closer to the Hawkes cabin. The town's expanding need for fresh game made hunting a far more difficult proposition for Hawkes. Before long, he complained to Eliza, all the wildlife would be driven out of the valley.

At first Eliza appeared to be blissfully unconcerned. The Lord, she kept telling him, would provide. Hawkes was skeptical. He believed in God, but One who was more conspicuous by his absence from the ebb and flow of human affairs. His God helped those who helped themselves. But like Cam, he knew better than to argue matters of faith with Eliza. That was a battle lost before it was even fought.

Then something happened that made the threat posed by Gilder Gulch very real to all of them.

Pretty Shield liked to collect serviceberries and chokecherries from the valley floor during the spring and summer, and often strayed far from home in this pursuit. One day while engaged in this activity, she happened to look up just as two strangers emerged from the tree line on the other side of a meadow. Startled, Pretty stood and stared for a moment, and the men did likewise. But then they started toward her—and Pretty wisely turned and ran. The men gave chase, whooping and hollering as though it was all great sport. Pretty Shield could run like a deer, and it didn't take her long to leave the men far behind.

She knew she had to tell someone what had happened, and she went to Hawkes instead of Cameron. "They are getting closer," she told the mountain man, after relating to him what had occurred in the meadow. "One day soon they will find this place."

Hawkes nodded. He shuddered to think what the two men might have done to Pretty had they somehow managed to catch her.

"Those two men," he told Eliza, "will go back to town and tell everyone that there are Indians in this valley, I expect."

"But is that so bad? Maybe it will make them stay closer to home."

Hawkes shook his head. "Not when there's gold involved. It will just make them trigger happy, and that means it has become much more dangerous for us now."

For the first time, Eliza really seemed to be listening and taking his concerns seriously.

"So we are going to have to move again," she said sadly, looking around at the cabin that she had worked so hard to turn into a comfortable home.

"I don't see as how we have much choice, Eliza. I'm really sorry."

She smiled at him, touched his bearded cheek with her fingertips. "You're blaming yourself again, aren't you? It wasn't your fault that you were accused of crimes you didn't commit, was it?"

"Well, no, but . . ."

"And you didn't force me to marry you."

"No."

"And have I ever once complained about the life that we've led?"

"You're not the sort to complain."

"Even if I were, I wouldn't be complaining. You know why? Because I am happy with my lot in life.

So, it's settled. We will move. But . . . where are we going to go, Gordon?"

Hawkes sighed. "West, I reckon. Deeper into the high country."

But when he told his son that they were pulling up stakes, Cameron balked.

"So you weren't even going to bother asking me what I wanted to do," said Cameron. "You make the decision and expect everyone else to go along. Well, maybe this time I don't want to move. Maybe I'm sick and tired of moving."

"It's the only thing we can do, son."

"I'm not the one who's running from the law. I don't have to leave this valley and I don't want to. And one more thing. I want to know why Pretty ran to you and told you about those men who chased her but didn't want to tell me about it."

"Maybe because she figured you would lose your temper and do something stupid. Like go after those men."

"I'm not a child anymore," snapped Cameron, fuming. "So you should all stop treating me like I am."

Hawkes was at a loss when it came to dealing with Cam. He didn't know what to do other than hope that his son suddenly came to his senses. Though eager to leave the valley to get his family out of harm's way, he took his time making the preparations, hoping Cameron would come around. But Cam showed no signs of having a change of heart, and finally in desperation Hawkes took Pretty Shield aside and asked for her help.

"Somebody's got to make him see reason," he told

her. "He sure won't listen to me. He seems bound and determined to go against me at every turn. I don't know what's gotten into him, frankly."

"Yes, you do know why he is this way," she replied, with a gentle smile. "It is because of me. You just do not want to say so."

"I reckon. Maybe." Hawkes was uncomfortable. That was a path he did not care to go down. "Can you talk to him, Pretty? Talk him into coming with us?"

"I will try. But I do not think it will do any good. He is a lot like his father. Very stubborn. It would be easier to make water run uphill than to change Cameron's mind once he has made a decision. I do not think he will go with you. He thinks it is time for him to go his own way."

Hawkes was crestfallen. Of course, as all fathers do, he had known that this day would eventually come. And, again like all fathers, he had dreaded its coming—so much so that he had denied to himself that it would ever really happen. Now that it was upon him he didn't know how to react. He didn't want to leave Cameron behind but he knew how dangerous it would be for Eliza and Grace if they all stayed.

Eliza was saddened, too, by the prospect of parting with her son, but she took comfort in her faith that God would look out for him, and she told Hawkes that it was time to give Cameron some room.

Hawkes still wasn't convinced—until a hunting party from the gold camp showed up close enough that he could hear their guns from the cabin. That made up his mind. The next day he loaded their belongings on a travois, put Eliza and twelve-year-old Grace on a horse, and said his good-byes to Cameron and Pretty Shield. He sensed that Pretty wanted to go with him, but she felt duty-bound to stay by Cam's side, and Hawkes was glad that someone would be here to take care of his son.

For several days after his family's departure from the valley, Cameron languished in a moody and silent depression. Pretty Shield thought, hoped, that he was going to change his mind about staying behind. Instead, she woke one morning to find him saddling his horse and announcing that he intended to pay Gilder Gulch a visit.

"You must not go," she told him. "It isn't safe."

"I can take care of myself. You should know that by now."

"We do not belong in such a place, among such people," she insisted.

"We? Who said anything about you going? No, you're staying right here. I'll be back in a few days."

Not giving her time to argue, Cameron swung aboard his horse and left the clearing where the cabin stood, never once looking back.

He had not gotten far down the trail when a sound made him turn around. Pretty Shield was running to catch up with him. He had thought that leaving her without a horse—now that his father was gone they had but the one horse between them—would discourage this kind of thing. But she was fleet of foot and could run all day with scarcely a rest if need be. Exasperated, Cameron sharply checked his horse and waited for her to catch up.

"I thought I told you to stay home," he said crossly.

"You can tell me whatever you want," she snapped back at him. "But I go where I please. And if you are going to that town then I am going too."

"You'll just make trouble for me."

"Then don't go."

"Why are you doing this? Because you're worried about me? Or is it because you promised my pa that you would look after me, like I was still a child."

"You are not a child. You are a man—a proud, stubborn fool of a man." She extended her hand. "Now, let me ride behind you—or will you make me run behind your horse like a good little squaw?"

Cameron cursed under his breath. Then he reached down to take her by the wrist and reluctantly helped her up behind him. Pretty Shield put her arms around his waist and held on as he kicked the horse into motion, and together they proceeded down the trail toward the valley floor and Gilder Gulch.

Pretty Shield's heart was filled with dread. She was certain that no good would come of this venture. But she knew how pointless it was to try to talk Cameron out of going. She wasn't sure if he had gold fever or if he was just determined to go against his father's wishes, to display his independence no matter what the cost.

But regardless of her fears she would stay with him, and do whatever she could to protect him, because he was the son of Gordon Hawkes.

Chapter Four

When the prospector named Jeffers raised him by tossing all the markers he had left into the pot—a hundred dollars' worth—Charles Devanor figured the odds in a heartbeat and decided that the man was pulling a bluff.

Jeffers had chased the other two players out of this hand with sheer bravado. Now he leered at Devanor—big teeth like crooked yellow tombstones in a gaunt face that bristled with an unkempt beard.

"I've got you whupped this time, gamblin' man," he crowed.

"Anything is possible," conceded Devanor.

He was lying. He didn't think it was possible at all that Jeffers had him beat, and he had two good reasons for thinking that way.

For one thing, the cards were against Jeffers. They were playing five card stud and the prospector had two jacks showing. It was possible that his hole card would give him another pair, but that was of no concern to Devanor, who had two pair himself, kings high. Jacks high would be the best Jeffers could do if he did have two pair. The other possibility—and this was the one that Jeffers was trying very hard to

46

sell—was that his hole card was a third jack. But the odds were against that being the case. A third jack had already been dealt to one of the other players; Devanor figured the fourth jack was still in the deck.

The other thing Devanor had going for him was the fact that he had been playing across a table from Jeffers for over an hour now. That was more than enough time for him to take the measure of any man. His livelihood depended on an ability to read an opponent and he was very good at it. He had seen Jeffers shift slightly back in his chair and look around the tent saloon on each of the three occasions when he had held the winning hand. He hadn't done that this time. Which told Devanor that Jeffers wasn't that sure about his cards. And if he wasn't sure, he wouldn't have bet everything—unless he was running a bluff.

"So what's it going to be, gamblin' man?" pressed Jeffers. "You in or out?"

"Well," drawled Devanor, "I'm staying in. Because I think you're trying to buy the pot."

He pushed a hundred dollars' worth of chips into the pile at the center of the table.

One of the other players, not sitting back and observing, let out a low whistle. "There must be better than four hundred dollars on the table."

"You're calling me?" asked Jeffers, staring at Devanor like he just couldn't believe what was happening.

"I'm seeing your hundred," corrected Devanor, "and raising you three hundred more."

He pushed more chips into the pot.

Joe Duff's tent saloon, as usual, was crowded. Every table was occupied. The bar—planks laid across hogsheads—was three deep with drinkers. The percentage girls could hardly make their way through the tables for all the men standing and drinking and talking. A constant din of loud voices filled the smoky confines of the dirt-floored, canvas-roofed watering hole. But the noise suddenly subsided as those in the immediate vicinity of Devanor's table turned to look at the game. And this stillness spread in quickly widening ripples away from the table, so that by the time the gambler had finished adding to the pot, Joe Duff's saloon was nearly as quiet as a church. Everyone was paying attention.

Duff's man, Wiley Roe, came to stand at Devanor's shoulder. Roe was the biggest man Devanor had ever seen, strong as a bull and dumb as a fence post, his hands big enough and powerful enough that Devanor had no doubt he could snap a man's spine as easily as if it were a dry twig. Devanor had an agreement with Duff; the saloonkeeper got twenty-five percent of the gambler's earnings. So Duff had a proprietary interest in Devanor—not just in the pot currently in question but also in making sure that Devanor didn't get killed by a poor loser. That was why Roe was here now—that and the fact that the brawny bouncer liked Devanor. The latter could only assume it was because he treated Roe with respect, which was more than could be said for Roe's employer. Devanor had seen people treat stray dogs better than Duff treated Roe.

Yet at the moment Devanor was in no mood to tolerate Wiley Roe's presence. "Go away, Wiley," he said curtly. "I don't need you. And you're blocking my light."

"Yessir, Mr. Devanor," mumbled Wiley. He lumbered away to watch the table from a discreet distance—if anything a man did who was seven feet tall and weighing in at three hundred pounds of bone and muscle could be described as discreet.

Jeffers was staring at the pot, the leer frozen on his face. He seemed to shrink in the chair and Devanor knew why. The prospector realized his bluff had been called and he was going to lose everything.

"I-I thought we were playing table stakes," muttered Jeffers, desperately looking for a way out.

"We are," replied Devanor, leaning back in his chair and taking one of his Mexican cheroots from the pocket of his black frock boat, clenching it between his teeth and lighting it with a match scraped to life on the edge of the table.

"Well then that hunnerd dollars is all I got left."

"I'm betting that's wrong. I'm betting you've got your claim deed on you."

Jeffers reached under his scruffy, blanket coat, then caught himself. "How do you know that?" he asked suspiciously.

"Educated guess. You just got back from Denver with it, didn't you? You wouldn't trust anyone else with it, I know that much. So you're bound to have it with you, and if you brought it to this table then I'm raising you, three hundred dollars against your claim."

"My claim's worth more than three hunnerd dollars—a lot more."

"So what if it is? You don't have anything to lose. You've got me whupped, remember?"

Jeffers looked at the other players, saw that he was

not going to get any support from them, and shook his head fiercely.

"No, this ain't right. Table stakes, that's what you said. Take that three hunnerd back."

"You brought the deed to the table," said Devanor coldly. "Now lay it out there, or forfeit the pot."

"You can't do this," protested Jeffers.

"Watch me," said Devanor, fastening cold dark eyes on the prospector.

Jeffers stood up so abruptly that he knocked his chair over. "I'm take my markers and cashing out."

"No, you aren't going to do that," said Devanor through a veil of blue cheroot smoke.

Jeffers had a pistol under his belt and he thought about using it—he telegraphed as much to the gambler with the flare of wild desperation in his eyes.

"Don't be a jackass, Jeffers," said one of the other players disdainfully. "He's got the drop on you."

Only then did Jeffers see what the other player had already noticed—that Devanor's right hand was under the table. The prospector couldn't tell whether the gambler actually had a gun in that hand or not, but he wasn't crazy enough to find out the hard way.

"The pot's yours," he growled. "You ain't getting my claim, though, you cheatin' son of a bitch."

"I didn't want your claim," replied Devanor, and curled his left arm around the pot to take it in. "I just wanted to see you sweat."

Wiley Roe reappeared, this time directly behind an unsuspecting Jeffers, and he grabbed the prospector roughly by the collar of his coat. "Mr. Devanor ain't no cheat," Roe rumbled menacingly.

Devanor smiled wryly. "And whether I'm actually

a son of a bitch is a personal matter between myself and my mother," he said, as Jeffers was hustled out of the tent saloon and hurled into the muck of the street.

A shuffling of feet and a murmur of voices that rose swiftly into the old familiar din accompanied the prospector's unceremonious exit, and the men in Duff's saloon returned to whatever had been of interest to them prior to the showdown at Devanor's table.

"Gentleman, I am going to take a break," Devanor told the other two players, and as he stood up they saw the bone-handled derringer that had been in his right hand disappear back into a pocket of the frock coat. Roe returned to gather up the gambler's winnings as Devanor went to the bar. The men there made space for him—and for Joe Duff. The big, bluff, rubicund black Irishman grinned happily at Devanor.

"You were a little hard on that fellow, weren't you, Dev?"

"Are you complaining about how I treat your customers?" Devanor motioned to one of the barkeeps, who produced a shot glass and filled it to the rim with brandy. The gambler rarely drank strong spirits, and never whiskey—especially the kind of cheap rotgut that Duff peddled to the rest of his clientele.

"Hell no. I'm making a big profit off of you. Best thing that has happened to me in a long while, you coming here to Gilder Gulch. But I want to make a lot more, you understand. So I would purely hate to see you push the wrong man too far and get yourself ventilated."

"It's gratifying to know that at least one person would mourn over my dusty grave."

Duff laughed—it was an ugly braying sound that tended to rub Devanor's nerves raw. "I would even pay for your pine box out of my own pocket, my friend."

"I didn't like him," said Devanor, by way of an explanation. "He annoyed me. And he was a lousy poker player."

"So you taught him a lesson he'll not soon forget." Duff nodded. "Only you should have taken that claim deed. You know, between the two of us we could own this hellhole in no time at all."

Devanor sipped the brandy down until the glass was half-empty. Then he drew on the cheroot, brought the glass up under his nose and let smoke trickle out of his nostrils and into the glass before inhaling it again, savoring how the smoke had captured the flavor of the liquor. It was a trick best done with brandy in a snifter, but there were no snifters in Gilder Gulch; Devanor was happy just to find the brandy.

"I have no wish to own any part of this hellhole," he told Duff. "I don't plan to be here that long, anyway."

"I aim to stay until they take the last nugget of gold out of the ground," said Duff. "Then, when that last nugget is in my pocket, I'll pull up stakes. But not before. I intend to make everything that's worth anything in this town mine."

"A worthy goal." Devanor finished the brandy and walked away from Duff without so much as a by-your-leave.

Reliable Wiley Roe had carried his winnings to The Banker—a balding, bespectacled man wearing a green eyeshade and sitting behind a plank table in the corner of the tent saloon. Another of Duff's employees, a burly half-breed with a scarred face and sporting a sawed-off shotgun and Bowie knife, stood guard over this man and the iron strongbox beneath the table. Devanor did not know The Banker's real name, and had never heard him called anything else. The Banker's job was to issue paper markers to prospectors who wanted to try their luck at poker or buck the tiger at Duff's faro table. The Banker would weigh the prospector's gold on his scales and write out the markers worth ten dollars each, each marker bearing the gold seeker's name. The Banker also exchanged chips for hard money and currency. He had a reputation for scrupulous honesty, so there weren't many who balked at this arrangement.

At The Banker's table Devanor cashed in his chips and paper markers and got his winnings—less Duff's twenty-five percent, which remained in the strongbox—in hard money and gold dust. The Banker never looked up from his work. He never spoke. He did not acknowledge anyone's existence. His world was wholly composed of gold and money, the scale, the strongbox, wooden chips and paper markers—nothing else seemed to matter to him.

Devanor put a twenty-dollar gold piece in Wiley Roe's ham-sized hand and left the tent saloon, pausing just outside to draw a deep breath of cold night air into his lungs, clearing his head and letting the ringing in his ears subside. The icy chill in his smoke-irritated lungs made him cough. The rutted, muddy expanse of Gilder Gulch's one and only street lay before him, and the darkness, thankfully, disguised the unsightly clutter of the structures that lined both sides of the street. As usual, his gaze was drawn to the snow-covered flanks of the high peaks, ghostly in the moonlight. Their presence always managed to calm him, soothe nerves set on edge by the tension and ugliness and bustle of the gold camp. There was only one other thing that could soothe him like that. And before he even thought consciously of her, Devanor began to walk north, trudging through the mud of the street. He glanced up to see a familiar figure sloshing toward him. Devanor couldn't help but wonder if Luther Harley's unsteady progress was due entirely to the treacherous footing, or if the newspaperman had resorted a little too often tonight to his whiskey flask.

"Mr. Devanor!" said Harley, delighted. He brandished a newspaper from under his arm. "My most recent masterpiece. As one of the handful of people in this town who can read, I want to make sure you get one."

Devanor took the paper. "So your Washington hand press finally arrived."

"Indeed. Somewhat the worse for wear, but the contraption functions. Rather like yours truly, I might add." Harley chuckled, amused with himself.

"The *Gilder Gulch Argus*," read Devanor. He scanned the full sheet, printed on a single side, with six columns of cramped type. Half of the page was occupied by Harley's editorial, the rest by a list of claims and the news that two men had died in the previous week. One, a notorious drunkard, had passed out on the street in the middle of the night and had been run over by a lumber wagon the following morning. The other had been found in an alley with his head bashed in and his pockets turned out.

"Hmm," said Devanor. "I wonder where our friends the Doone brothers were on the night that poor soul met his untimely end?"

"I am given to understand that they had staked a claim about a mile upcreek. Read my editorial, if you please."

" 'Gilder Gulch has been in existence for less than six months, and already boasts of more than its fair share of scoundrels, cutthroats, confidence men, and women of ill repute, human predators who find in the gullible, ignorant heathens who populate this mountain Sodom easy and willing prey.' "

Harley grimaced. "It just gets better. I learned long ago the value of editorial abuse to attract a readership. People like to be chastised."

"I'll read the rest a little later, Luther. The night is young and I have some preying yet to do. How much do I owe you for this?"

"Nothing, nothing at all. Though I would point out that a yearly subscription is a mere twelve dollars. You can pay me at your convenience. And do read it, Charles. I mention Joe Duff's place later in the piece."

"In flattering terms, I'm sure," said Devanor dryly.

"But of course. Happy hunting." Harley moved on down the street, wobbling uncertainly through the mud.

Devanor continued in the opposite direction. Near the edge of town he turned down an alley between two buildings and came upon a row of shacks. Walking past them, he was propositioned by a woman lounging insouciantly in a doorway.

"Looking for a good time, mister?"

The gambler did not respond and moved on. Bawdy laughter issued forth from one of the shacks. A man stumbled out of another, tugging his suspenders up onto his shoulders. Devanor sighed. This was where the prostitutes of Gilder Gulch plied their trade; every shack was occupied by at least one of Harley's "women of ill repute." Some local wit had already given this seedy row of shacks a nickname— Paradise Alley. Working here, suspected Devanor, was more hellish than heavenly, though.

Reaching the last shack, he noticed with dismay that the door was closed. Sounds of a man in the grips of passion came from within—a sound Devanor did not want to hear. He walked on into the darkness, far enough so that he did not have to listen. There he stopped and waited, his back turned to Paradise Alley, feeling slightly sick to his stomach, wishing he could forget all about Alice Diamond, purge thoughts of her completely from his mind; wishing he could go back to his room at Gilder Gulch's so-called hotel and sleep until dawn, but knowing that sleep would elude him if he did not see her face and hear her voice. So he had to stay, had to wait, had to suffer.

Fortunately he did not have to wait too long. Ten minutes passed and then he heard a door creaking open on stiff whang leather hinges, and turned to see a man emerge from the last shack. He did not see the gambler standing in the darkness, but turned in the other direction, returning into the heart of the gold camp. Yellow lamplight spilled out of the shack's open doorway, and Devanor hesitated only a moment before starting forward. He was nearly there when a shadow fell across the lamplight and then he saw her, standing in the doorway, clad in a long golden wrap made of silk and adorned with scarlet Chinese dragons on the shoulders. She heard him, peered into the darkness, and when she recognized him her features softened and her body relaxed. She was afraid of something—he had already detected a fear that pervaded everything she did and said—something that she thought would come one day out of the shadows of her past and destroy her.

"Oh, it's you," she said, and she sounded pleased.

"Evening, Alice." He leaned against the front wall of the shack within arm's reach of her. The scent of her perfume washed over him; the smell of her always made him light-headed, but he did not want to get any closer for fear that he might smell other men on her, too. At the same time, his arms fairly ached to hold her.

"I'm sorry you had to wait," she said.

"No, it's quite all right. I don't mind." Devanor marveled bitterly at how ludicrous that sounded—of course he *did* mind, very much minded, and Alice was no fool—she knew he did, and why. But for some reason they had to continue playing the charade.

"Have you had any luck tonight?" she asked, groping for a safe topic of conversation.

"Yes, I've been lucky. I'm glad I decided to come to Gilder Gulch."

"So am I," she said, looking away as she said it. "But in your case I guess luck doesn't have much to do with it, does it?" she asked.

Devanor smiled. "Well, a little luck never hurt."

She pulled the wrap tighter around her throat. "It still gets awfully cool at night. Do you . . . would you like to come inside?"

Devanor glanced past her at the narrow rumpled bed that took up nearly half of the space in the small, one-room shack, and shook his head. "No, I don't think so. I just came by to see how you were doing. I won't keep you standing out here."

"It's all right. I'm glad to see you."

He nodded curtly, suddenly feeling the urge to escape. This was too discomforting to suit him. "I had better be going."

"Oh." He could hear the disappointment in her voice. She started to say something else, but stopped herself and managed a smile.

Devanor touched the brim of his hat. "Good night, Alice."

"Yes, good night," she said wistfully.

He turned away, then felt so much revulsion for his own cowardice that he stopped and turned back to face her.

"Alice . . ."

"Yes, Charles?"

She was so pretty, he thought, her delicate beauty in such stark contrast to the ugliness of Paradise Alley.

"Alice, there is a spare room at the hotel. I will get it for you. I would like for you to stay there, not here. This place . . ." He made a stiff gesture to incorporate all of Paradise Alley. "This place is not for you. It bothers me that you're here."

"Bothers you?" Her smile turned cold. "Why should it bother you? This is where I belong."

"If I have offended you, it was not my intent. But I have to disagree. You do *not* belong here, Alice."

"I am a prostitute, Charles. There is no point in denying it. I am among my own kind."

"I wish you would at least consider my offer."

"I doubt they would allow me to conduct business at the hotel," she said dryly.

"No, they would not. But you wouldn't have to."

"Oh, I see. So you want to *keep* me. *That's* what you are suggesting."

"No, it's not like that at all—"

"Yes, it is exactly like that. You would pay for my room, my meals. What else would you be paying for?"

"That's not what I . . ." He didn't know, in his anguish at having angered her, what to say to set things right between them. He was a man seldom at a loss for words, and when it did happen it was usually disastrous.

"But that's what it would be, Charles."

"Not the way I see it. I would not expect—I mean, I would never take advantage . . ." He could see that it was no use, and gave up. "All right then," he said stiffly. "My apologies. I will not bother you again."

"You're not a bother," she said, softening.

"Good night to you." Devanor turned on his heel and walked away with long quick strides, feeling like an utter fool, his cheeks burning with humiliation, angry at himself for the weakness that she caused in him.

It was still early. Joe Duff's tent saloon would be packed for hours yet. There would be plenty of gold seekers there willing to test their luck against his skill with the pasteboards. But Devanor wasn't in the mood. Because his thoughts were clouded, his emotions in such turmoil, he would not be able to play up to his game.

He went instead to the gold camp's one and only hotel—a long, narrow log structure, hastily erected like everything else in Gilder Gulch, consisting of a claustrophobic common room and a hallway providing access to a row of small private rooms. Devanor's room, like the others, had a single window that offered a view of a muddy alleyway, and a bed made of green lumber built into one corner. The bed sported a lumpy horsehair mattress covered by a frayed linen sheet and a thin quilt. These were the best accommodations Gilder Gulch had to offer. The only other place in town was a big tent down the street that could house three dozen customers on cots lined up so close together that a man had a hard time walking between them. Devanor paid dearly for the privacy afforded him by the hotel room—the weekly rate was highway robbery considering that the same amount of money would buy a comfortable, well-furnished suite in a respectable San Francisco hotel. But privacy was important to him, and never so much as at this moment, when he wanted nothing whatsoever to do with another human being.

Lighting a kerosene lamp that stood on a crate in the corner, the gambler stretched out on the bed, hands behind his head, and stared morosely at the low ceiling, listening to the muted noises of the gold camp and debating whether the only recourse left open to him was to leave this place in the morning. That seemed to be the only hope for his peace of mind. Gilder Gulch had nothing to offer him now except money, and suddenly money wasn't that important to him anymore.

Eventually he dozed off. A tapping on the door startled him awake. He swung his long legs off the bed, and two strides carried him to the door. As an afterthought he slid a hand into the pocket of his frock coat—the pocket that contained the over-and-under derringer. Opening the door, he gaped in surprise at the sight of Alice Diamond, wrapped up in a long dark cloak. She was the last person he had expected to see. He had supposed his visitor would be one of Duff's men, come to see why he wasn't at work making a profit for the Irish saloonkeeper.

"I have reconsidered your offer," she said forthrightly. "Is it too late to take you up on it?"

"Of course not. Please, come in."

She entered his room, moved to the center of it, then stopped and looked around with a bemused expression on her face. She turned to face him, and smiled.

"You don't have to leave the door open, Charles. I'm not a lady. I don't have to worry about my honor, nor do you have to be concerned about my virtue."

"You are a lady to me."

Startled, she gazed at him in wonder.

Devanor closed the door.

"I reacted foolishly when you made that kind offer," said Alice. "And I want you to know why I reacted that way." She sat on the edge of his bed; he leaned against the wall next to the door. "My story is not an unusual one, I suppose," she continued, looking at her hands which rested on her lap, fingers interlaced. "My parents were desperately poor. When my father died, he left my mother all alone. I was the eldest of eight children, so I did what I could to help. I became the mistress of a wealthy man. He had been after me for quite some time. He provided not only for me but for my entire family. But eventually he grew tired of me. Some men want only what they can't have, not what they do have. I was passed from one man to another. Then there was Philip. He made the mistake of falling in love with me. There was a quarrel. Philip was killed, and the man who kept me was placed on trial for murder. He was acquitted, of course. He was a very important man. Philip's family blamed me more than they did him. And they were not without influence. All the publicity shamed my mother terribly. Well, no, she was already ashamed; the publicity just displayed her shame for all the world to see. When I could take it no longer, I ran away. I came out here. I became what I am."

She paused in her dispassionate narrative, looked up at him and seemed to Devanor to look very much like a little girl hopelessly lost, vulnerable and afraid.

"You've never told anyone else this, have you?" he asked.

"No. So, that's why I reacted to your offer the way

I did. And now that you know all about me, if you want to take back that offer I will understand."

"The offer stands. But why did you change your mind, Alice?"

"Because you're in love with me."

It was not an answer Devanor had expected, nor the one he had wanted to hear, but he could not deny that it was true. He pushed away from the wall.

"I will go arrange for the room," he said.

"There is no need for you to go to that expense," she said. "Unless you mind sharing a . . . room with me."

She looked shyly away from the intensity of his gaze. It was not, of course, just the room she was offering to share.

"No, I don't mind at all. Should we go get your things?"

Alice stood up. "That can wait until tomorrow," she said, then walked over to the kerosene lamp, bent down and blew out the flame.

Chapter Five

It seemed to Pretty Shield that Cameron was as excited as a boy with a new toy when he rode into Gilder Gulch. She, on the other hand, was quite afraid—though she refused to show it. Cameron appeared clueless to the possible dangers of the gold camp, and that worried her most of all. He was blind to the risks involved in coming here, so that Pretty, who had always felt safe in his presence, now found herself cast in the role of protector. This was a heavy burden, made doubly so by her commitment to Gordon Hawkes to see that no harm came to his only son.

Naturally they were the subject of a great deal of curious attention by the denizens of Gilder Gulch. A buckskin-clad mountain man and Indian woman were not exactly common sights in the boomtown. And Pretty could sense that much of the scrutiny focused on her had more to do with the fact that she was female than that she was an Indian. But for the dozen or so calico queens of Paradise Alley, women were more rare than gold here—a shortage keenly felt by the two hundred men in and around the camp.

There was, as usual, a lot of activity at Joe Duff's

tent saloon, so Cameron gravitated in that direction, dismounting in front of the place and untying his rifle from the saddle.

"You stay here and watch the horse," he told Pretty.

"What are you going to do?"

"Just find out what's going on. This looks like a good place to do that."

"Cameron . . . ," she began, but he was in no mood to listen to any more of her dire warnings, and turned his back on her to enter the saloon.

Pretty slid off the horse, feeling much too exposed. Gripping the reins, she leaned her body against the animal's withers. It was the only living thing in Gilder Gulch that she did not at this moment feel threatened by.

Inside the tent saloon, Cameron stood and took in the sights and sounds and smells, jostled roughly by men passing in and out of the watering hole, and conscious of the looks thrown his way by some of the clientele. A thick-shouldered, redheaded man came up to him, grinning broadly.

"Haven't seen you around before," said Joe Duff.

"My first time here, that's why."

Duff gave Cameron's buckskins a closer survey. "Name is Duff. You can call me Joe. This is my place. Where are you from, anyway?"

"I'm from around here."

"Got any gold on you?"

"No, not yet. Where do I get some?"

Duff laughed. "You just stake out a claim, my friend, and start panning or digging."

"Oh."

"But then you come back here to my place and spend it all on bad whiskey and worse women, okay?" Duff slapped Cameron on the back with bruising joviality and laughed again.

"Has anybody around here struck it rich yet?"

"Well, I dunno—let me think about that." Duff looked around, brows furrowed as he pretended to give the query serious thought. "Yeah, I know one person who has. Me!" And again he laughed. "Come on now, belly up to the bar and have a drink."

"I don't have any money to pay for a drink."

"Since you're a newcomer, this one is on the house. But keep in mind that it's likely to be the last thing you get for free in Gilder Gulch!"

Duff made way for them both through the usual press of men congregated at the bar. He ordered a shot of whiskey for Cameron, which one of the barkeepers instantly produced. Cameron hoisted the glass and hesitated, looking at the amber liquid contained therein with some trepidation.

"What's the matter?" asked Duff. "Something floating in there that shouldn't be?"

"No, it's just that, well, I've never had real whiskey before."

Duff gaped in astonishment. "Well, then, my friend, it's time you started to live it up! Now drink her down."

Cameron nodded. "I'm with you all the way," he said, and knocked back the shot. Gasping, he put the empty glass down and gripped the edge of the plank bar in a white-knuckled grip as the liquor flamed in his throat and exploded in his belly.

"Well?" asked Duff. "How was it?"

Cameron nodded again, trying to catch his breath. "Good," he wheezed.

"A lot more where that came from. A man can get anything he wants around here—as long as he's got the gold to pay for it." Duff gave Cameron another hearty slap on the back. "See you around, my friend," he said, then plunged into the crowd of men.

Cameron lingered a few moments at the bar, taking in the melee that surrounded him. It was a novel experience for him, and an intoxicating one. Most of his life had been spent in isolation. Once a year his father had taken them to visit Fort Bridger, or an Absaroke Crow village—Gordon Hawkes had a good relationship with the Crows that went back a long way. During those all too brief summer sojourns with the Indians, his one and only opportunity to associate with people outside of his family, Cameron had fraternized with the Absaroke youth. Unfortunately, he had fraternized too intimately with a Crow maiden named Walks in the Sun. Their love for each other had led to a sexual encounter that had enraged Walks's family, and many of the other Crows as well, with the result that the ties between Gordon Hawkes and the tribe were severely strained. Cameron, for all intents and purposes, was banished from the tribe.

All that had happened a couple of years ago, and since that time Cameron had not been around anyone besides his family and Pretty Shield. Joe Duff's clientele were a rough and rowdy lot, loud and boisterous and sometimes violent—and they smelled bad, too— but Cameron could overlook all these shortcomings in his excitement to be among his own kind. He wanted to be accepted into this group, and to do that

67

he needed gold. That was obvious to him, as was what he had to do: take Joe Duff's advice.

He went outside to find three men loitering in front of the tent saloon, looking covetously at Pretty Shield, who was desperately ignoring them. They were whispering to one another and grinning lecherously, and Cameron bristled at their behavior. But he chose not to confront them. He had not come here to make enemies.

"We should leave this place," Pretty told him as he reached the horse and took the reins from her hand.

Cameron tied his rifle to the saddle and mounted Indian fashion without touching foot to stirrup. Once aboard the horse, he extended a hand to Pretty and helped her up behind him. He didn't say anything, just spared the three men a glance before turning the horse up the street.

Pretty Shield was relieved. They were leaving Gilder Gulch, and not a moment too soon in her opinion. She wondered what had happened to Cameron inside the tent saloon. Why was he so taciturn now? She supposed that she would find out in good time. Until then she made her own assumptions—that Cameron had gotten his wish; he had seen the gold camp firsthand and had not liked what he'd seen, and now they would go back into the mountains where it was safe.

They rode north along the creek, swinging wide around the numerous claims that prospectors had staked out along the stream. Not long ago the banks of the creek had been lined with trees and brush. Now all that had been cleared away, replaced by hastily thrown together shanties and lean-tos. A slope Pretty remembered as once being covered with a stand of beautiful aspen trees was now a muddy field of stumps. The creek that had once run as clear as crystal was now murky and soured. Men worked in it, panning for gold or using rockers. They stopped what they were doing when they heard Cameron's horse, and took up their weapons, watching warily as Cam and Pretty passed by. The boundaries of the claims were usually marked in some fashion—with crude signs or posts or piles of stone. The claims were not uniform in dimension. Each man or group of partners who staked a claim took whatever he or they thought could be defended from interlopers. The only law here was the law of the gun, and if a person trespassed on another's claim he could expect a violent response.

Cameron and Pretty rode about a mile along the creek before the claims began to thin out. Farther on there were still claims to be seen, but they were separated by stretches of undisturbed streambed. Below a bend in the creek, Cameron stopped the horse and took a long look around. Pretty wondered what he was doing, but said nothing. Finally Cameron nodded satisfaction and said, "This will do."

"What do you mean?" she asked, puzzled.

He didn't answer, swinging down off the horse and starting to work piling up water-smoothed stones into a pyramid about two feet high. Pretty stared at him with growing horror, reluctantly acknowledging to herself what Cam's labors meant. Once he had finished with the first pile, he took thirty long, measured paces along the creek and then proceeded to build another pyramid. Done, he stood and looked from one pile of stones to the other and again nodded.

"If I can't defend this piece of ground against all corners then I don't have any business being here," he said, more to himself than to Pretty.

"You *don't* need to be here," she replied, "and neither do I!"

His expression was one of ambivalence. "You don't have to stay. I would just as soon you didn't. Remember, I didn't want you to come along in the first place."

Dismayed, Pretty shook her head. "What has happened to you, Cameron? Why are you acting this way?"

"This is what I want to do. I'm going to do what I want for a change." Seeing how hurt and bewildered she was, he softened, walked back to where the horse stood and put his hand on Pretty's leg just above the knee. "I wish I could make you understand, Pretty. There's a whole world out there, a world full of amazing sights and big opportunities. Why should I be a prisoner of these mountains just because my father is?"

"Because you belong in the mountains, not here, not out there in the white man's world."

"Why not? I want to go places. I want to see things. Have things. I want to be somebody. This is as good a place as any to start." Cameron paused, studied her face and sighed. "I can see I'm not getting through to you. I've just felt trapped for a long time, Pretty, and I want to live for a change."

"I do not know why you need *things*," she said.

"You have these mountains to live free in—and you have me."

Cameron's half-smile twisted with bitterness as he turned away. "The mountains do not belong to me—and neither do you. Do us both a favor, Pretty, and go."

She sat there in the saddle for a moment, sorely tempted to follow his suggestion, wondering if she should find Gordon Hawkes and tell him what Cameron was doing and persuade him to come here and take his son away from this place, by force if necessary.

But she could not bring herself to leave Cameron alone, and so she dismounted.

"What do you think you're doing?" he asked.

"What does it look like? I am staying here with you."

Cameron was annoyed. "If you stay, I don't want to hear any more about how we should leave. We'll go when I have enough gold in my pocket to get us somewhere. Is that understood?"

Tight-lipped, Pretty Shield nodded.

"Okay then." In spite of himself, Cameron was glad she had decided to stay. He realized that her presence here might attract trouble—he kept thinking about those three men leering at her in front of Joe Duff's tent saloon. But he loved Pretty Shield, and would have been lonely without her, even though there were risks involved in her staying, even though she annoyed him at times. And even though he knew she loved his father, not him.

"It's settled," he said. "Let's get to work. We have a lot to do."

* * *

Cameron didn't know the first thing about hunting for gold, but he could be a quick study when he wanted to be. There was no point in going to one of the prospectors located along the creek and asking for help. Assuming he wouldn't be gunned down before he could get close enough to say hello, he doubted that any man embarked on the search for gold in and around Gilder Gulch would take the time to give lessons to a greenhorn like him.

The only thing left to do was to learn by watching. After hastily erecting a lean-to to provide himself and Pretty Shield with some shelter from the unpredictable spring weather, Cameron set about observing other prospectors on their claims. He used all the skills his father had taught him to get close enough to see what he needed to see without being spotted. There wasn't much doubt in his mind what would happen to him if he was discovered. They would figure him for a claim jumper or robber and start shooting without wasting any time on questions.

Cameron also returned to the gold camp, spending some time nearly every day loitering in Joe Duff's tent saloon and listening to the prospectors talk. He soon learned that one could not just take up space at Duff's place—if you didn't have hard money or gold to spend on whiskey or women, or to lose at the games of chance, you didn't stay long. One of Duff's men would show you the door, and none too gently if you protested at all. Cameron had come to Gilder Gulch without even two coins to rub together, but he knew how to improvise. Each time he came into the gold camp, it was with fresh-killed game.

Food was scarce in Gilder Gulch, and much of the game had been scared off. But he always managed to bring something in—white-tailed jackrabbit, or snowshoe hare, once even a mule deer, and occasionally marmot or muskrat; the hungry gold seekers weren't picky. Joe Duff, always attuned to the possibility of profit, paid him for the kills, then butchered them out and sold the meat at top dollar, secure in the knowledge that Cameron would spend all that he had been paid in the tent saloon. And he was right about that. Cameron spent his earnings freely, investing in information.

He learned a great deal.

He found out that placers—locations in a streambed where gold tended to accumulate, like the one George Jackson had found and which had resulted in the birth of Gilder Gulch—were popular because it was relatively easy for a prospector without capital or equipment to collect the gold. But a placer miner had to know what he was looking for; mica, or fool's gold, was often found in placers. Unlike mica, gold was soft. It would not break when hammered. You could bite into a pure gold nugget and leave teeth marks.

The one essential tool that a placer miner had to have was a pan, one about twelve to fifteen inches in diameter at the top, less than that at the bottom, and a few inches deep. Cameron got his hands on one and gradually learned the art of using it. You filled the bottom with sand and then added water; spinning the pan, you let the water slosh out, carrying the sand over the rim a little at a time. In a few minutes all that remained in the bottom of the pan was a soggy residue prospectors called the "drag." Spreading the residue out, the placer miner might find, if he was lucky, tiny specks of gold. These were extracted from the drag with the tip of a knife. Cameron learned that he could work about fifty or sixty pans of sand a day. But it was monotonous toil, squatting in a cold mountain creek for hours on end. Quite by accident, he had picked a good spot to do some prospecting. Within his claim markers was a gravel bar where gold accumulated as the waters of the creek swept around the upstream bend. A week's worth of work produced about a half quart of gold dust, which was worth around two hundred dollars at the going rate. Cameron was bone-tired, but elated. From his point of view, two hundred dollars was a lot of money.

Learning of Cameron's good fortune, one prospector suggested that they partner up, insisting that there was probably a "pay streak" below the gravel bar on Cam's claim. Gold gradually sank through sand and gravel to the bedrock underneath, forming a rich layer that could be as little as a few feet beneath the surface of the bar. He would need help to get to it, said the prospector. The creek had to be diverted away from the bar, which then had to be excavated. A lot of work, more than one man could handle, but probably well worth it. Locating the pay streak would likely net them thousands of dollars in profit. Cameron was intrigued, but he wasn't interested in sharing.

He decided instead to build a sluice. It was Joe Duff who told him to make one—a wooden trough built at a slant of about thirty degrees; at the high end was a hopper covered with wire mesh. Using a bucket or shovel, the miner poured loads of the gravel through the mesh into the hopper—the mesh eliminated larger debris. Then bucketloads of water were poured in to divert the material out of the hopper and down the trough, which sported strips of wood called riffles across the bottom. The water washed the sand down the trough and out the lower end, while gold-bearing drag was caught by the riffles. This was then panned. Cameron became convinced that he could work his claim much more efficiently that way, and collect gold far more quickly. He could construct the sluice from available timber—all he needed was some wire mesh. Joe Dull found some for him, and Cameron felt then as though he was really in business.

Others apparently thought so, too. Cameron began to see strangers lurking like vultures in the vicinity of his claim. He was pretty sure they were up to no good, and soon decided that it was no longer safe to go into Gilder Gulch, for that would mean leaving Pretty Shield by herself to guard the claim. And while she was as brave as any person he had met, and plenty scrappy in a fight, he wasn't sure she could handle a claim jumper.

On the other hand, it wasn't safe to send Pretty into the gold camp to pick up supplies, either. And someone had to hunt for game—an endeavor which inevitably took Cameron far from the claim, thanks to the scarcity of the wildlife in this valley.

A few days without coffee, sugar or flour for biscuits finally convinced Cameron that he had to risk it—he would go into Gilder Gulch one more time and purchase enough supplies to last them for the rest of their stay here, which he figured was only a matter of weeks. Pretty was happy to hear that, though she wasn't too happy about being left alone.

"There is a man who has been watching me," she told him. "He always stands over there." She pointed to a spit of land around which the creek made its bend about a hundred yards upstream.

This was news to Cameron. "Are you sure? I've never seen him."

She gave him a withering look. "Yes, I am sure. I do not see things that are not there."

"Well, how can you know that he's watching you? Maybe he's interested in my claim."

"I know. I can feel his eyes on me."

Cameron grimaced. "I have to go into town, Pretty. I'm leaving you my pistol. If this man—or anyone else—steps foot on the claim, just shoot him. Don't worry, I'll hurry. It won't take long. I'll be back before you know it."

And hurry he did. Returning to the claim, he was relieved to find that nothing had happened. "Did you see that man while I was gone?" he asked Pretty.

"No, not yet," she replied.

The next day Cameron saw him. The man stood for about an hour exactly where Pretty Shield had said he would be, at the bend of the creek. Cameron tried to ignore him. On the following day the man was back again. Annoyed, Cameron tried to stare him down. The man didn't seem to care that he had been discovered. He left the spit of land in his own good time, heading up the creek. Cameron noticed that he had a game leg. The next day he was back yet again. It was as though he was daring Cameron to do anything. Cameron worked at the sluice—he was in a hurry to take a few thousand dollars' worth of gold out of the gravel bar and then get out. But the stranger's presence nettled him. When he could take it no longer, he threw down the hatchet with which he was trimming boards for the trough and snatched up his rifle.

Pretty Shield had gone into the lean-to in order to remove herself from the stranger's view. Now she came out, alarmed. "What are you doing, Cameron?"

"I'm going to have a talk with that man," he said.

"No, don't do that, please . . ."

But, as usual, he would not listen, and angrily waded up the creek, making a beeline for the place where the stranger was standing.

The man held his ground. He was broad in the shoulder, with yellow hair and a gaunt, beard-bristled face, cruel lips and cold blue eyes. He was dressed like any other man in Gilder Gulch—stroud trousers tucked into mule ear boots, a red flannel shirt stained with dirt and sweat, his features shadowed by the low brim of a Kossuth hat.

"Who the hell are you?" asked Cameron curtly.

The man's smile was as chill as the north wind in the heart of winter. "The name's Mitchell Doone—if it's any business of yours."

"Ordinarily it wouldn't be. But you appear to be mighty interested in *my* business. Now, why is that?"

Mitchell Doone looked Cameron up and down with faint contempt lurking in his eyes.

"It ain't your business I'm interested in. Me and

my brothers already have a claim up the crik a piece."

"Then why do you keep standing here? Go work your claim and leave me alone."

"Don't go telling me what to do, boy. What I'm interested in is your squaw."

"She's not a squaw."

"She's an Injun gal, isn't she?" Mitchell's smile broadened into an unattractive grin. "Tell me something. Is it true that Injun women got no hair anywhere on their bodies?"

Cameron scowled, his temper flaring out of control. "I want you to stop bothering us, you hear?"

Mitchell didn't seem to. "I'll give you a good price for her."

"She's not for sale, damn it!"

"Then how 'bout we just rent her out for a night or two? Me and my brothers would make good use of her. See, I like to share with my brothers. But not to fret—we'd turn her back to you in pretty good condition. Just a little worn out, maybe . . ."

Cameron slammed the stock of his rifle into Mitchell's chest, hard enough to knock the man down. Snarling like a wild animal, Mitchell got back up spoiling for a fight, grabbing for the pistol stuck under his belt. But his game leg slowed him just a little—and he caught himself staring down the barrel of Cameron's long gun. Trembling with rage he fought hard to control, Mitchell Doone very slowly took his hand away from the pistol.

"What's your name?" he hissed.

"Cameron Hawkes."

Mitchell nodded slowly. "I like to know the names of the men I kill."

"I see you around here again, you could be the one who gets killed."

Mitchell sneered at that. "Oh, you'll see me again. You can bank on that."

"Get going."

Mitchell Doone turned and sullenly limped away.

Cameron waited until the man was out of sight. Then he crossed the creek, returning to his claim.

"Please, Cameron," whispered Pretty. "Let us go away from this place now! Please!"

"Not yet," he said curtly, and put down the rifle to continue working on the sluice.

Chapter Six

Three days passed and Cameron saw no more of Mitchell Doone during that time. He tried to tell himself that he never would, either—that Doone had decided not to press the issue and would leave well enough alone. But Cameron just couldn't quite convince himself of this. There was something about Doone that scared him—and there wasn't much that could rattle Cameron Hawkes. He wasn't real sure what that something was. He knew one thing, though: Doone was not the kind who would forgive and forget having been knocked down and humiliated. When he did come back, it would not be just for Pretty Shield. He would come for a reckoning with Cameron.

Cameron spent those three days finishing his sluice box. On the third day he put it into operation, and in a single afternoon harvested more gold than he had done in a couple of weeks of panning.

"Just one more week," he told Pretty. "Maybe ten days. Then we'll have enough gold and we can leave."

"Enough gold for what?" she asked, plainly skeptical.

"Why, enough for us to live in style for a spell, anywhere we have a hankering to be."

Pretty stared at him as though she didn't even know who he was anymore.

"I do not want to live in style. I want to live the way we have always lived, in the mountains. I do not want to live in the white man's town. I do not belong there."

"Well, maybe I belong there. Maybe that's what I want."

"You just think you want it because you have never had it. You have no idea what it is like."

"Oh, and you do? When was the last time you lived in a white man's town?"

"I have never done that. But I know plenty about white people. Enough to be sure I do not want to live among them."

"No, the only white person you really want to have anything to do with is my father."

Angered, Pretty Shield left the lean-to and went down to the edge of the creek.

Regretting his harsh words, Cameron went down to join her a few minutes later, and apologized.

"Tell me the truth, Pretty," he said, plaintively. "I need to know. Why are you still here, really?" His voice ached with emotional anguish, for he thought he already knew the answer. He just needed to hear it from her own lips. He thought that maybe that would free him from the hold she had over him.

"Because I care about what happens to you, Cameron," she said wearily.

"You sure it's not because you can't have my father, so being with me is the next best thing?"

She hit him, and he was caught completely off guard. It wasn't a slap—she balled up a fist and spun around quick as lightning, throwing a punch that connected squarely with his jaw and rocked him back on his heels.

"Damn," he muttered, rubbing his jaw. "Why in the hell did you do that, Pretty?"

"To teach you that you should be more careful with your words," she snapped.

"No, I think you hit me because I spoke the truth and you don't like the truth any more than I do," he said sadly. "Well, when I'm done here, I'm thinking about going down to Denver. Then maybe on to Santa Fe. Or St. Louis. I'm not sure yet. But I know one thing. I want to see what's out there. I expect I will come back to the mountains, all in good time. But first I want to see the world. Now, I know you don't want to do that. And I don't want you to come with me, anyway. What I want is for you to go now. Go tell my father that I'm well. Tell him what I aim to do, if you like. And tell him and my ma not to worry, that they will see me again."

She didn't say anything, but simply stood there for a moment and stared at him with a lost expression on her face. Cameron wanted to tell her how much he loved her, but he couldn't, because he really wanted her to leave. He wanted that not only because of the threat posed by Mitchell Doone, but also because it hurt so much, every time he looked at her, to know that he loved someone who did not love him back.

Finally she silently turned away, returning to the lean-to. This time he did not follow her, sitting instead on the bank of the creek in the cool twilight, trying to get used to being without her. In the long run he figured he would be better off alone. At least then he would not be confronted by a daily reminder of these humiliating circumstances in which he found himself. That was, after all, what he was trying to escape.

As the day drew to a close—the third day since Cameron's confrontation with Mitchell Doone—storm clouds began to gather, cloaking the jagged peaks that enclosed the valley. Cameron took one look at the menacing, black-bellied sky pregnant with rain and knew that one hell of a tempest was brewing. In the springtime, mountain storms struck quickly and with ferocity. There was little to be done in terms of preparing for the onslaught; Cameron knew the wisest course would be to get to higher ground, but that would mean abandoning his claim.

The angry clouds hastened the coming of night, and spectacular bolts of forked lightning stabbed violently at the earth, followed by thunder that boomed so loudly it sometimes hurt his ears. Cameron made sure his horse, made nervous by the noise, was hobbled and securely tethered before crouching in the lean-to with Pretty Shield. Bad storms were one of the few things that frightened Pretty, and in spite of the emotional turmoil they had just put themselves through, Cameron smiled and put an arm around her and tried to assuage her fears. He met with indifferent success on that score, though.

The first few drops of rain began to fall, large and heavy—and a few minutes later the storm struck in all its fury, the leading edge a maelstrom of whipping winds driving the rain in sheets, sometimes nearly parallel with the ground. Under such conditions, the lean-to provided no shelter at all. In seconds Cameron and Pretty Shield were drenched. Only when lightning flashed could Cameron see farther than an arm's reach away, but the lightning struck quite often, the attendant thunder so loud now that it made the very earth tremble.

Cameron watched with growing alarm as the creek in front of the lean-to began to rise at a rapid rate. He realized that he would lose the sluice box located at the water's edge, and he was helpless to do anything about it. Sure enough, the debris-filled waters surged higher and higher and made the sluice box teeter precariously on its stilts; and then another lightning flash revealed that it was gone. But Cameron had a bigger worry—the rising waters were getting closer to the lean-to.

A bolt of lightning struck so close that its flash was blinding. Cameron could feel its heat. Pretty cried out, and the horse tethered nearby screamed, a shrill, unnerving sound.

"Stay put!" Cameron told Pretty, and as the thunder pealed like a volley of musket fire, he burst out of the lean-to into the teeth of the storm. The wind tore at him, howling in his ears, the rain pounding against him. He peered into the darkness, stumbling in the direction of the horse, sloshing through ankle-deep water. More lightning gave him enough illumination to see that the horse was lying on its side. He rushed to it, knelt, lay a hand on it and in disbelief felt no life within. Had the horse been struck by the lightning bolt? Had it struck that close? He ran his hand down the animal's shoulder to its neck and felt something hot and wet and sticky. He waited for the next lightning flash with his heart pounding in his chest—and when it came he saw the big bloody gaping wound. Lightning had not done that. This was man-made butchery.

"Pretty," he gasped, and then louder: "Pretty!"

He whirled, and in the lightning's brilliance he saw Mitchell Doone, a hand ax in his hand, advancing on the lean-to. Cameron realized then that Doone had killed the horse, using the hatchet—and that the man was not finished killing.

"No!" roared Cameron, and groping for the knife sheathed in his belt, he rushed forward. Brandishing the hand ax, Mitchell turned to meet the charge. That placed him downstream while Cameron was facing upstream—so when yet again the lightning flashed, it was Cameron who saw, to his astonishment, a wall of water hurtling toward them, surging around the bend in the creek, careening against a tree-strewn slope and crashing down on the site of his claim. At the same instant he saw Pretty coming out of the shelter and he shouted at her to run for her life, but she could not hear him over the roar of the water and the rain and the thunder, all joined for an instant in an unnerving cacophony. Too late she saw the wave, taller than a man, and then it struck the lean-to, smashing it into kindling, and slamming into Pretty as well, and then Mitchell Doone, sweeping them both off their feet, carrying all before it.

Cameron had only seconds in which to react. But he knew that at best Pretty was a poor swimmer, so he altered course in mid-stride and lunged for her even as the wave bore her past him. He managed to grab her arm just as the water hit him and knocked him off his feet, hurling him downstream. The front of the flood wave passed in advance of him, and for an instant he and Pretty floundered in a shallow trough before a second surge picked them up and carried them onward. Cameron kept a tight grip on Pretty's arm and kicked strongly for the slope a few yards to one side, not fighting the powerful current so much as trying to use it to help him in his struggle for the slope. Finally, with great relief, he felt the ground beneath his feet and at the same time reached up to grab the low-lying limb of a birch tree. Turning over on his back, he dug in his heels and crawled out of the water on his back, pulling Pretty out with him. He did not rest until they were about ten feet up the slope from the edge of the water that rushed and roared past at high speed. It seemed to him that the floodwaters were no longer on the rise. And was it his imagination or did the deluge seem to lighten suddenly into a steady downpour? Lightning was still flashing constantly, but the leading edge of the storm had passed.

Nothing remained of his camp. The lean-to was gone, as was the sluice; he had lost his rifle, even his knife, in the floor. Cameron wondered how the claims downstream would fare. Probably no better. And what of Gilder Gulch? The gold camp lay directly in the path of the flash flood. Some would say, mused Cameron, that Nature was trying to eradicate the ugliness that man had wrought in this valley, that the storm and the flood were meant to purify through destruction. Pretty Shield, for one, would buy into that notion. Cameron wasn't so sure. All he was sure of was that he had less now than when he had come here. At least he and Pretty were still alive.

Exhausted, he lay on his side in the mud as Pretty huddled close beside him. She was shivering from the cold. He put his arms around her and pulled her body closer to him and shut his eyes. In the morning he would consider his situation and wonder about what came next. Now all he wanted to do was rest.

His final thought was of Mitchell Doone. The last he had seen of the man, he was being swept away by the floodwaters. He could only hope that Doone had drowned. Cameron soon drifted off.

Pretty's scream jolted him awake—just in time to see, in the gray gloom of an overcast dawn, the snarling rictus of Mitchell Doone's mud-splattered face and the hatchet sweeping down toward him. In that split second Cameron instinctively moved his head aside, just enough to save his life; it was not a conscious reaction, there was no time for that. The edge of the hatchet's steel head gashed his skull before biting deeply into the earth, shearing off some of his hair. Cameron flailed out, knocking Mitchell's arm aside, and whipsawed the man's legs out from under him. Mitchell fell, growling in incoherent rage, keeping a grip on the hatchet. Rolling away, Cameron got to his feet and yelled at Pretty to run. He didn't have time to see if she obeyed him—Mitchell was charging, the hatchet raised. Cameron feinted uphill then hurled himself downslope, rolling on a shoulder and coming up in a crouch. At his feet lay a length of shattered tree limb, as thick around as his arm and about as long. He grabbed it as Mitchell, veering, kept coming at him. Doone expected him to dodge to one side again, but this time Cameron lunged forward, slipping under the downward sweep of the hatchet, throwing up an arm to deflect Mitchell's misjudged blow, and at the same time thrusting the jagged end of the limb into Doone's midsection as hard as he could. The hatchet glanced off Cameron's back as it slipped out of Mitchell's hand. Doone staggered backward, groping at the limb that now jutted out of his middle. He stared at Cameron in blank surprise.

"You've killed me, you son of a bitch," he said.

Then he turned, as though to simply walk away—and Cameron could see the bloody jagged tip of the limb protruding from the man's back.

Mitchell Doone took one step. Then suddenly his legs buckled and he pitched forward to lie facedown in the mud.

"Is he . . . dead?" asked Pretty Shield.

Only then did Cameron realize that she hadn't heeded him, and hadn't run. He picked up Doone's hatchet and advanced cautiously, reaching down to grab Doone by the shoulder and roll him over. Mitchell's sightless eyes stared, unfocused, at the brightening sky. Cameron felt for a pulse at Doone's neck and wrist. Only then did he relax, lowering the hatchet and drawing a ragged breath.

"Yes, he's dead."

Pretty looked around. She saw no one. "We must go now."

"Go where?" Cameron glanced disapprovingly at his hands. They were shaking. It had been a very close call. He felt warm blood dripping down the side of his face.

"Anywhere. *But we must leave this valley now!*"

Cameron stood over the body of the man he had killed, trying to come to terms with what he had done, struggling to think rationally. That was a most difficult task after having just killed a man.

"Wait," he said. "He mentioned that he had brothers."

"That is why we must run, Cameron. Before his brothers find out what has taken place here."

"If we run, they'll come after us. I don't have a horse anymore, Pretty. I have no other weapon but this." He lifted the hatchet for her to see. "We wouldn't stand much of a chance."

"We will have no chance at all if we stay."

"This was self-defense. I had to kill him. No, I can't run away. I won't. I'm going to take the body into Gilder Gulch and tell everyone exactly what happened."

She stared at him, fists clenched in pure frustration. "Please, Cameron. Listen to me just this once. We go now and they will not be able to catch us. Not in these mountains that we know so well. On foot we can go places that they cannot follow on horseo. We will leave no trail. *We can get away.*"

"You just don't get it, do you?" he rasped. "My father lives the life of a fugitive, apart from the rest of the world until the day he dies, because he was accused of two murders he did not commit. If I run now, they will think I murdered this man. And then I will have to live as my father does. And that is no life at all!"

Approaching him, Pretty Shield reached gingerly for the wound on his head. But he moved away, and when she persisted he grabbed her wrist and gazed earnestly into her eyes.

"Pretty," he said, his voice soft but his tone firm. "I will tell you this one more time. I want you to go. Like we talked about before, only now it's more important than ever that you do as I say."

"I cannot leave. I have seen all that happened. I can tell them what you say is true."

He nodded. "Yes, that may be true. But if it goes badly, I don't want you around. I don't want to have to worry about you. I have enough to worry about."

She set her jaw in a stubborn line that by now Cameron knew all too well.

"Then leave with me," she said. "That is the only way you can get me to go—if you go, too. But if you stay, then I stay."

This time Cameron did not ask her why.

In spite of his head wound, Cameron managed to carry the corpse of Mitchell Doone draped over one broad shoulder the long mile into Gilder Gulch.

Where the gold camp stood, the valley was broader than upstream in the vicinity of Cameron's claim, where the slopes closed in on both sides of the creek. The flash flood had dispersed over the bottomland and hit the camp with much diminished force. Still, several of the town's flimsy structures had been wrecked, and the street resembled a lake of mud strewn with debris. Every claim above the town had been obliterated, and some of those below, as well. Many men milled around aimlessly, stunned by their sudden misfortune. Most of them assumed at first that the dead man Cameron carried had fallen victim to the natural disaster. Three men gathered in a knot of conversation on the street watched Cameron's progress for a while before wading through the muck to intercept him. Cameron stopped, staring at them with eyes dulled by pain and exhaustion. Pretty Shield had been trailing along behind; now she came up to stand close at Cameron's side, watching the three men with the wariness of a hunted animal.

"Who is that?" asked one of the men, nodding at Cameron's burden.

"His name was Mitchell Doone," replied Cameron.

"One of the Doone brothers?" The man glanced at his companions, then went around behind Cameron to lift the dead man's head so he could get a look at the face. "What about Chandler and Harvey? What happened to them?"

"Those are his brothers?" Cameron shook his head. "I don't know anything about them."

"So what happened?" asked one of the other men.

Cameron looked him straight in the eye and said, "He tried to kill me so I killed him instead."

The man who had asked the question glanced at Pretty Shield. Cameron thought, *He knows why it happened—because of her. He believes me, too. That means he knows what kind of man Mitchell Doone was.*

"You'll have hell to pay when Chandler and Harvey Doone find out," predicted the man, and there was pity in his eyes.

"It was in self-defense," said Cameron, making a weary gesture with an arm as heavy as lead to indicate his own head wound.

"Well, that's what you say," said the man who had spoken first.

"What he says is the truth," said Pretty.

"Yeah. Like I should believe an Injun."

Cameron walked right through them, and they parted to let him pass. Spotting Joe Duff standing in front of his tent saloon with a tall, lean, black-haired man in a mud-splattered black frock coat, he angled across the street in their direction. The two men stopped talking as he drew near. A few feet away from them, Cameron shrugged the burden off his shoulder. Mitchell Doone's corpse sprawled in the mud.

"Jesus Christ," muttered Duff, noticing the gaping hole in the dead man's midsection. "Don't leave that here, Hawkes! I don't know what to do with it and it's very bad for business."

Charles Devanor glanced at the saloonkeeper with faint contempt.

"That's too bad," said Cameron crossly. "I'm sick and tired of carrying him."

"That's one of the Doone brothers, isn't it?" asked Duff.

"Mitchell Doone," said Devanor, nodding. He looked curiously at Cameron. "Did you do that to him?"

"I had no choice. It was him or me. He wanted Pretty Shield here and he found out he was going to have to kill me to get to her, and that's what he tried to do. Now he's dead."

"Looks like he came close, though," observed Devanor, peering at Cameron's head wound.

"It looks worse than it is." Cameron glanced over

his shoulder. More men had joined the trio who had stopped him in the street, and he could tell that he and the body of Mitchell Doone were the subjects of their very animated conversation. "Mr. Duff," he said, "I brought the body into town—that should prove I'm telling the truth. I didn't run, because it wasn't murder. But . . . well, I'm not sure how many people here are going to believe that."

"I believe you," said Devanor, "because I knew Mitchell Doone."

"It doesn't matter if I believe you or not," said Duff. "There are two other Doones and they're the ones you have to worry about, my young friend. You killed their brother, and whether you were justified or not won't matter to them."

"He's right," concurred Devanor. "You need to get out of here."

"That is what I told him," said Pretty. "But he will not listen to me."

Devanor smiled. "Most men are too pigheaded to listen, ma'am, even though a lot of times women make more sense than they do."

"I lost everything in the flood," said Cameron. "And he butchered my horse. I need to buy a rifle, some powder and shot."

"You got anything to buy those things with?" asked Duff.

Cameron nodded. He pulled from under his shirt a small rawhide pouch that was tied around his neck. "I've got maybe a hundred dollars' worth of gold dust right here."

"Well, scaring up a rifle and some powder and shot around here will take a little doing," said Duff.

"Tell you what. I have a tent out back. Keep some extra stores in it, and sleep out there most of the time, too. You two can stay in there until I see what can be done for you."

"How long will that take?" asked Pretty.

Devanor could tell that the Indian woman had the right idea—she wanted to get out of Gilder Gulch right now, not a day or even an hour from now. The gambler was of the opinion that her instincts in this regard were right on the money. The buckskin-clad fellow named Cameron Hawkes was either naive or stubborn to the point of foolishness. Whatever the reason, he was taking a terrible risk. But Devanor kept his mouth shut.

"Not long," said Duff. "Don't worry. You can rely on me."

"And what about this?" asked Cameron, indicating the corpse at their feet.

"I'll have one of my men take care of it," said Duff. "Now, you two get on back to the tent and stay out of sight." He turned to enter the saloon.

As Cameron and Pretty started to move away, Devanor said, "I think there is one thing you should know."

"What's that?" asked Cameron.

"Duff was wrong about one thing. You cannot rely on him."

Cameron stared a moment at the gambler, then gave a curt nod, took Pretty by the arm and walked away.

Chapter Seven

It didn't take long for Chandler Doone and his brother Harvey to appear in Gilder Gulch in search of their missing brother. And since the recent arrival of Mitchell Doone's corpse was already the chief topic of conversation in the gold camp, surpassing even the damage done by the flood, the two surviving Doones were quickly directed to Joe Duff's tent saloon.

At first Duff had wanted to remove the body as far from his place of business as humanly possible. But just as he was about to order Wiley Roe to remove the unsightly carcass, Duff, ever the businessman, had an inspiration. So he had Roe carry the body inside his establishment and place it on the bar. This drew quite a crowd of spectators, evidence, if any was needed, of Joe Duff's uncanny business acumen. When Westerners congregated, whiskey was bound to flow, and as he had expected, Duff was doing a brisk trade in the usual rotgut.

There the body lay, in state, and covered up to the neck by a blanket when Chandler and Harvey arrived.

The crowd—which had become more boisterous in direct proportion to the amount of cheap whiskey

Duff's bartenders dispensed—fell abruptly and completely silent. Duff mused that it was suddenly as quiet as a church in his bucket-of-blood saloon. As if by magic, a wide corridor appeared between the saloon's entrance and the bar where the body lay, as the men parted to give the Doones an unobstructed path. Nobody knew exactly what to expect from Chandler and Harvey when they found out what had happened; consequently, everyone wanted to give the two men plenty of room.

The brothers scanned the crowd with cold blue eyes which finally came to rest on the blanket-draped corpse. All the observers present noted that Harvey appeared more dumbfounded than shocked, as though he just could not comprehend that Mitchell had drawn his last breath. Chandler, on the other hand, looked like he was ready to explode from barely restrained fury. His face drawn into taut, grim lines, he led the way through the crowd to the bar. Harvey fell in behind him almost reluctantly, like he really didn't want a closer look at what lay under that blanket.

Duff was behind the bar, and he noticed that both of his barkeeps unconsciously shrunk back at the approach of the Doone brothers; Duff couldn't blame them—his instinct was to do the same thing. But he stood his ground.

"Hello, Chandler. Harvey," he said. "This is a tragic day. My sympathies to both of you."

Chandler gazed at his dead brother's features for a very long time—or rather it seemed a very long time to Duff. So long that the saloonkeeper felt compelled to break the uncomfortable silence in hopes of easing the mounting tension.

"I had him brought here because, well, we didn't know what else to do," explained Duff. "And I knew how many friends would want to pay their last respects." He made a gesture that incorporated the crowd.

Chandler looked up long enough to spare Duff a withering glance. "Mitchell didn't ever have any friends," he said. Lifting the blanket, he turned momentarily pale when confronted by the sight of the gaping hole in his brother's chest. "God damn it," he rasped. "God damn it, I want to know one thing. *Who did this to my brother?*"

"Cameron Hawkes," said Duff. "He claims that it was in self-defense. He's got a pretty nasty wound himself where, apparently, your brother tried to split his head open with a hatchet."

Chandler glared at him and Duff raised his hands as though fending off a physical attack.

"I'm just telling you what Hawkes told me," added the saloonkeeper hastily. "There weren't any witnesses."

"Now, now, Mr. Duff. That's not what I heard."

All heads turned to Luther Harley, who had entered the tent saloon previously unnoticed, since everyone's attention had been riveted to the scene at the bar.

"And just exactly what have you heard?" asked Chandler.

"That in fact there was a witness. An Indian woman."

"Who says so?"

"She says so, Mr. Doone. She says that your brother was bothering her and Hawkes intervened. Soon thereafter, your brother decided to get even with Hawkes. And now he lays there, evidence incontrovertible that vengeance is a two-edged sword."

"Who told you all this, Harley?" asked Duff.

"Your business associate—and my friend— Charles Devanor."

Harvey's lips curled into an ugly snarl. "You can bet that anything that tinhorn says about us is a lie. Hell, he tried to kill Chand here before we even got to Gilder Gulch."

"Hmm." Harley smiled dryly. "Speaking of witnesses, I was a witness to that particular contretemps. And I believe Mr. Devanor was simply trying to teach a lesson in the courtesy a man should show a woman. Regardless, I might add, of her profession."

"What you said about Mitchell is a damned dirty lie," growled Chandler, pulling the blanket up over his dead brother's face. "He wouldn't want nothing to do with no stinking squaw. No, I'll tell you what really happened. He was murdered, pure and simple."

A murmur ran through the crowd. The men, it seemed to Harley, preferred Chandler's rendition.

"Now, just a moment," said the newspaperman. "Why would this man Hawkes have designs on your brother's life?"

"For his gold. Why else?" Chandler turned to Duff. "You find a sack of gold on the body?"

"Well I . . . I thought you would rather I did not disturb the body."

"You disturbed it enough to put it on display here. Well, I'm sure the gold sack is gone."

"Cameron Hawkes did show me a sack of gold," said Duff. "He said it was his,"

"Where I'm from, it's simple," said Chandler. "An eye for an eye, and that's it. This Hawkes feller killed my brother. So now I'm going to kill him."

Some of the men in the crowd nodded enthusiastically and voiced their approval. The kind of Old Testament law that Chandler was espousing was something they could understand. Harley surveyed the crowd and thought, *These men are angry. The flood wiped out a lot of them, or at the very least set them back. They have been hit hard and they want to hit back. And since they can't take their frustrations out on the mountains, they're looking for a more convenient target.* He knew none of these men truly cared that Mitchell Doone had been killed. And they weren't backing Chandler because they liked him. If anything, they feared him. Rumor had it that the Doone brothers were indifferent prospectors, at best—that they preferred looking for gold in the alleys of Gilder Gulch after dark. And perhaps, mused Harley, that was another reason the men were inclined to support Chandler. They were just too afraid to stand up to him. Who wanted to get in the way of Chandler Doone and his quest for vengeance?

"We're with you, Doone," shouted one man in the crowd.

"Yeah, I say we get a rope and hang the murderer!" shouted another, his voice slurred from too much of Joe Duff's snakehead whiskey.

Chandler glowered. "I don't need nobody's help to do what I got to do."

"Hold on there," said Harley, wishing he was as inebriated as some of the others in the tent saloon so that he might not have felt the pricking of his conscience. He had to stand up for law and order and reason or never look at himself in the mirror again. Devanor had labeled him a crusader, a man with a fondness for lost causes, and only in being that could he find any self-worth. Though reluctant to do so, Harley had to speak up. Because the gambler had been right all along.

To his surprise, the crowd quieted and gave him their attention, and Harley had to wonder if it was possible that he had more influence with these men than he had previously thought.

"There is a right way to go about this," he told them. "A man has been killed. The killer should be tried. His guilt or innocence must be established in a court of law."

"A trial?" A man in the back of the crowd laughed derisively. "Hell, how we going to have a trial? We don't have a courthouse. We don't even have a judge."

"The Territory of Kansas has circuit judges, and while none have seen fit to come through here yet, we can send for one. We will hold Hawkes in custody until the judge can get here and preside over a proper trial."

"That will take too long!" piped up the one who had suggested getting a rope. "Let's hang Hawkes and be done with it. That's what I call swift justice!"

"That isn't justice at all," insisted Harley. "It's cold-blooded murder."

"Like Chandler said, it's an eye for an eye," argued the man.

"Damn it!" roared Chandler. "I said it before—I don't need no help. There'll be no trial and there'll be no hanging, either. There's just going to be a reckoning." He turned to Duff. "You know everything—or like to think you do. I bet you can tell me where Hawkes is."

"Yes, I know right where he is," said Duff, smiling submissively. "I have him."

Chandler's Remington Army revolver seemed to materialize in his hand. He pointed the gun at Duff, thumb resting on the hammer, a finger on the trigger.

"Then you better hurry up and tell me where he is. I'm not a patient man."

The color drained right out of Duff's face. He knew Chandler Doone was a dangerous man—but the death of his brother made him completely unpredictable, as well. The pistol in his face, Duff realized, was no idle threat. Chandler was hurting and he wanted to hurt someone back, and he wasn't going to be too particular about how many someones that amounted to.

Swallowing the lump that had suddenly formed in his throat, Duff said, "He's out back. I'll . . . take you to him."

He headed for the tent's rear exit, followed by Chandler and Harvey, and the crowd of men surged after them. Luther Harley saw that he had no chance of getting through the mob, so he turned to leave by the front flap—and saw Wiley Roe standing there with a scowl on his craggy face.

"Wiley, do you know where Devanor stays?"

"Yes, sir, I know."

"Then go get him. Tell him to come here right away. And for God's sakes, hurry, man!"

Wiley Roe hesitated. "I dunno if I should—"

"Look, I know you take orders from Duff. But there's going to be bloodshed and it has to be stopped and I don't think I can do that by myself. Don't you understand?"

The big man just stared at him, seeming not to comprehend what the urgency was all about, and a dismayed Harley had to assume that Roe really didn't have much of an idea about what was going on.

"Never mind, Wiley. It's okay." Harley smiled reassuringly—and fleetingly thought how odd it was that he was treating a man who stood seven feet tall and weighed three hundred pounds like a small child.

The newspaperman left the saloon and hurried around back. The crowd of onlookers had already encircled the tent that Duff used for storage, and they could smell blood; the men were shouting, a mad, guttural sound, the words all but unintelligible to Harley. He braced himself and plowed resolutely into them. By the time he had worked his way to the front, he felt like he had been in a fistfight and gotten the raw end of the deal. He arrived just in time to see Chandler emerge from the tent, his face crimson with rage. Duff was standing there with Harvey Doone beside him, and Harley noticed how the saloonkeeper seemed to physically shrink under Chandler's furious gaze. Chandler raised the Remington and for an instant Harley thought he was going to shoot Duff. Instead, Doone laid the barrel of the revolver hard across Duff's face. The saloonkeeper went down hard. He grabbed his face and blood oozed between his fingers.

"What game are you trying to play?" rasped Chandler, looming over the fallen man.

"I-I don't know what you're talking about!" mumbled Duff.

"He's not in there!" roared Chandler. "You said he would be in that tent and he ain't. You said you had him. You goddamn liar. I'll show you what happens to people who get crossways with me." And with that Chandler aimed the pistol at Duff's head and thumbed back the hammer.

The crowd instantly fell silent.

"For the love of God," whimpered Duff.

"No!" shouted Harley. "Put that gun down, Chandler."

Harvey Doone glanced malevolently in the newspaperman's direction. "You keep your nose out of this," he muttered, " 'less you want to be next."

Harley scanned the grim, hushed crowd. "Are you all just going to stand there and let him commit murder? And you call yourselves men?"

"By God," roared Chandler, "I'm getting tired of you, Harley!" And he suddenly swung the revolver around to draw a bead on Harley's chest. Paralyzed with fear, Harley watched as Chandler's finger whitened against the trigger—and the realization that he was about to die battled with utter disbelief that this was actually happening.

"Pull that trigger, Doone, and you're a dead man."

Chandler turned his head slowly to see Charles Devanor standing within the circle of spectators. Wiley Roe stood behind him—though a moment before Roe had been in front, clearing a path for the gambler through the circle of onlookers, elbowing them aside with as much effort as other men would have exerted to swat a fly.

"Stay out of this, Devanor," warned Chandler. "It ain't none of your business."

"I'm making it my business," replied the gambler, his voice as hard as cold steel.

Chandler noted that Devanor's right hand was dangling straight down by his side, the hand concealed from Doone's view by the frock coat. He could only assume that in that hidden hand Devanor had the bone-handled derringer that Chandler was already acquainted with.

"I'll kill you, Devanor," he said. "I've wanted to ever since—"

"Yes, I know," said the gambler, his tone one of complete disdain. "Ever since your lesson in manners. So you're going to kill Duff and Harley and me. You're going to be very busy, Doone."

"I'll deal with anybody who gets in my way."

"Well, the man you really want is long gone."

Chandler stood, blinking, as though he was unable to understand what Devanor was trying to say to him.

"What do you mean gone?" asked Harvey.

"I mean gone. Departed. Left town."

"You helped him, didn't you, you son of a bitch," gasped Chandler.

"Yes, as a matter of fact I did."

"He helped a murderer escape!" came a voice of protest from the midst of the crowd. "He ought to be the one with a rope around his neck!"

"Is that you, Jeffers?" inquired Devanor, with a smirk on his dark, angular face. "Now, if you get rid of me, who would you bluff at poker?"

"Go to hell, Devanor!"

"Oh, I'm on my way. All in good time, though. Why don't you come with me, Jeffers? And Doone, you're invited, too. Maybe we can have ourselves a game of chance with the Devil himself."

Luther Harley gaped at Devanor. Confronted by the vengeance-seeking Doones and a hostile crowd, the gambler was actually trying to provoke a fight! Harley couldn't believe it. There was something raw and edgy about Devanor all of a sudden, as though he was in the grip of some kind of suicidal madness, and whatever it was, wherever it came from, it made Charles Devanor the most dangerous man Harley had ever seen—and that included Chandler Doone.

Everyone else sensed it, too. Even Chandler. The wild and reckless disregard that Devanor displayed—for the lives of anyone there, and his own life, as well—in a way evened the odds that had been stacked against him, so that Harley had to wonder if this lethal insanity on the gambler's part was not a bold ploy, a brilliant piece of acting designed to do precisely that. But somehow the newspaperman didn't think this was an act. He'd caught a glimpse of this darker side of Charles Devanor once before, on the journey here from Denver, when Devanor had tangled with Chandler Doone for the first time. The fatalistic gambler courted death as a release from some terrible burden on the soul, surmised Harley. Or perhaps as recompense for a monumental sin committed in a carefully guarded past? *I don't think I'll ever find out the truth,* mused Harley, *because he's going to get his wish. He's going to get himself killed before I can unravel the mystery.*

Ploy or not, Devanor's attitude saved his life. It made everyone present think twice about taking him on—and on further reflection no one, not even Chandler Doone, and especially not Jeffers—wanted to test the gambler's resolve. The crowd, only a moment ago aroused into violent mob action, was suddenly subdued, even ambivalent.

"Which way did he run?" asked Chandler coldly. "Was he mounted? Was he armed?"

"I have no idea where he went," replied Devanor. "All I wanted to do was get him away from here, and I accomplished that."

"He killed my brother!"

"Yes, that's right. No one denies it. But Hawkes had no choice. It was self-defense."

"You don't know that. That's just what he says. You weren't there."

"No, I wasn't there," admitted Devanor. "But I know what your brother was like, so I believe the story Hawkes told."

Chandler's eyes narrowed into slits. "You had better be careful what you say about my brother." He turned his attention to the crowd. "I'm going after Hawkes. Who wants to go with me?"

"How are we going to find him?" Harvey asked his brother.

"We'll find him," rasped Chandler. "Now, come on. We're wasting time. The longer we stand here the farther away he gets."

With that Chandler walked away, his strides long and full of angry purpose. Luther Harley was forgotten. So was Joe Duff. Harvey followed his brother; he had been following Chandler all his life, had even followed him out of their mother's womb, and he didn't know how to do anything else. Most of the crowd followed Chandler Doone, too. For some of them the prospect of participating in a manhunt seemed like great sport, a way to forget their troubles. For others, Cameron Hawkes had become the focus of their frustrations. Oddly, catching him had become as personal for the crowd as it was for the Doone brothers.

Devanor watched them go, then pocketed his derringer and offered Joe Duff a hand as the saloonkeeper struggled unsteadily to his feet.

"You better have that head of yours looked at," advised the gambler. "You're bleeding pretty badly."

"Like you care," said Duff crossly. "God damn it, Dev, you nearly got me killed."

"How do you figure?"

"You now what I mean. You came here and talked Hawkes into leaving, and all the while I thought I had him and I told Chandler Doone I did, and when it turned out I didn't, Doone was all set to kill me instead." Duff paused to draw a long breath. "God damn you, that's all I got to say."

Devanor smiled dryly. "I suspected you were up

to something. I didn't think you'd go so far as to hand him over to Doone, though, you sneaky bastard."

"Well, I . . ." Duff shrugged, suddenly defensive. "I didn't have much of a choice."

Luther Harley snorted at that.

"So what did you do?" Duff asked the gambler, studiously ignoring the editor of the *Gilder Gulch Argus*. "Did you give him a gun and a horse, for crying out loud?"

"Forget about Hawkes. He's gone. It's over. You can't make any more profit off this."

"You should mind your own business," snapped Duff. "Stick to playing cards. It's just healthier for you that way." He glowered next at Wiley Roe. "Who are you working for now, anyway? Him or me?"

"Wiley was just protecting your twenty-five percent," said Devanor. "So ease off."

"I would really appreciate it if you would stop telling me what to do!"

"If you'd do the right thing, I wouldn't have to keep telling you."

"I did the right thing—for me. Or tried to." With a gesture of pure disgust, Duff terminated the discussion and walked away.

With a doleful glance in Devanor's direction, Wiley Roe followed his boss back into the now empty tent saloon.

"Well," said Harley. "I guess I owe you my life."

"You don't own me anything," replied Devanor crossly.

"Why are you angry at me? Maybe it's because you didn't get your wish."

"What are you talking about?"

"You're still alive, my friend."

Devanor gazed bleakly at the newspaperman. "Don't try to play the hero anymore, Luther," he said. "You're not cut out for it." He turned and walked away.

Chapter Eight

When they left Gilder Gulch, Cameron and Pretty Shield headed north, making for the Hawkes cabin at the other end of the valley. From there it would be a fairly easy climb to a pass that would take them out of the valley altogether, the same route his father had taken only a month earlier. He didn't dare risk leaving the valley by the pass to the south; that was the trail connecting the gold camp with the Horseshoe Pass station and the outside world, and from what Cameron had heard it was well traveled. His object was to get out of the valley as quickly as possible—and undetected. He had to assume that everyone he would meet was a potential enemy, so he had to avoid all contact.

Everyone except the gambler, Devanor. Cameron still wasn't quite sure why the man had helped them. From some comments that Devanor had made about the Doones, Mitchell in particular, he assumed it might be because of some festering antagonism that existed between the gambler and the Doone brothers. But then there was something else behind Devanor's helping hand.

"Why are you doing this for us?" Cameron had asked him.

"Because I know about places like this," replied Devanor. "You'll get no justice here. I've seen an innocent man hanged before and I don't want to see it again, if it's all the same to you." With a troubled expression, Devanor looked away as he spoke, and it seemed to Cameron as though he was reliving something in his past that he would have preferred to forget.

Devanor had provided him with a horse and a pistol; he didn't say where he had gotten these things or how much he had paid for them. One thing was sure: Both the animal and the firearm had seen better days. The horse was a swayback mare at least a decade old, and had not known a saddle in a good long while. That didn't really matter, since Devanor had been unable to find a saddle for sale anyway. And the vintage pistol was a single-shot percussion; the gambler had acquired some powder and shot to go with it. Such things—really, all things—were scarce in Gilder Gulch, and sold at a premium.

"I'll pay you back somehow," Cameron told him. "I always pay my debts."

Devanor nodded. "That's an admirable trait. Now get the hell out of here."

As they rode north away from Gilder Gulch, Pretty Shield, astride the plodding mare behind Cameron, often checked their back trail. Cameron knew she was very apprehensive. So was he. He could only hope that if the Doone brothers set out in pursuit they would head in the opposite direction, toward

Horseshoe Pass, assuming that their prey had used the trail.

One of the Doones did just that. At Chandler's behest, Harvey took six men and headed down the trail that everyone who came to Gilder Gulch had to take to reach their destination. Everyone except Cameron Hawkes. Several of the prospectors in the hunting party told Chandler that they were pretty sure Hawkes had come down from the north, down out of the mountains. Maybe he lived up there, and maybe he would be heading home.

The problem for the mob was a shortage of mounts. In Harvey's group, some of the men rode double. Those who chose to go with Chandler could scare up only two horses and six mules between them. Chandler refused to let any of his men ride double; that, he said, would just slow them down too much. Eight men could come with him and no more. Someone suggested drawing straws to see who got to go along. Chandler curtly dispensed with such time-consuming nonsense. He picked the eight men at random, Jeffers among them. It really didn't matter to Doone if they were the best eight for the task at hand. He would have just as soon gone after Cameron Hawkes by himself. Whether the eight men chosen stuck with him to the bitter end or not was a matter of supreme indifference to him.

There was, however, one man Chandler did want along—the half-breed who worked for Joe Duff. It had been bandied about Gilder Gulch that the breed had once been an army scout, and rumor was that he had also spent time as a manhunter after his scouting days with Phil Kearny's Army of the West during the war with Mexico ten years ago. It was said that he could track a ghost across water.

"I want you to tell your man to ride with me," Chandler told Duff. "You owe me that much."

Duff didn't think he owed Doone a damned thing. All he wanted at this point was to be rid of the whole stinking mess. But he wasn't about to stand up to Chandler; he was in no real hurry to be clubbed with a pistol again. So the saloonkeeper spoke to the half-breed.

"He says he'll do it," the saloonkeeper reported back to Chandler. "But it will cost you a hundred dollars for his services."

Chandler grimaced. "And what do you get out of that? Your usual twenty-five percent, I guess, right?"

Duff shook his head. "I want no part of this."

"He'll get his blood money—as soon as he finds Hawkes for me."

A short time later, Chandler Doone was riding north with the breed and eight other men. Even with the breed along, Chandler didn't know how they would find the trail of the man he was after; assuming Hawkes had even come this way.

Late in the day they came upon the tracks of a single-shod horse. They followed it along the rain-swollen creek for an hour before the breed called a halt. He dismounted, knelt down and studied the ground. The rider of the horse whose tracks they had been following had also dismounted here.

"This is not the man you want," the breed told Chandler.

"How can you be so sure?"

113

"This one wears boots. I have seen the man you are after. He wears moccasins."

Some of the other men cursed. They had been on a wild goose chase for the past hour. But Chandler didn't appear all that upset. "Then we just keep looking."

"If we don't catch him soon, he'll get out of the valley and then we'll never be able to find him," complained Jeffers.

"I'll find him," replied Chandler. "No matter how long it takes."

They camped that night a dozen miles up the valley from Gilder Gulch. While the others were brewing up coffee at the crack of dawn the next morning, the breed saddled his horse and rode up the western slope, disappearing into a stand of aspen. Jeffers wondered aloud where he thought he was going, but Chandler didn't look like he was even paying attention. Doone lingered in camp as the sun rose to paint the high snowcapped peaks in brilliant orange, and the others, saddle sore from the previous day, didn't complain about the dalliance. Several hours later the breed reappeared.

"I think I have found their trail," he told Chandler, and pointed at the high reaches to the west. "They are going up there. I think they are trying to go over the mountain."

Without a word Chandler went to his horse, swung up into the saddle and rode out. The others scrambled to break camp and follow.

The mare was old and slow, and as they began making the sometimes steep ascent from the valley floor, Cameron had to wonder if they would not make better time on foot. Often he had to dismount and lead the horse over the rougher spots during the climb. But he didn't make a definite decision until he happened to look down from one vantage point and see the men who were in pursuit. They were about a mile away, yet there was no doubt in his mind who they were and what they were about.

Getting back aboard the struggling mare with Pretty Shield, Cameron urged the horse onward until, a short time later, he found what he was looking for—a log which was all that remained of a once tall and stately lodgepole pine. He steered the mare to an end of the log and stopped it there; at his bidding Pretty slid down out of the saddle onto the log. Cameron followed suit, then whacked the mare on the rump. Snorting, the offended horse lumbered away. Cameron watched, willing the animal to keep moving. To his relief the mare continued on and out of sight, angling downslope—the path of least resistance. He turned to take Pretty by the hand. They walked to the other end of the log—a good seventy-five feet—and then jumped to the ground and headed straight up the slope.

An hour later, the breed led Chandler Doone and the other men from Gilder Gulch past the log, following the tracks of the mare. But a little farther on the breed checked his horse and dismounted to take a closer look at the sign. Finally he straightened and scanned the slope behind them.

"What the hell is the matter now?" asked Chandler.

"This horse we follow—it carries no riders."

"What? How can that be? How can you be sure?"

The breed looked at Doone with ill-concealed disdain. "Anyone could see that the tracks made by the horse are not as deep now as they used to be. This means no one rides."

"Then they got off somewhere back there." Chandler angrily threw a thumb over his shoulder. "And you missed that, didn't you? I thought you were supposed to be the best at this kind of thing."

The breed did not reply. He got back on his horse and wheeled the animal around and headed back the way they had come.

Chandler and the others had no alternative but to follow.

When he reached the log, the breed again checked his horse. He eyed the log for a moment, then rode to the other end.

"They got off the horse here," he told Chandler, pointing at the log. "Then they walked along to this end." He gestured uphill. "They have gone that way."

"How long ago did this happen?"

The breed pursed his lips and made an educated guess. "One hour ago, no more than two."

"And now they're on foot," said Chandler, gloating. "By God, now I've got him!"

The breed merely shrugged. He wasn't so sure of that.

With strong legs and strong lungs, Cameron and Pretty Shield made good time. Now that he knew there was pursuit, Cameron abandoned any hope of returning to the cabin, and instead headed straight for the high pass that would take him out of the valley. And since they were on foot, Cameron chose the steepest and most difficult route, thinking that in this way he would slow down his mounted pursuers, or even force them to abandon their mounts altogether.

Then came the fall. They were nearly to the rim of a tree-covered ridge when a rock gave way under Cameron's weight and pitched him down the slope, head over heels. His foot caught against an exposed tree root but his momentum carried him on, and he gasped at the stab of pain as his ankle snapped. A moment later his fall was abruptly and painfully broken by a tree. He lay there moaning and dazed until Pretty Shield could reach his side. When she rolled him over on his back, he winced.

"Broke my ankle," he said through clenched teeth. "Think I-I busted a rib, too."

Pretty didn't say anything. He looked into her eyes and saw that she knew what he did—that this was as far as he was going to go for a while.

"Leave me, Pretty. Go on," he said calmly.

"Just rest a little," she said. "Then we will both go on. I will help you. You can make it."

"No. I can't make it and we both know that. You go get help. I'll be okay here. I think we've thrown them off. They won't find me now."

Pretty Shield scanned the slopes below. She had seen no sign of their pursuers since they'd abandoned the mare. But that didn't mean the men who were after them weren't still on their trail.

"I will stay with you," she decided. "I will set your ankle."

"Damn it, Pretty," sighed Cameron. "For once I just wish you would do what I tell you! If you go now, you could be through the pass by nightfall. Just go get my father and bring him back. Will you at least do that for me?"

Again Pretty Shield surveyed the slopes. And then she nodded. "I will do what you ask."

Cameron breathed a gusty sigh of relief. "Well, it's about time!" He managed a smile. "Pretty, I didn't mean what I said before, when we had our big fight. About how I thought you were only staying with me because you couldn't have my father. And how I didn't want you around. I've always wanted you around, Pretty. Except for now, of course." He grinned at her.

She smiled back, halfheartedly. "I will set your ankle before I go."

She did it quickly and deftly, and he hissed through clenched teeth at the jolting pain, and then she leaned closer and kissed him on the lips, a soft and lingering kiss good-bye.

"Go," he said, his voice husky with emotion, "and please be quick about it, okay?"

"I will come back soon," she promised.

Putting on a brave front, Cameron nodded and watched her go. She ran like the wind upslope and paused once at the rim to look back. Standing there, framed against the majestic peaks beyond, she raised her hand. He waved back. Then she was gone.

Somehow Cameron knew that he would never see her again.

*　*　*

In spite of the pain, Cameron dozed off, only to be abruptly awakened by the braying of a mule and the answering nicker of a horse. Looking down the slope, he saw Chandler Doone and nine other men about a hundred yards away. The one in the lead, a swarthy man with long black hair, was scanning the slopes above. Cameron recognized him as one of Joe Duff's men. So Devanor had been right—Duff was not a man who could be trusted. At first Cameron couldn't tell if the breed had spotted him or not—he lay partially concealed behind the tree that had broken his fall.

Down below, the breed turned to Chandler Doone. "I will take my one hundred dollars now," he said.

"The hell you say. You'll get paid when this job is done."

"I have done my job. The man you seek is up there." The breed nodded at the wooded slope.

"What?" Chandler peered up the slope. "Where? Where is he?"

"He is there. I have found him for you. Now you will pay me what we agreed on."

"Later, later," rasped Chandler, dismounting and drawing his Remington pistol.

"Not later. Now."

Something in the breed's voice made Chandler turn to look at him—and it was at that point that Doone realized the breed was pointing a sawed-off shotgun in his general direction. The breed wasn't exactly aiming it right at him, but the message was clear. At such close range, a double-barreled blast from the scattergun would cut him clean in two.

"You've got a lot of nerve pointing that damned thing at me, you bastard," said Chandler, astonished.

"I am finished here. You will do what you came here to do. I want no part of it. I do not kill people unless I am paid to do it."

Grimacing, Chandler produced a pouch that jangled with the hard money it contained. This he tossed to the breed, who caught the pouch deftly, weighed it in his hand and nodded his satisfaction. Mounting his horse, the breed rode away without another word.

Chandler glanced at the others. "Well, what are you waiting for? Hawkes is up there. This is what you rode all this way for. Let's go get him."

Jeffers and the rest of the prospectors seemed suddenly less enthusiastic. "What if he's got a gun?" asked one.

"What if he does?" Chandler sneered at them. "Oh, I see. You've all got a yellow streak down your backs. Why didn't you say so?"

Stung by his contempt, the men sullenly dismounted. All of them had brought along at least one gun—a rifle, a pistol or a shotgun.

"You," said Chandler, pointing at one of them. "You stay with the mounts. The rest of you spread out and follow me."

He started up the slope. Seven of the Gilder Gulch men fanned out in a ragged line and began to climb as well.

Wincing, Cameron managed to sit up and lean against the uphill side of the tree. He checked the cap and load of the percussion pistol Devanor had given him. His only hope was to bring down a couple of the men, and by so doing discourage the rest. He had killed before—when he and his father and Pretty Shield had been trying to escape the Dakota Sioux who had held Gordon Hawkes captive. Just the thought of taking life again made the bile rise in his throat. But it had come down to this—his life or theirs.

When the men were halfway up the slope, Cameron aimed and fired at the big, redheaded one in advance of the others. The pistol kicked in his hand. He narrowed his eyes against a drift of stinging powdersmoke. The bullet missed the big man in front but hit another who was coming along behind him. This man cried out in pain. Flinging up his arms, he toppled backward to roll down the slope. Cameron ducked back behind the tree as several of his adversaries returned fire. With steady hands Cameron swiftly reloaded the pistol.

"Come on!" roared Chandler, seeing the others falter. He waved the Remington menacingly. "Damn you all—I'll shoot you myself if you don't keep going!"

They took the threat seriously—and charged clumsily up the hill. They didn't realize that Chandler was letting them precede him this time. Their attention was wholly focused on Cameron's place of concealment. First one of them, then another, and another, paused to fire at the tree. Most of them missed their mark.

Cameron had been shot at before. He calmly finished reloading, took a quick look around the tree to spot his next target—and fired.

The bullet hit the man high in the shoulder, spinning him around. The wounded man lost his footing and slid downhill twenty feet. Groaning, he crawled behind a tree, clawing at his shoulder with bloody fingers.

Chandler had been waiting for Cameron to show himself, and when he did, Doone brought the Remington up and pulled the trigger. The bullet glanced off the tree sheltering Cameron. A sliver of bark gashed Cameron's forehead. He wiped the blood out of his eyes and quickly reloaded.

But when he pulled the trigger this time, the old percussion pistol misfired.

Cursing, Cameron managed to get to his feet, leaning heavily against the tree, gasping at the pain this effort caused him—he couldn't take a deep breath due to the cracked rib. He spun away as another bullet hit the tree inches from his face—spun right into the stock of a rifle wielded by Jeffers, who had put on a burst of speed to circle around behind Cameron.

Bright red blood spewing from his nose, Cameron fell sprawling, fighting to remain conscious. The world was bobbing around him—a world of pain and hopeless despair. He felt himself being lifted roughly to his feet and then there was more pain as he was slammed against the tree trunk. His knees gave out, but the man who had him by the front of his buckskin hunting shirt would not let him fall—instead, he slammed Cameron into the tree again, even harder this time.

"Look at me," hissed Chandler. *"Look at me!* You

know who I am? You killed my brother, you son of a bitch. *You killed my brother!"*

Cameron managed to focus on Chandler Doone's face. It was twisted into a snarling rictus of rage. Spitting a mouthful of blood, Cameron said, "He deserved it."

"You're a dead man."

"I know," said Cameron calmly. "And so are you."

Chandler pulled the trigger. He had the barrel of the Remington pressed into Cameron's chest, so the revolver's report was muffled. He let go of Cameron's shirt and, together with the men of Gilder Gulch, watched the lifeless body tumble down the slope.

For a moment no one said anything. From somewhere way off in the distance came an eagle's cry.

Jeffers glanced at Chandler. Slump-shouldered, his face blank, Doone just stood there staring at the body of the man he had slain, which had finally come to rest halfway down the slope. Feeling sick to his stomach, Jeffers looked at the others, and could tell by their expressions that they felt as he did: empty, nauseated and fervently wishing at this moment that they were anywhere else but here, at this place, a part of this madness.

"It's over," said Chandler, his voice dull. "My brother has been avenged. Now he can rest in peace."

Jeffers just shook his head and went down to check on the two men Cameron had shot. One was dead; shot through the neck, he had bled to death in a matter of minutes. The second man, though seriously wounded and still carrying the slug deep in his shoulder, would survive. Jeffers rounded up some help and carried this one down to the bottom of the slope where the horses and mules were being held. He was trying to bind up the wound when Chandler Doone and the rest of the men arrived. Chandler went straight to his horse and climbed into the saddle. He did not acknowledge the presence of the others, just kicked his mount into motion and rode away. The Gilder Gulch men silently watched him go.

Eventually one man spoke up. "What do you reckon we ought to do with the dead?"

"Take them back with us," said Jeffers.

"Even Hawkes?"

"Yes, him too."

For another moment they just stood there, listless, and not looking one another in the eye. Jeffers mused that they all looked like schoolboys who had been caught red-handed doing something inexcusable.

"I'll say one thing for Hawkes," muttered one of them at last. "He died game."

Jeffers could do nothing more than curse.

Chapter Nine

As was his custom, Luther Harley was burning the midnight oil when he got the unexpected visit that, looking back on it later, he realized had fundamentally turned his world upside down.

The newspaperman lived and worked in a small one-room log cabin at the south end of the gold camp's one and only street. It was barely big enough for his Washington hand press, a cot and a small kneehole desk. But that didn't matter to Harley. The place suited him. He had never been overly concerned with creature comforts or material things. The only thing that he really cared about was his work. And usually he did the lion's share of that at night. He was too busy during the day roaming the gold camp, watching its denizens, making note of their activities, looking for something of interest to put into the next edition of the *Argus*. Then, too, he normally drank a good bit as the day wore on, and frequently reached for his flask while working at the press or at his desk, so that he usually slept the morning away.

The knock on the door startled him. Rarely did he have any visitors, especially at such an hour. Curious, he went to the door and opened it.

A tall, wide-shouldered man in buckskins stood there. He had sandy hair and beard, and piercing blue eyes. They were the most haunted eyes Harley could remember ever having seen. A rifle in a fringed and beaded doeskin sheath was cradled in the man's left arm. This man was clearly no gold hunter.

"Can I help you?" asked Harley.

"My name is Gordon Hawkes," said the man, "and I've come for my boy."

Stunned, Harley took a step back. "My God," he gasped. Staring at the face of the man before him, he experienced a profound dread that chilled him to the bone. He thought, *I am literally looking into the face of Death.*

Hawkes stepped into the cabin, and only then did Harley realize that the mountain man was not alone—a young Indian woman had been standing behind him. She walked inside, too.

"I know you," said Harley, peering at her. "I saw you in town once, with Cameron Hawkes. That means you're the one Mitchell Doone was . . ."

He stopped, mortified by his insensitivity as he saw the guilt that she carried, and knowing that he had only made it worse.

"Yes," said Pretty Shield, softly. "I am the reason all of this happened."

Harley suddenly had an overwhelming desire for a good stiff drink. He went to his desk and resorted to the flask, taking two big gulps of the whiskey it contained.

"I know that my son is dead," said Hawkes, his voice husky and hollow. "Pretty took me to the place where she last saw him. There was a fight. Men died. It was ten against one."

"Yes, yes." Harley nodded. "Men died. Two of them. Your son and a fellow named Johnson that your son killed."

"Pretty told me everything that happened."

"Right. I for one believe your son killed Mitchell Doone in self-defense. But Mitchell's two brothers were bound and determined to have their revenge. There was no talking them out of it."

"But you tried anyway?"

Again Harley nodded. "For what it's worth, yes, I did. I tried to make the case that your son deserved a fair trial. But we have no law here, Mr. Hawkes, and such things as trials are a nicety that most of the men in this town did not appreciate."

Hawkes stepped closer, and in spite of himself Harley cringed. Being in proximity to the mountain man was like standing too close to the edge of an abyss. This was a dangerous man—made even more so by grief and rage.

"I want you to do two things," said Hawkes. "One is for me, the other one is for yourself."

"Yes?" Harley battled mightily against the urge to reach for the whiskey flask again.

"The first is, tell me where my son's body is buried. The second is, get out of town as soon as you can."

"Get out of town? Mr. Hawkes, I assure you that I was not one of the men who—"

"I know that. But when I'm done, this town will not be here anymore."

"You're angry, and you have every reason to be,

God knows. But revenge will profit you nothing, Mr. Hawkes!"

The mountain man's eyes narrowed into slits, and Harley could almost feel the heat of the barely contained fury that burned within them like coals in a banked fire.

"Don't preach to me," said Hawkes. It was not a protest, but rather a warning.

"I'll take you to where your son . . . rests," said Harley, and reached for his rumpled coat.

The gold camp's cemetery was south of town—a fact for which Harley was grateful, because it meant he did not have to accompany Gordon Hawkes through the gold camp. If Hawkes had anything to do with it, there would be some blood shed, and Harley wanted to at least postpone that from happening. He didn't think he could prevent it—didn't think even God Almighty could do that.

In its eight months of existence, Gilder Gulch had gone a long way toward filling up the plot of land located on the outskirts of town that had been chosen as the site for its bone orchard. The cemetery had been partially enclosed by a stone fence, rocks piled up a couple of feet high on two sides, but whoever had begun that project had abandoned it halfway to completion. By Harley's estimation, twenty-eight men had died in and around the gold camp—that number included Mitchell Doone and Cameron Hawkes. This number did not include several people it was believed had gone missing somewhere along the trail from Horseshoe Pass; it was presumed those individuals had met with foul play, but their bodies had never been discovered.

Some of the graves had crude markers—crosses or slabs of wood. And most had been covered with rocks. Coyotes had taken to excavating some of the burial sites as soon as they were occupied. They were also seen with increasing frequency lurking around the edges of the gold camp and prowling along the creek where the claims were located, scavenging for food, bringing down an occasional mule. And every now and then, usually very late at night, one might be spotted loping across the street or between the buildings right in the middle of Gilder Gulch.

A half moon seemed to be balanced on the shoulder of a high peak to the west, providing enough illumination to see by. Harley led Hawkes and Pretty Shield to a mound of stones in a corner of the cemetery. He stopped some distance from it and gestured lamely.

"This is it," he said. "I'm truly sorry, Mr. Hawkes. Truly sorry."

Hawkes stood and stared bleakly at the grave. "There's no marker," he muttered.

"No. Charles Devanor and I paid for the coffin, however. It was well constructed, I assure you."

"Devanor?"

"The one I told you about," Pretty told Hawkes. "The one who tried to help us."

Hawkes nodded, but didn't say anything. Harley could sense that it was all the man could do to maintain his composure. It was, decided the newspaperman, entirely too difficult to watch a father grieve over the final resting place of his son. Harley had never been married, never had children, and he could only imagine the torment Hawkes was suffering.

"Well," he said, "I'm sure you would like to be alone now, so I'll be going." He turned away.

"Harley."

"Yes?"

"Don't forget the second thing I want you to do."

Harley nodded and walked away.

He went straightaway to the gold camp's hotel, hoping to find Charles Devanor there. On his way, he paid little attention to all the activity in and around Joe Duff's tent saloon—there was nothing unusual about a raucous crowd being there well into the early morning hours. Two men were fistfighting in the middle of the street, such a commonplace occurrence that nobody was bothering to watch. Over in Paradise Alley someone was shooting off a pistol. Harley assumed the shootist had spotted a coyote or was drunk enough to use the moon for target practice. He doubted that one of the fallen angels who plied their trade in Paradise Alley was the target; women were too rare a commodity to kill.

His knock on Devanor's hotel room door was answered by Alice Diamond. Her eyes were sleepy and her hair was mussed and she was pulling around her a golden wrap adorned with crimson Chinese dragons.

"My apologies, Miss Diamond, for waking you. I would not call at such an hour unless it was very important. I must speak to Devanor. Is he here?"

"He must still be down at Joe Duff's."

"I'm sorry to have bothered you." Harley turned to go. Alice touched his sleeve to detain him.

"What is it, Mr. Harley? Has something happened?"

"No, but something is about to. Not to worry, though. Good night."

Harley retraced his steps and headed for the tent saloon. Devanor was at his usual table, playing five-card stud and methodically cleaning out three luckless prospectors. Harley shook his head—these men never learned. It didn't seem to matter how often they lost to the gambler or how much gold dust he took from them. They always came back for more, flirting with Lady Luck again. But then, as the newspaperman had told Devanor months ago, when they had first made each other's acquaintance, that kind of insane optimism, or compulsive risk taking, was part of the gold seeker's nature. It was their weakness, and could Devanor be blamed for exploiting it? Harley thought he could be, just as Joe Duff could be blamed for exploiting the miners' fondness—or call it weakness—for whiskey. The prostitutes of Paradise Alley allowed themselves to be exploited for profit; Harley supposed that made them somewhat less predatory than a saloonkeeper or a gambler.

Giving the tent saloon a quick survey, Harley saw neither of the Doone brothers. He slipped through the crowd and reached Devanor's table just as the gambler won a substantial pot with two pair, queens high. One of the other players swore fervently under his breath and pushed his chair back from the table.

"That finishes me," he muttered, and got up.

"It's been a pleasure," said Devanor, raking in the pot.

"For you, maybe" was the gold seeker's sour reply.

Harley settled into the vacated chair. Devanor glanced up and registered mild surprise.

"Come to bet the Gilder Gulch *Argus* on a turn of

the cards?'' asked Devanor, smiling. ''Or do you plan to harangue me again on the evil of my ways?''

''I need to talk to you, Charles.''

''You have to play to sit at this table, Luther.''

''I mean I need to talk to you privately. It's important.''

Devanor took a closer look at the newspaperman's face. Luther Harley wasn't a man easily rattled, but something had rubbed the man's nerves raw tonight.

''Well, it's about time I called it a night anyway. Thank you, gentlemen,'' he told the other two players. ''Better luck next time. Luther, wait for me outside. I have to see The Banker.''

Harley went outside while Devanor took his chips and paper markers to The Banker and cashed out. A few minutes later the gambler emerged from the saloon and, glancing at the peaks above them, brandished a Mexican cheroot. Harley struck a match and lit the cheroot for him. That put him close enough to whisper and be heard, which was a good idea since men were continually entering and leaving Joe Duff's establishment.

''The young man named Cameron Hawkes, that Chandler Doone killed,'' said Harley. ''His father is here.''

''Really.''

''Yes, really. And he's come for revenge.''

''Do you blame him?''

''You don't understand, Charles. What he said leads me to believe that he intends to destroy this town.''

Pondering this news, Devanor puffed on the cheroot for a moment. Harley backed up a little—he had seldom smelled anything more foul than the gambler's Mexican cigars.

"Well," said Devanor, at long last, "that would be a big job for just one man."

"Yes. But if one man could do it, it would be this one."

Devanor smiled faintly. "I believe he's got you spooked, Luther."

"He scares me, yes. As much as Chandler Doone ever did. Maybe more. Hawkes means what he says, Charles. And he advised me to get out of town immediately."

"Are you planning to take that advice?"

"Of course not. But I thought you might want to get Miss Diamond away from here."

"Thanks for telling me this, Luther. But I'm curious. If you believe what this man has told you, why *aren't* you leaving?"

"I would betray my professional ethics if I ran away from a story like this," said Harley, and laughed. Devanor thought the laugh sounded a little forced, and more than a little nervous. The gambler had to wonder if that was Harley's real reason for staying. Surely there was more to it than that.

"I think it's just wild talk from an angry man," said Devanor. "No one would be crazy enough to take on a whole town and try to destroy it single-handedly. No, he's here for the Doones, and to be perfectly honest with you, Luther, I wish him all the best in that endeavor."

"So you're intent on staying, too."

Devanor nodded. "I couldn't possibly pass up an opportunity to see Chandler Doone get what's coming to him. Now, you should go home and get some sleep, my friend. Believe me, Gilder Gulch will still be standing when morning comes. I'm not sure that's a good thing, necessarily—but it will be."

Harley grimaced. Get some sleep? That, he mused, was easy enough for Devanor to say.

He hadn't actually met Gordon Hawkes. Yet.

Joe Duff usually slept in the tent behind his saloon, and more often than not he slept late. Sometimes business did not slack off for the night until only an hour or two prior to dawn, and while Duff could have left the peddling of bad whiskey and the running of his games of chance to others, he normally supervised everything himself. Making money was what he lived for, after all. And Duff knew he had a good thing going in Gilder Gulch. The gold camp saloon was his ticket to great riches. And for someone like Duff, born dirt poor and afflicted ever since with lousy luck, getting rich had become an obsession.

The one thing Duff didn't have to worry about was the strongbox in which much of his profits were kept. The box accompanied The Banker to his room in the Gilder Gulch hotel, and The Banker was always accompanied by Wiley Roe and the half-breed, who stood guard over the room, sleeping in shifts.

Profits had been so good, in fact, that The Banker had cut a hole in his hotel room floor and placed another, larger, iron box underneath, in which a lot of the gold dust, currency and hard money now belonging to Duff was hidden. According to The Banker's meticulous accounting, there was about fifty thousand dollars' worth of profits in the box. The Banker had suggested having most of the profits transported east under guard, to be deposited in a bank where, he said, it would be safer. But Duff was reluctant to let the saloon's profits, even a dollar's worth, out of his reach. "When we get to one hundred thousand dollars," he told The Banker, "I'll take it to a bank myself." The problem with that, as Duff saw it, was the length of time such a task would keep him away from the gold camp; after all, the nearest bank as far as he knew was in Santa Fe, or maybe St. Joseph, Missouri.

The Banker merely shrugged. It was Duff's money, and whatever Duff wanted to do with it was all right with him. All he cared about were numbers. Numbers were reliable. People were not. Numbers made sense to him. With their foibles and weaknesses and irrational fears, people never had.

Although he did not have the money and gold with him at night, Duff took the precaution of sleeping with a pistol. A man was a fool to go unarmed on the frontier—and that was doubly true in a lawless gold camp. So on the morning following the arrival of Gordon Hawkes in Gilder Gulch, Duff was very surprised to wake up and find himself with an uninvited guest in his tent—but even more surprised when he groped for the pistol that was no longer where it should be.

"Is this what you're looking for?" asked Hawkes, holding up the gun.

Sitting up on the narrow cot which served as his bed, Duff stared at Hawkes and tried to put on a brave front. This buckskin-clad man looked as wild and unpredictable as the mountains from which he had obviously come.

"Who the hell are you?" he asked. "And who do you think you are, barging into my tent like this?"

"The name is Hawkes. And that answers your second question, doesn't it?"

"Hawkes." Duff got very pale. "Cameron Hawkes . . ." His voice failed him as the immensity of the peril in which he found himself hit home.

"Cameron was my son."

"I had nothing to do with that, I swear to God!" blurted Duff.

"Maybe, maybe not. But from what Pretty tells me, you know the names of the men who killed Cameron."

"Pretty? Who is . . ."

Hawkes was sitting on a cask, just inside the tent flap. Now he leaned forward, Duff's pistol in his hand, a sheathed rifle laid across his lap—and there was an almost feverish intensity to his gaze that made Duff forget what he was saying.

"The Indian woman who came here with my son. Now—I want those names. I know about Chandler Doone, but I want them all."

"You want them all dead."

Hawkes nodded.

"Nine men rode with Chandler Doone," said Duff. "You're planning to take them all on?" The saloonkeeper shook his head. "You must be loco."

"Give me the names."

Duff felt suddenly very cold. He began to shiver. It wasn't fear—or so he tried to tell himself. Even in early summer the mountain mornings could be chilly.

"Jesus Christ, Hawkes," he said. "I can't do that! Besides, those men didn't really do anything. It was Chandler Doone who took your son's life."

"Those men helped."

"If I told you what you wanted to know, I would be finished in this town."

"I see. So you're an honorable man—when it comes to saving your own life." Hawkes looked down at the pistol and at that point Joe Duff could no longer fool himself: He was trembling with fear and for good reason. Hawkes was thinking about killing him. "And your business," continued the mountain man, "means that much to you, that you'd rather die than ruin it."

Duff realized that this was his moment of truth. *You have fifty thousand dollars,* he told himself. *Tell him what he wants to know. Stay alive! Take what you've made so far and get the hell out.*

But he had waited his whole life for this chance, this golden opportunity the likes of which would not likely present itself again. For once he was in the right place at the right time and he had been the first one to get here—and now this son of a bitch was ruining everything. It just wasn't fair! Fifty thousand dollars was a lot of money. But it wasn't enough. Not nearly enough to make up for a lifetime of hard-scrabble poverty and a string of business disappoint-ments, of being treated like dirt by people who thought that they were better than he just because they had more money in their pocket than he did. And it wasn't even close to what he knew he could take out of this gold camp, given a chance—at least twice that amount and probably much more. This was a rich gold strike and the placer miners had hardly begun to harvest it.

If I leave now, mused Duff, bitterly awash in self-pity, *I might not be a nobody anymore, with fifty thousand dollars—but I won't ever be the kind of somebody I deserve to be.*

"I'm not giving you the names of those men," he told Hawkes. "You can kill me if you want to, but I won't do it."

Hawkes drew a long breath and stared bleakly at the saloonkeeper for a moment that seemed to Duff to drag on forever.

Then, without another word, the mountain man stood up and left the tent.

Joe Duff stared at the tent flap in disbelief. At first he was grateful that Hawkes had spared his life. But before long he was just angry. Pulling on his boots, he stepped out of the tent and saw his pistol on the ground. Picking up the weapon, he shoved it under his belt and made up his mind that the first order of business today was to go tell the Doone brothers about Gordon Hawkes. Chandler and Harvey would make short work of the mountain man. Then they could bury the bastard, right next to his son.

Accompanied by Pretty Shield, Hawkes left Gilder Gulch and rode up into the foothills above town. At the end of a wooded ridge he found a rocky promontory which provided a good view of the gold camp and the ugly clutter of claims along the creek. He settled down among the rocks and watched—and waited.

But what was he waiting for? wondered Pretty Shield.

She was afraid to ask. Afraid, really, even to speak to him. It wasn't anything that he had done that made her feel this way. He had not placed any blame whatsoever on her for what had happened. Yet she *knew* she was to blame. If it had not been for her, Cameron might still be alive. This was obvious and irrefutable as far as she was concerned. And it had to be obvious to Hawkes as well. Either he knew it and was not willing to speak of it—or he would come to that realization eventually.

Pretty was not afraid of being physically harmed by Gordon Hawkes. Although Cameron's death had wrought a profound change in him, she believed that she still knew the man well enough to be certain that he would not harm her. No, what she feared—and it would be far, far worse than physical harm—was that Hawkes would send her away, no longer able to look at her, or tolerate her presence. And who could blame him for feeling that way, after what had occurred?

So it was only natural that she tried to be as inconspicuous as possible and not speak unless spoken to.

It was almost too much for her to bear to be back in this dreadful place. She had broken down and wept upon returning to the hillside where she had abandoned Cameron to meet his death, alone. She did not often indulge in crying. And Hawkes—he had not wept at all. He had not to her knowledge shed a single tear, even though he had known the truth when he saw the blood and the bullet-scarred trees and the disturbed ground marking the places where men had fallen. These things had told him the whole story, and he could reconstruct the event as well as if he had been an eyewitness. And while he did not cry, Pretty could tell that he wept inside. And knowing that tore at her heart. She could not bear to see the man she loved so stricken with grief.

She did not want to be here, but she had to be. Not that she thought she could do anything that would come close to putting right what she had done. But she was bound to Hawkes more now than she had ever been. The bonds of love were strong, as they had always been. Added to them now were the bonds of guilt.

Hawkes remained at his post on the rocky promontory all day. Only when night fell to cloak the valley in darkness did he stir. Then he went to his horse and untied the blanket roll from the saddle.

"We'll camp here," he told Pretty.

She nodded. "I will get some wood for a fire."

"No. No fire tonight." Hawkes studied her face, knowing that she wondered what he was planning—knowing, too, that she would not dare ask. "We'll stay here tomorrow. Give them a chance to come to us. If they don't, I'll have to go down and get them."

Pretty spread her blankets a few feet from where Hawkes was lying. The night was cool; it would grow cold by the early morning hours. She recalled the nights they had spent together in a Dakota lodge, when he had been a captive of the Sioux. For a long time he had remained true to his wife, but finally he had succumbed to his loneliness and desire, and the days and nights that had followed that surrender had been the happiest of Pretty's life. Since then not a night had gone by that she hadn't wanted to be in his arms, that she hadn't ached to open herself up to the pleasure and fulfillment of his caresses. She didn't think she had ever felt more lonely and more in need of another human's touch than she did this night. But she could not approach Gordon Hawkes. He would probably reject her advances, and she did not want to suffer rejection. And if he did not reject her—well, then she would only be multiplying her guilt. So Pretty Shield rolled up in her blankets a few feet away from where Hawkes lay and watched him, wondering if he would be able to sleep, knowing that she herself would not be able to.

Chapter Ten

Though he had been presiding over poker games until three o'clock in the morning, Charles Devanor woke at the crack of dawn. He lay very still and relished the warmth of Alice Diamond's body, luxuriated in it, the feel of her hip and shoulder pressed against him, the scent of flowers wafting faintly from the fetching disarray of her chestnut brown hair. Watching her sleep, Devanor's thoughts turned—as they had been doing a lot since Luther Harley had informed him of the arrival of Gordon Hawkes—to leaving Gilder Gulch.

He had told Harley that, in his opinion, the mountain man's threat to destroy the gold camp was not something to be taken seriously. And he had assured the newspaperman that he had no intention of leaving because he relished seeing the Doone brothers—Chandler in particular—being brought down. But lying here next to the woman he loved, Devanor was having second thoughts. Again. He had them each time he saw Alice. He had gotten too much into the habit of thinking only of himself. Whether Gordon Hawkes prevailed or not, there was one certainty: There would be more violence in Gilder Gulch. Probably a lot more than had been the case before. And did he really want to take the chance that Alice might somehow become a victim of that violence?

Devanor was an extremely patient man. Patience was a virtue he had cultivated because it was an asset— make that a necessity—for the able poker player. In his opinion, poker was a game of stamina as much as skill. Impatience led to recklessness, and recklessness was a recipe for disaster. Especially against capable opponents, the successful poker player had to be able to wear down his adversaries, had to be able to play his best game over a long period of time with a minimum of mistakes, had to be able to recover from an occasional setback without getting desperate to recoup, and to accept the occasional small triumph without falling into the trap of thinking that *now* was the time to press the issue, before his opponent was really weakened sufficiently. Winning was all about endurance, all about knowing how to wait until the right moment to deliver the coup de grâce. The successful hunter was patient enough to wait until he had the best possible shot. The principle applied to the successful gambler, as well.

So it was that even though he had made up his mind to pose a very important proposition to Alice— one that would fundamentally affect the rest of their lives—Devanor was able to restrain himself from waking her. He lay there quietly, propped up on an elbow, gazing fondly at her face, so beautiful in the childlike innocence of repose, not marred in sleep by the anguish that lingered in her eyes and at the corners of her mouth when she was conscious, an anguish that was the consequence of a tragic past. *What is more important to you?* Devanor asked himself. *Her happiness, or your desire to see vengeance wrought upon the Doones?* The answer was simple enough.

He lay there, very still so as not to disturb her slumber, for nearly an hour. Eventually she began to stir, and Devanor smiled tenderly as her eyes fluttered open and she focused on his face. She smiled back at him, a languorous curl of the lips stirring his desire for her as she stretched beneath the quilt they shared, and almost purred in pleasure. Devanor resisted the urge to give in to passion, to kiss her and hold her and possess her and lose himself in her embrace. Resisted, even, when she curled an arm around his neck and pulled his lips down to hers. *I had forgotten how to make love,* she had once told him. *And I had forgotten what it felt like to be made love to. You've reminded me, Charles. You've brought me back to life.* Now that he had awakened this part of her, she was ver nearly insatiable, and was inclined to seize every opportunity, and considering the hours he worked in the tent saloon, they did not come with any regularity. Right now she wanted him, pressed her lithe body insistently against him, and he could feel the heat of her soaring passion through the thin muslin nightdress that she wore.

Reluctantly he curtailed the passionate kiss and, his lips so close that they brushed against hers as she spoke, murmured, "Have you ever been to San Francisco?"

Alice pulled her head back and gazed earnestly, curiously, at his face. "No, I never have."

"I think you would like it. There is much to do and see there. I get the feeling sometimes that you're bored here, Alice, and I don't blame you if you are. San Francisco would like you very much, too. You would be the most beautiful woman there."

She smiled. "Flattery, sir, will not get you anything that you have not already had, Charles."

Devanor chuckled. "And I would have to work much less in San Francisco. I could find any number of high-stakes poker games. I could make as much in a single night there as I do in a whole week here. Which, of course, means I could spend a great deal more time with you. I know it can't be much fun sitting in this room all by yourself at night while I'm at Duff's place."

Alice nodded. At night she was a virtual prisoner in the hotel. The gold camp was never a safe place to take a stroll, day or night, but it only became that much more hazardous after sundown. She seldom went out without him, for if she did it was inevitable that she would be accosted by men who, in some cases, remembered her from Paradise Alley and assumed she was still selling her body. Only once had she been so accosted when in Devanor's company, and the gambler had been quick to chase the offender off.

"You've been to San Francisco, then, I take it," she said.

"Yes. I spent a few years there. It has become quite a city. Even has an opera house, you know. Theaters, good restaurants—you name it and San Francisco has it. And if it doesn't, it will soon have it."

"Sounds wonderful. But why did you leave, Charles? Why would you trade a place like San Francisco for a place like this?"

He hesitated, brow furrowed. "That's a long story."

"I've got all the time in the world."

"Why don't I tell you," he said, "on the way to San Francisco?"

"Then I have another question for you—and maybe you'll answer this one." She grinned at him. "Why do you want to leave Gilder Gulch all of a sudden? Does this have anything to do with Luther Harley? He came here last night looking for you. Said he had something important to talk to you about."

Sitting up, Devanor ran his fingers through his tousled black hair and realized that he needed to be as candid as possible with Alice. She was too perceptive, and would not be easily put off.

"Remember that young man who killed Mitchell Doone? The one that Chandler Doone tracked down and shot to death, in turn?"

"Yes, of course I remember. A terrible, terrible business."

"His father is here."

"Here? In Gilder Gulch?"

"Well, no one seems to know exactly where he is at the moment. But he's close by. And he has come to exact revenge."

"Against Chandler Doone, right? Surely not against you, Charles. After all, you tried to help his son."

"This man Hawkes told Luther that, in effect, he blames the whole camp for what happened. He's declared war on us all."

"And that's why you want to leave so suddenly."

"I don't want you to be in danger, Alice."

"I don't see how I am, not from Hawkes."

"He seeks vengeance. An animal in great pain will strike out at anything. Nothing, no one, is safe around this man in his present state of mind."

"I see." Alice thought it over. "Charles—why do you hate Chandler Doone so? It can't be entirely because of what happened in that wagon when we were all coming here."

He stared at her. "Damn it," he said, and then smiled, "I sometimes think you're too smart for your own good."

"You really must tell me," she said softly. "Why do you want to remain such a mystery to me? I've told you all about myself, my past, my mistakes. I trust you—don't you trust me?"

Devanor lay back down with a long sigh, put his hands behind his head and stared at the ceiling. It was her turn to prop herself up on an elbow and look down at him. She reached out and traced his jawline with her fingers, her touch as light as a feather. Ringlets of chestnut hair fell across her cheek.

"I suppose I will have to trust you," he said, somber. "Trust you to still want to be with me after you have learned the truth."

"Of course I want to be with you, Charles. I want to be with you forever."

He took a moment to find the right words. "I hate Chandler Doone because he reminds me of the men in the mob that hanged an innocent man in San Francisco."

"You were there? You saw this happen?"

"Oh yes, I was there," said Devanor bitterly. "I

wish to God I hadn't been. But then if I hadn't been there, the hanging would never have taken place."

"I don't understand. What are you saying?"

"In the last few years, as San Francisco grew larger, there has been a lot more crime. And while they do have peace officers there, they haven't been able to maintain law and order very well. So some of the citizens finally banded together and formed a vigilance committee. They proceeded to take the law into their own hands. They dispensed justice without worrying about little things like trial by jury.

"One night, a man was killed in cold blood. He was just a harmless old drunkard, but someone gunned him down in an alley on the Barbary Coast. A pistol was found near the body. The gun belonged to a man named Andrew Roberts. The vigilantes seized Roberts and hanged him that same night."

"You said he was an innocent man?" she asked, still confused. "If he was innocent, what was his pistol doing beside the body?"

"Yes, he was innocent. I know he was."

"How could you know that?"

Devanor glanced at her and then quickly away. "Because he was playing poker with me the whole night. He couldn't have committed the murder."

"You tried to tell those vigilantes that, didn't you?"

"Of course." Devanor sighed. "But you cannot reason with an angry mob. Those men smelled blood. They wanted revenge. But they called it justice. Funny part of it was, some of the same men who hanged my friend Andrew had been known to kick and curse that old drunk while he lived. They didn't care *then* if he lived or died."

She gazed at him, trying to read him, sensing that there was still something he wasn't telling her. "Is that why you left San Francisco, then?"

Devanor nodded. "I had to get away for a while, you see."

"Poor Charles," she said, touching his lips with the tips of her fingers. "You feel badly because you couldn't stop those men from hanging your friend. That's why you helped Cameron Hawkes, isn't it? Because you didn't think you had done enough that night in San Francisco."

"Yes, I suppose that's true. I could have stopped it."

"No, you couldn't have. No one man can stop a mob."

"I could have."

"You really should stop punishing yourself."

"Those vigilantes didn't care about justice. What they did wasn't really about right and wrong. It was about fear. They were afraid, you see. Afraid for their businesses, their families, their own lives, because of the crime running rampant in the city. And when people are afraid they lash out—sometimes blindly."

"Yes, I know they do. I've seen it."

"Now Chandler Doone will be afraid. Afraid of this man Hawkes. Oh, he'll never admit as much. But I expect he will try to hide behind this town. And so Hawkes is going to start a war. And I want to take you out of here before it gets out of hand."

"You're ready to go back to San Francisco?"

"I would like to take you there, Alice. If you'll let me."

She thought it over for a moment. Devanor was confident that she would say yes. After all, she wasn't happy here in Gilder Gulch. So he was very surprised by her response.

"I'll go with you, Charles. But . . . not just yet."

"Not yet? Why not? Why on earth would you want to stay here even one more day?"

"That's not it at all," she said, looking away. "But . . . well, there is a dangerous and unpredictable man out there somewhere. Right now I just think it would be safer for us if we stayed right here."

"So you don't want to go to San Francisco. Is that it? We can go somewhere else. Santa Fe. St. Louis. Anywhere you want, Alice, How about London? Or Paris? You name it."

"No, I would love to see San Francisco with you. I don't care where we are as long as we're together."

"Do you mean that?"

She smiled at him. "Yes, I mean it."

"I would not let anything happen to you. You don't have to worry about Hawkes."

"But I do worry. And not for myself. I simply couldn't bear it if anything happened to you, Charles. I wouldn't know what to do. And I . . . I don't want to go back to the way it used to be."

Devanor relented. He was convinced that staying in Gilder Gulch would be far more hazardous to their health than trying to leave the valley, and he was confident that he could get Alice safely away. But she was afraid to risk it, and he decided not to press the issue, at least not for the moment.

Alice kissed him, and her passion ignited his own, and they made love—and for a while at least Devanor forgot all about Gilder Gulch and Chandler Doone and the mountain man named Hawkes. He even stopped dwelling on the fact that he had not been able to bring himself to tell Alice the whole truth about what had happened that night in San Francisco.

Because he was too afraid that if she knew the truth, she would leave him.

Late that morning Devanor arrived at the tent saloon and walked in on Joe Duff, standing on the bar and exhorting about two dozen of the gold camp's denizens to take action against the menace posed by Gordon Hawkes.

"I'm telling you," said Duff, "that this man is a danger to us all. No one is safe as long as he's alive. You're not safe anywhere, not even in town. I mean, he was right there in my tent, for God's sakes. He could have cut my throat while I was sleeping."

Standing behind the crowd, and speaking over the murmurs of its members, Devanor asked, "And why didn't he, I wonder?"

Duff peered suspiciously at the gambler. "Because he wanted the names of the men who rode with Chandler Doone."

"Which you refused to provide him."

"Of course I refused! Damn right I did. Even on pain of death I wouldn't betray my friends and neighbors."

"No," muttered Devanor, with a smirk, "you

wouldn't do that. That would be very bad for business."

"What did you say?"

Devanor spoke louder. "I'm just wondering why Hawkes didn't kill you after you refused to cooperate."

Duff scowled. "How do I know? We're dealing with a crazy man here. There's no telling what he'll do. All the more reason to go out and get him before he kills somebody."

Devanor shook his head. "You would be playing right into his hands if you did that."

"What do you mean?" asked one of the miners in the crowd.

"Because if you go out after him you're taking the fight onto his ground, and it will be on his terms. I suspect that this man has lived in these mountains for years. Most of you are lowlanders. He's a highlander, so to speak. And he is by nature a hunter and a fighter. He would have to be to have survived out here on his own. He could strike you down and you might not even see him while he's doing it."

"We made pretty short work of his boy," said another. "That wasn't too hard to do. I reckon we could handle the father, too, if we were of a mind."

"You think so, do you? I would remind you that the boy killed one man and almost did for a second. And he was badly hurt at the time. Sure, I suppose if every man in this valley went up into the mountains after Hawkes you would get him eventually. But I'd be willing to bet that some of you, maybe a good many of you, would never come back again."

"You tried to help the Hawkes boy," said one man,

his manner truculent. "Why are you trying now to help the father? That's what I'd like to know."

"I'm saying this is between Hawkes and the Doone brothers. It doesn't have to be any of your business. Go work your claims and let them settle it between themselves."

"Hawkes told me he wants *all* the men who rode with Doone," said Duff. "That means he wants them all dead."

"Were you one of those men, Joe?"

"You know I wasn't."

"Then you don't have anything to worry about, now do you?"

"You're a loner, Dev. You always have been and you always will be. You don't care about anyone else. But I do, and I say we all had better stick together. I for one will not stand by and let some lunatic murder my friends."

"We're with you, Joe!" shouted someone in the crowd, and most of the other men voiced their support, too.

Joe Duff waited a moment, basking in the approval of these men.

"We've got no law as such in Gilder Gulch," he then said. "No sheriff and no judge. It's up to us to keep the peace here and to protect ourselves. This man Hawkes is a killer. We have every right to go after him."

"Kill him before he kills us!" shouted someone.

Duff held up a hand to abbreviate a roar of approval for that sentiment. "But we've got to get organized. It won't be easy to find this man. Devanor is right about one thing: Hawkes knows these mountains. One thing we know is that he's here, in this valley, somewhere. He's close by. So we'll put together search parties and cover every inch of ground. Now, all of you go and tell your friends what we're going to do. We'll meet back here in three hours. Bring your guns and all the ammunition you can carry."

"What about our claims?" asked a prospector. "Who's gonna watch over them while we're gone?"

"Let it be known that the vigilance committee will deal with claim jumpers very harshly," replied Duff. "We will hang them."

Devanor shook his head. "That's just fine," he said to himself. "Another vigilance committee."

As the men poured out of the tent saloon, Devanor sat down at his usual table. Wiley Roe brought him a deck of pasteboards. The gambler thanked him, examined the cards, and then began to shuffle them. He glanced up as Joe Duff jumped down off the bar and approached the table, flush with success.

"You're a fool, Dev," said the saloonkeeper cheerfully. "You try to stand in the way of this and you'll get hurt. Maybe worse than hurt, if you know what I mean."

"You're the fool, Duff. While your vigilantes are out hunting for Hawkes, who is going to bring in the gold? You've bought into twenty-five percent of nothing."

"The gold can wait. This can't."

Devanor shrugged. "And where are the Doones? Where do they fit into all of this?"

"I warned them about Hawkes, personally. Chandler told me to mind my own business. Said he would take care of Hawkes in his own way and his own time."

"That's not what this is all about anyway."

"What do you mean by that?"

"This is about you, Duff. About power. You wanted to run this town from the very beginning."

Duff planted his knuckles on the table and leaned forward. "And maybe if you don't like that you should leave."

Devanor smiled, unruffled. "Oh, believe me—I would if I could. But that's no way to talk to the 'best thing that ever happened to you.' Care to play a friendly game of cards?"

The gambler flicked a pasteboard across the table at Duff. The saloonkeeper turned it over to reveal a ten of spades.

"You should be careful, that's all I'm saying," said Duff. "Your luck could run out."

He turned and went back to the bar to have a drink from his private stock.

Devanor turned the next card up and laid it on the table in front of him. It was a queen of hearts.

"It hasn't run out just yet," he murmured.

Chapter Eleven

From his vantage point, Gordon Hawkes watched as men rode out of the gold camp. He was a couple of miles away as the crow flies, but he could estimate that there were about ten to twelve men in each of the four groups that left Gilder Gulch that afternoon. One group rode south down the trail that led to Horseshoe Pass. A second rode north along the creek, up the valley, in the direction of the cabin that Hawkes had abandoned two months earlier. One rode east into the foothills. The fourth headed west for the wooded slopes below the rocky promontory where Hawkes had been keeping a tireless vigil for the past twenty-four hours.

Grim, he turned to Pretty Shield. "They've finally decided to make a move," he told her. "You'll be staying here."

"I want to come with you."

"Can you identify the men who rode after my son? Do you know this man Chandler Doone by sight?"

"No. I never saw any of them close enough to know what they look like."

Hawkes nodded. "Then you can be of no help to me. Only a hindrance. You will stay."

"But I want to help! I want to . . . to do *something.*"

He looked at her a moment, his expression one that was impossible for her to decipher. "Maybe there will be something you can do, later. But right now there isn't. And I don't want you to come with me."

Pretty Shield simply nodded.

He started to turn away, and then thought of something. "And if you try to follow me, Pretty, I'll tie you up and leave you."

Hawkes climbed into the saddle strapped to the back of his mountain mustang and rode away. Pretty didn't try to follow.

Angling down the slopes, Hawkes intended to intercept the group of men who were coming his way. When he knew they were near, he found a hiding place for his horse in a thicket at the top of a rock ledge about twenty-five feet high. He got down on his belly at the rim of the ledge, the Plains rifle beside him, and waited. As he had calculated, the hunting party passed almost directly below him. They were taking the path of least resistance in their slow, meandering descent. There were eleven men in the group, and by the looks of them they were all prospectors. All but two of them were riding mules; the other two were mounted on lowland horses that were struggling to make the climb, far less surefooted than the plodding mules or the mountain man's half-wild mustang. The men carried a wide array of weapons—pistols, shotguns, hunting rifles, knives, and hatchets. Hawkes noticed that one of them had an odd-looking rifle with a short, narrow barrel. He had not seen the likes of such a gun before.

Once the men had passed his position and were

out of sight among some trees, Hawkes returned to his horse and mounted up.

He shadowed the Gilder Gulch men for the better part of an hour. And though they were very watchful, they never knew he was there. By then the sun had long since sunk below the western high reaches and the valley was filling up with night shadow. The hunting party decided to make camp in a high meadow. Wood was collected, a fire built, coffee put on to boil. The mules and horses were put on a picket line and allowed to graze in the tall verdant grass that the meadow had to offer. Hawkes left his mustang some distance away and slipped in closer, unseen and unheard. He expected there to be at least one sentry posted. To his surprise, there were none. All the men were gathered near the fire. He could hear their voices droning in conversation from his place of concealment at the edge of the meadow, but could make out only an occasional word. He was downwind from the mules and horses, so they did not detect him. He could smell the coffee brewing, and then the beans and biscuits that the men cooked up for supper. Hawkes figured he could drop two or three of them by the light of the fire before the rest could scatter into the darkness. Then, in the dark, as they crashed through the brush in panic, he could account for several more. But that kind of slaughter was not what he was after. So he just waited, biding his time.

The Gilder Gulch men were tired. After supper some of them turned in immediately. Others had a smoke and talked awhile longer among themselves. The fire was allowed to die down. The stars were out in force by then, bathing the meadow in a dim, ghostly blue light. Finally Hawkes spotted what he had been hoping for. One of the men, the one who carried the peculiar long gun, walked away from the camp. He checked on the picketed mounts and then began to roam along the tree line, circling the meadow slowly.

At last, thought Hawkes. A sentry.

Still he waited, motionless. Several times the sentry passed within a few yards of where he lay, but remained blissfully ignorant of the mountain man's presence. Hawkes was waiting until the camp settled down—until he felt fairly sure that the other men were sleeping. And waiting served another purpose; after over an hour of patrolling the meadow the sentry became less alert. Not that it would have made much difference—alert or not, he would not have heard Hawkes when the mountain man finally decided to make his move.

Drawing a Bowie knife from its sheath, Hawkes waited until the sentry had passed by his position before getting up and moving in behind the man. He held the knife by its blade and struck at the back of the head with the bone handle, hard enough to knock the man out cold. The sentry went down without making a sound. Hawkes crouched beside the unconscious man and looked in the direction of the camp. All remained quiet. There was no alarm. Sheathing the knife, the mountain man picked up the sentry's rifle and, grabbing the man by the collar, dragged him into the woods. Well out of sight of the camp, he hoisted the man over a shoulder, stopped to pick up the strange gun and his own Plains rifle, and returned to the place where he had left his horse.

When the sentry came to and found himself lashed securely to the trunk of a tree, his wrists bound tightly together with rope, he saw a bearded, buckskin-clad man sitting cross-legged on the ground near a crackling fire just a few feet away, methodically sharpening the blade of a big knife on a whetstone. The sound the blade's steel made as it passed back and forth over the smooth stone grated on his nerves.

"Please," he gasped, choking on his fear. "Please don't kill me."

Hawkes looked up from his work. He put the knife back in its sheath, picked up the sentry's rifle, which lay on the ground beside him, and stood up. The sentry tried not to tremble too much as the mountain man drew near. Hawkes held up the gun.

"I've never seen one of these," he said.

"It's a Joslyn, Model 1855, breech-loading carbine," said the man quickly. "Some folks call it a needle gun."

Hawkes pulled a ring located on the top of the stock, raising a metal strap to expose the carbine's breech. "So you load here and not down the barrel."

The man nodded. "It's a fifty-four-caliber, made in Connecticut. I bought it off a sailor in California last year."

Hawkes lifted the Joslyn's stock to his shoulder and sighted down the barrel. "Can't be too accurate at long range."

"I don't know. I'm . . . I'm not a very good shot anyway."

Hawkes lowered the carbine and looked at the man impassively. "What's your name?"

"Malone. Benjamin Malone."

"I guess you know who I am, since you're out here trying to kill me."

"No! I mean, yes, I know who you are. But we're not trying to kill you. No."

"Really?" Hawkes smiled, but there was nothing friendly about his expression. "Then why did you bring this along?" He held the carbine up.

"Look here," said Malone, his voice pitched higher than normal. "All I know is they're saying you aim to kill every man in Gilder Gulch. I'm just trying to protect myself, that's all."

"Not every man. Not unless I have to. All I want are the men who were there when my son was killed. You weren't there—were you?"

Malone stared at him, his features a portrait of fear.

"I swear, I was not one of them."

"Then all you have to do is tell me their names."

"I—I can't do that. If they found out, they'd . . . they'd cut my throat."

Hawkes laid the carbine down, drew the Bowie knife and stepped closer. Malone made a guttural noise when he felt the razor-sharp cold steel against his Adam's apple.

"You mean like this?" asked the mountain man.

"For the love of God," whispered Malone.

"I'll ask you one more time. Their names."

"I don't know all of them, I swear it!"

"Then give me the ones you do know."

"Chandler Doone—he's the one who killed your son. Joe Duff's hired hand, the half-breed, tracked your boy down, but he wanted no part of the killing, so Doone paid him off and he rode out."

That won't save him, thought Hawkes. *If this is true, the half-breed killed Cameron as surely as if he had pulled the trigger himself.*

"You know more of them than that," he said, and increased the pressure of the blade against Malone's throat.

"Tom Jeffers! He was there. And . . . and Bill Radcliffe. Josey Crane. Ed Beechum, but Ed was the one your boy killed. And there was John Mellock. Mellock got shot, too, in the shoulder. The wound got infected and he's still laid up in a pretty bad way."

"There were three others."

"Yeah, but I'm not sure who they were. Might not still be around, for all I know."

"But the ones you named—they are still around, right?"

Malone nodded. He was nauseous with fear, and it was all he could do to keep from throwing up.

"Any of them ride up here with you today?"

"Yeah. Josey Crane. God help me."

Hawkes took the knife away from the man's throat. Blood oozed from the thin two-inch-long cut the knife's edge had made.

"God helps those who help themselves," he said.

Turning, he picked up the Joslyn carbine and kicked dirt over the fire, stomping out the embers. Without the fire's light Malone could scarcely see anything. The late-rising moon was a mere sliver, and the night sky was concealed from his view by the canopy of the grove of trees in which they were located. Hawkes was merely an indistinct form moving in the darkness, moving without making any sound, and that in itself was enough to unnerve Malone.

"What are you going to do to me?"

"Nothing," said Hawkes. "Unless I find out you've been lying."

"I ain't lying. But . . . but you're not just going to leave me out here like this, are you?"

"I've got some work to do," replied Hawkes. "When I'm done with it I'll come back and cut you loose. And then you're going to get out of this valley and never come back. Right?"

"I'll go. Don't worry. Let me go now."

"I'll be back."

"You're going after Josey Crane, aren't you? But what if you get killed instead? Then what happens to me? You can't just leave me here!"

There was no answer from the darkness. All Malone could hear were sounds he thought were being made by a horse moving away. He struggled in vain against his bonds. "Hawkes! Hawkes, you can't—" Abruptly he clamped his mouth shut, fearful that if he made too much noise the mountain man would come back and cut his throat just to keep him quiet. That was something he felt sure Hawkes could do—and experience no qualms in doing.

The men from Gilder Gulch began to rouse themselves at daybreak. The first man out of his blankets turned his attention immediately to building up the fire, stirring the banked coals and adding some kindling. At this elevation, even in summer, dawn could be a bone-chilling affair. Only when he had the fire going did the man, sitting on his heels and holding his hands close to the flames, scan the meadow. When he didn't see the sentry, he frowned and stood up and took another look around. Then he muttered a curse.

Coughing up night-gather, Josey Crane sat up and looked at the man. "What the hell is wrong with you, Joe?"

"Who the hell is supposed to be standing guard?"

"Malone took the first watch," replied Crane, pulling on his boots. "He was supposed to wake Armstrong up after four hours."

"He didn't do that," said a third man, also standing now to survey the meadow. "Where could he be?"

"I'll tell you where," groused Joe. "He's curled up out there somewhere, sound asleep!" Cupping hands around his mouth, he bellowed: *"Malone, you lazy bastard!"*

A shot rang out, just as a bullet plowed through the fire Joe had so painstakingly brought to life a moment before, showering his trouser legs with embers. Joe yelped and flung himself to the ground. Shouting, the other men rolled out of their blankets, grabbing boots and hats and guns and falling behind their saddles—the best available cover in the middle of the high mountain meadow. Another shot rang out, the bullet kicking up dirt as it struck the ground near the fire.

"Where's it coming from?" roared Armstrong.

"Over yonder," said Crane, gesturing at the tree line on the uphill side of the meadow.

"Is it Hawkes?" shouted another of the Gilder Gulch men.

"Now, how the hell would I know that?" asked Joe, noticing that one of his trouser legs was smoldering, and throwing dirt on it.

"It has to be him," said Crane.

Everyone ducked as another gunshot rang out.

"Where the hell is Malone?" asked Armstrong.

"Could be he's dead," said Crane.

That made everyone stop and think for a moment. Minutes crawled by in silence. It eventually occurred to them that quite some time had elapsed since the last shot was fired. Crane took the chance and raised his head to quickly scan the tree line.

"It's too damn quiet," muttered Armstrong. "I don't like this."

"Maybe whoever it was is gone," said Joe, but he said it without much conviction.

The shrill whinny of a horse, followed by another gunshot and then the thunder of shod hooves, whipped their heads around. They looked toward the picket line in time to see the mules and the horses galloping off into the trees.

Cursing again, Joe leaped to his feet as though to give chase.

"Joe, get down, you fool!" shouted Crane.

Another gunshot—and Joe was spun around. Clutching at his bullet-shattered elbow, he lost his footing and fell, writhing in pain, cursing louder than ever now.

"Stay down!" yelled Crane. "All of you—keep your fool heads down."

"Can't be just one man," said Armstrong. The first shots had come from the west, the uphill side of the meadow, while the mules and horses had been located on the downhill side of the camp. Armstrong doubted that a single man could have been shooting at the camp from one side and then made it all the way around to the opposite side in order to run off their mounts in such a brief span of time. "Maybe it's Injuns, Johnny," he said. "A war party on the prowl for horses—or scalps."

"Just keep down," snapped Crane, and glanced across the camp at the wounded man. "Hang on in the camp, Joe, just hang on."

"You in the camp!"

Crane couldn't tell where the voice was coming from. He exchanged looks with the other Gilder Gulch men hunkered down behind their saddles.

"Who are you and what do you want?" called Crane.

"You know who I am."

"It's Hawkes," hissed Armstrong. "Has to be. Damn sure ain't no redskin, that's certain."

"What do you want?" yelled Crane.

"I want Josey Crane. The rest of you can go. Just leave your guns and walk away."

The blood seemed to freeze in Crane's veins.

"Jesus," muttered Armstrong. "He wants you, Josey, on account of you riding with Chandler Doone."

Joe had crawled back to his saddle. Resting his head against it, he squeezed his eyes shut for a moment, took a deep breath and tried to conquer the pain that wracked his body.

"What are we going to do?" asked a man named O'Fallon.

No one replied.

"Well, maybe . . . maybe we should do like he says," said O'Fallon.

"Shut the hell up," growled Joe. "I ain't gonna run away with my tail tucked. Josey's a friend of mine. We stick together, that's what we do. Damn it, there are ten of us and only one of him!"

"Yeah, but we're not the one he's after," protested O'Fallon. "Why should we all get killed for something we had nothing to do with?"

"You yellow coward," rasped Joe. "Because Josey would stick with you if the shoe was on the other foot, that's one reason. But go ahead, run. See how far you get."

"He . . . he said we could go. Meaning he wouldn't shoot."

"He shot me, didn't he?"

"Maybe he thought you was Josey," said Armstrong.

"He doesn't know which one of us he's after," replied Joe. "You're as dumb as a fence post, Armstrong, I swear."

"Wait, Joe," said Crane. "I think O'Fallon is right. I think you should all get out of here. It's me Hawkes wants. I don't care to see any of you get killed on my account. Especially not you, Joe."

"Why don't we all make a run for it?" suggested another of the Gilder Gulch men.

"Run?" Joe snorted. "I got a better idea. Why don't

we all rush him? He couldn't hit more than a couple of us before we got to him."

"We don't know where he is," said Crane. "He moves fast, too, and I haven't seen a sign of him yet."

"I don't know about the rest of you," said O'Fallon, "but I'm getting the hell out of here." Rising to his knees, he held his rifle high overhead. "Hawkes! I'm walking away! Don't shoot!" He tossed the rifle aside, waited a moment, and then stood up.

"I ought to shoot you myself," growled Joe.

"No," said Crane. "No, let him go, Joe."

"I'm sorry, Josey," said O'Fallon. He hesitated, looking at the rest of the men—all except Joe and Crane. He didn't dare look either one of them in the eye. "What about the rest of you? Are you gonna stay here until he picks you off one by one? I don't know about you men, but I came here to strike it rich—not end up six feet under with my mouth full of dirt."

Several of the others stood up and threw down their weapons. Joe watched them in disbelief. Josey Crane wasn't paying them any attention, though. He was peering over his saddle, scanning the tree line, hoping for just one glimpse of Hawkes, just one clear shot.

"My God," said Joe as the rest of the men stood up and discarded their guns. Armstrong was the last one. "Well, I knew you were dumb," Joe told him contemptuously. "But it never occurred to me that you had a yellow streak."

"Come on, Joe," said Armstrong. "I'll get you back to town before you bleed to death."

"You go to hell. I'm staying right here."

"Get going, Joe," said Crane. "Get that arm tended to."

"You deaf, Josey? I said I was staying. I don't run out on my friends. And no loco mountain man is going to run me out of this valley, either."

Armstrong turned to the other seven men standing. "Okay, let's go."

They headed downhill, away from camp.

"Well, Joe," said Crane, "if you're staying, I've got an idea."

"Let me hear it."

"Hawkes shot you. He saw you go down. May be that he figures you for dead. That could work in our favor."

Joe nodded. "I think I know what you've got in mind. Just get him in close, Josey, and I'll plug the son of a bitch."

Crane snugged a pistol under his belt at the small of his back. "Well, here goes," he muttered, and got up on his knees, holding his rifle high over his head, just as O'Fallon and the others had done. "Hawkes!" he shouted. "Don't shoot. I'm Crane. But I didn't shoot your boy and I don't want to die."

A minute passed—the longest minute of Josey Crane's life. He half expected to be shot down, and even found himself hoping that Hawkes was a good enough marksman to make it quick and painless.

Then he saw a bearded man in buckskins emerge from the trees, walking toward the camp with a Plains rifle racked on one shoulder.

"Here he comes," said Crane out of the side of his mouth. "And it looks like he's alone, Joe."

Joe lay with his back to Crane, unmoving. "Keep your nerve, Josey. We'll get him."

Hawkes stopped about twenty paces from where Crane was standing. The mountain man glanced at Joe, then fastened cold blue eyes on Crane.

"So you're Josey Crane, then," he said.

"That's right. You going to shoot me down in cold blood?"

"Maybe. But first, tell your friend to get up, slow and easy."

"He's dead. You killed him."

Hawkes smiled coldly. "I hit him right where I meant to."

Crane's expression gave him away. Reaching back for his pistol, he shouted at Joe. Rolling over, Joe fired his own pistol, but the shot went wide. Sweeping the Plains rifle down, Hawkes pulled the trigger. His bullet hit Joe squarely in the chest. An instant later Crane was dropping into a crouch and aiming his pistol at the mountain man. Throwing down the empty rifle, Hawkes whipped his Bowie knife out of its sheath. Crane fired just as he threw the knife. The bullet grazed the mountain man's shoulder. Crane lowered the pistol and stared in disbelief at the knife, which had penetrated to the hilt right below his sternum. He clutched the handle with a trembling hand, then dropped his pistol and grabbed the knife with the other hand as well. Looking blankly at Hawkes, he pulled the knife out, doubled over, blood drooling from between his lips, and pitched forward on his face.

Checking his shoulder, Hawkes was relieved to see that the wound was minor. His next order of business was reloading the Hawken rifle. That done, he checked Josey Crane for any signs of life. There was only a faint pulse to be found. Hawkes didn't bother checking Joe—he knew the other man was gone. He sat on his heels beside Crane and waited. A few minutes later, curled up in a fetal ball, clutching his midsection, Josey Crane breathed his last. *One down*, thought Hawkes. *Eight to go.*

Squatting there beside the corpse a little while longer, Hawkes wondered why he didn't feel satisfied with what he had done. He had hoped that at the very least he would feel a little less of the pain brought on by the loss of his son, which ached so terribly and with such constancy within him. Or perhaps a little less of the horrible emptiness that he had tried to fill up with rage. Instead, he had taken two lives, and now he felt worse rather than better.

Eliza had warned him. She had told him that it would be this way. She had known that if Cameron was dead, Hawkes would want vengeance.

"Every time you take a life you kill a little piece of yourself," she had said. "And no matter how many lives you take you will never be able to put right what went wrong."

But he had not heeded her. The problem was, he thought, that Eliza really didn't understand. He *had* to do something, because he had not done what he should have before—namely, to somehow prevent Cameron from going to the gold camp in the first place. It was a sin of omission that he had to wash away. He had failed Cameron once. To simply walk away from this would be tantamount to failing his son a second time.

He glanced at the face of Josey Crane, frozen in a grimace of pain, the sightless eyes staring in vacant shock. This man had seen his son being killed. Hawkes didn't think he would be able to let go until all the men who had seen that outrage were dead. No one must live to tell that tale.

Wearily, Hawkes got to his feet and glanced skyward to see that the first buzzard was already circling. Soon the sky would be filled with them, and eventually they would descend to begin the process of removing any trace of the sin he had committed here on account of the sin that had been committed against the flesh of his flesh.

Returning to where he had tied the mountain mustang, Hawkes rode back to where he'd left Ben Malone. He steered the horse right up to the tree to which Malone was lashed and, using the Bowie knife, cut the prospector's bonds. Malone made no sound. He dared not say anything. He didn't have to ask if Hawkes had found Josey Crane—from the expression on the mountain man's face, he had a pretty good idea about what had happened.

Hawkes didn't say anything either. Sheathing the knife, he rode away into the darkening woods. Malone watched him go, rubbing his raw and bleeding wrists, before starting down the mountain. He had no intention of going back to Gilder Gulch. Once he hit the valley floor, he was heading down the trail to Horseshoe Pass—and he was *never* coming back to the mountains again.

Chapter Twelve

On the following day thirty men went up into the mountains to recover the bodies of Josey Crane and Joe Harris—and, they thought, probably Ben Malone's as well. Taking note of all the goings on for the special edition of the *Argus* he planned to print that night, Luther Harley thought it odd that everyone involved seemed certain that this was no rescue party, that Crane and Harris and Malone were dead. Armstrong and O'Fallon and the other men who had walked into the gold camp late yesterday had told their story—and then to a man packed up their gear and left town, heading down the south trail that would take them out of the valley. Apparently everyone assumed that the three men left behind had met their end at the hands of the wild mountain man Gordon Hawkes.

Gilder Gulch was gripped by fear. How else to explain the necessity of thirty men to go up and recover the bodies? And why else were men leaving the gold camp in droves? In addition to O'Fallon and the seven other men who had abandoned Crane and Harris to their fate, at least twenty other gold seekers hit the trail for Horseshoe Pass that same day. At this rate, mused Harley, Gilder Gulch would be a ghost town within a fortnight. He decided to go see what Joe Duff had to say about that.

As expected, he found Duff in the tent saloon. What wasn't expected was the fact that the watering hole—what Harley sardonically dubbed the cultural center of Gilder Gulch—was virtually empty. The Banker was at his post in the corner, with the strongbox and his shotgun-toting guardian, the half-breed. Devanor was at his usual table, playing a desultory hand of solitaire. Duff was behind the bar talking to a bartender. When Harley came through the tent flap, Duff stopped in mid-sentence and glanced anxiously in his direction—then recognized the newspaperman and relaxed. Harley nodded at Devanor in passing— the gambler nodded back with a wry smile—and headed for the bar.

"Good morning, Mr. Duff. Pretty slow in here today."

Duff glared at him. "I don't need anybody to stand there and hold the bar up for me, Harley. You want to buy a drink or not?"

"Well, it's a little early yet, even for me." Harley chuckled.

Duff planted his elbows on the bar and leaned forward with a sneer on his lips. "You look like you're enjoying all this, Harley. Crane and Harris had a lot of friends, so I'd be careful if I were you, and not look too happy about things."

"A lot of friends indeed. Are you by chance including the eight men who left them to face Hawkes? I would venture to say your vigilance committee isn't working out quite the way you expected. But this is what comes of taking the law into your own hands."

"You think you're so damned smart. I'm beginning to think you're on this crazy mountain man's side in all this."

"Not at all," replied Harley, suddenly very serious. "Which is why I have sent word to the United States Army about what's transpiring here."

"The *Army*?"

"That's right. I gave letters to three of the men who left town this morning. Each said he would deliver his letter to the officer commanding at Camp Collins. I expect at least one of those letters to reach its destination."

Duff was caught completely by surprise. Slowly a scowl darkened his features. "We don't need the damned Army to take care of us. We can handle one man, for God's sake."

"Can you? Are you sure about that? You know, Duff, I'm a bit surprised you're not thanking me for taking the initiative on this."

"Why would I want to thank you?"

"Because without the Army's protection this town is going to dry up and blow away. And if that happens, how are you ever going to become a rich man?"

Duff looked around the nearly empty tent saloon, reconsidering.

"You're not doing this for my sake, though," he said. "That's for damn certain."

"Of course not. I did it because I don't want to see any more lives lost."

"I think that was a good idea you had, Luther," said Devanor, without looking up from his cards.

"The Army might decide to look into this matter of the death of Cameron Hawkes."

Duff looked askance at the gambler. "Why are you still here, anyway? Seventy-five percent of nothing is nothing."

Devanor laughed softly. "Very true. I'm still here because—well, because I can't leave just yet."

"Haven't seen the Doone brothers around town," remarked Harley. "I wonder if they are on the way to Horseshoe Pass themselves."

"They won't run," said Duff confidently.

"Chandler Doone is no fool," said Devanor. "That's plain to see, as he knew better than to join your vigilance committee, Joe."

"Or maybe," said Harley, "he's content to let Mr. Duff and his committee do the fighting—and the dying—for him."

"You're calling him a coward?" asked Duff, astonished. "You wouldn't do that to his face, I bet."

"Luther already stood up to him once," Devanor told Duff. "That's one more time than you have, Joe."

Duff made a dismissive gesture, signifying that he was done with the conversation, and left the bar to walk over to The Banker's table. Harley sat down across from Devanor.

"I still say you should leave Gilder Gulch, if only for Miss Diamond's sake," said the newspaperman.

"I offered to take her out of here. But she won't go."

"Why not? What's to keep her here?"

Devanor shrugged, continuing with his game of solitaire. "She says because it's safer here, as long as Hawkes is out there, somewhere."

Detecting something in the gambler's tone of voice, Harley said, "But you think there's another reason. You don't believe her."

"I don't know what that other reason would be. But since you've summoned the Army, I suppose peace will be restored soon enough. That's assuming, of course, that the Army comes."

"They will. This is the richest strike this side of California. Oh yes, the Army will come, mark my words. There's talk, you know, of creating a new territory out of the western portion of the Kansas Territory. And then a new state. A *free* state, I might add. With the current unpleasantness back East regarding slavery and its expansion, such considerations are of the utmost importance. Yes, my friend, the Army will be here."

"Why, Luther, I'm impressed by your ability to see things in the broader perspective."

"Everything is connected, didn't you know? Well, I had better be on my way."

"I don't suppose Hawkes stands much of a chance, then, once the Army does get here."

"You sound a little disappointed, Charles."

"Just an observation, really. I'm not taking sides. I have but one concern now—Alice's safety."

"Well, the Army won't be here for a while," said Harley, rising from the chair. "There's still time for a man like Hawkes to do plenty of damage. Good day."

"Good day to you, Luther."

When Tom Jeffers rode out to the claim worked by Chandler and Harvey Doone, located about a mile up the creek from the gold camp, his stated purpose was to inform the brothers of what had transpired in the first clash between the vigilantes and Gordon Hawkes. But he had an ulterior motive as well. Like Luther Harley, some of the men in Gilder Gulch were wondering why Chandler and his brother—but particularly Chandler—were apparently disinterested in doing anything about the threat posed by the mountain man.

He found the brothers working a sluice box, and he noticed that they labored with rifles within reach, and he didn't think it was claim jumping that they were concerned about. The Doones weren't very good hosts—Jeffers had to ask if he could partake of the contents of the coffeepot that was balanced on stones rimming a still smoldering cook fire. Chandler begrudgingly gave the go-ahead, though it was obvious he would have preferred that Jeffers turn around and go right back to town.

After pouring himself a cup of the pungent black brew, Jeffers sipped, made a face at the bitter taste and said, "I guess you've heard that some men went up into the mountains to find Hawkes. They didn't all come back. We found the bodies of Josey Crane and Joe Harris. No sign of Ben Malone, though. We may never find his body."

He glanced at Chandler and saw that Doone was supremely indifferent to the news.

"Josey Crane rode with you when you went after Cameron Hawkes," said Jeffers, thinking that perhaps Chandler did not realize who he was talking about.

"Did he now? I don't recall asking him to. I didn't ask any of you to ride with me, as a matter of fact."

"That's true. But we did ride with you, because we thought it was the right thing to do."

Chandler threw back his head and laughed. "The right thing to do? You don't have to lie to me. You and the others came along because you wanted some excitement. Well, now you've got more than you bargained for, haven't you?"

Jeffers was too afraid of Chandler Doone to let his outrage show. "You think what you like. Fact is, you killed Cameron Hawkes and now his father is here seeking revenge, and two, probably three men are already dead and a lot of people are wondering what you aim to do about it."

"I'm not going to do a damned thing about it," snapped Chandler. "Not until Hawkes comes after me or my brother."

"You don't understand. He's got a stranglehold on this town. A lot of the men are leaving on account of what's happening."

"What do I care? That just means there'll be more gold for me—and anybody else who has the guts to stay put."

Jeffers sighed. "Okay. I see how it is. You're waiting for somebody to ask you all nice and police. I'll be the one, then. We need your help, Chandler. Way I figure this, you could be the only one who could take Hawkes on and come out the winner."

"Oh, so you think that just because you and your friends rode with me that now I should help you with your problem."

"It's not just my problem, it's our problem. You,

me, Harvey and everybody else around here. And we wouldn't have this problem at all if you hadn't killed Cameron Hawkes, you know."

Jeffers knew right away that he had made a mistake. Chandler Doone's face turned dark with anger. Moving with startling quickness for such a big man, he took two long strides and kicked the cup of coffee out of Jeffers's grasp. Fearful, Jeffers fell backward off the log upon which he had been seated, thinking that Chandler meant to do him harm.

"That was an eye for an eye, damn you," rasped Chandler, looming over the prospector with fists balled up. "Are you forgetting what he did to my brother Mitchell?"

"No. No, of course not."

Chandler reached down and gathered a handful of Jeffers's shirt and heaved the man to his feet, then gave him a rough shove.

"This thing is between me and Hawkes. I don't blame him for coming after me. It's an eye for an eye with him, too. I didn't ask you and the others to get involved, but you did anyway, and now if you've got a problem, it's of your own making and not mine so you'll just have to deal with it. You got that?"

"Yeah, I got it."

"Then don't you ever come crawling to me no more."

Trying to muster up at least a little of the dignity he had just lost, Jeffers brushed off his dust-covered, coffee-stained clothes, cleared his throat and nodded. "Thanks for the coffee," he said dryly, and went to his horse.

Chandler watched him ride away, then snorted

and shook his head. He glanced at his brother. Harvey had been leaning against the sluice box, his massive arms folded across his chest, solemnly watching the exchange between Chandler and Tom Jeffers.

"You got anything to say?" snapped Chandler.

Harvey shrugged. "I just don't cotton to standing around here and waiting for Hawkes to show up, that's all." He looked around. All he saw were green mountainsides and gray peaks with snowy caps framed against a blue sky. It all looked peaceful enough. But there was a man out there, somewhere, who wanted his hide. "I can't shake the feeling that I've got a rifle sighted down on me every minute," he added.

"Don't worry about that. You can bet that Hawkes will want to be looking you straight in the eye when he kills you, Harvey."

"How do you know that for sure?"

"Because he ain't no coward. I can tell you that right now, without ever having met the man."

"If you say so," said Harvey dubiously.

"I say so." Chandler hefted his saddle and headed for the horse tethered nearby. Both the horse and the saddle had been some of his earliest acquisitions following his arrival in the valley. He had killed their previous owner, who had been traveling alone on the trail in from Horseshoe Pass. The man hadn't been a prospector; he had looked more like a tinhorn gambler. Not that it mattered to Chandler Doone what his chosen profession had been. He had dragged the body well away from the trail and left it for the coyotes and the buzzards—and as far as the horse and saddle were concerned, he had let it be known around the gold camp that he'd found them. Nobody had the nerve to call him on it.

Chandler had figured that he needed a good horse for those roundabout late night trips into Gilder Gulch that he sometimes made. Being at best an indifferent placer miner, Chandler was convinced that the quickest route to riches was to prowl the shadows of Gilder Gulch with knife and pistol and relieve careless prospectors of their gold dust or nuggets. It was, after all, the same kind of lucrative activity he had engaged in in other places, and the main reason he had come to this valley in the first place. He wasn't averse to panning for gold, but he wasn't about to depend on that alone to pay his way. Ordinarily he didn't kill his victims—except on the rare occasions when he got careless and let them see his face. More often than not they were drunk, and as a result unaware of his presence until he was knocking them into unconsciousness with the butt end of a pistol. That done, Chandler would rob the man and ride out of town, circling up into the foothills to avoid all the claims that lined the creek.

"Where are you going, Chand?" asked Harvey.

"Jeffers drank the last of our coffee. I'm going into town to get some more, and a few other things." Chandler threw the saddle over the horse's back and began to cinch it down. "You look after the claim until I get back. I won't be gone too long."

It wasn't the gold in the creek that Chandler was worried about; his main concern was the stash of stolen loot he had buried under that log over by the campfire. There was several thousand dollars' worth of hard money and gold dust in that cache, ten times what he and his brother had taken out of their unproductive claim. There was even a gold pocket watch that Chandler figured was worth nearly a hundred dollars.

Harvey didn't like the idea of being left alone for any amount of time, not with a proven killer stalking the valley looking for the men who were responsible for his son's death.

"Well, what if Hawkes shows up while you're gone?" he asked.

Chandler grinned sourly at him. "Ask him polite like if he'll be so kind as to stick around until I get back."

"That isn't funny."

"No, it isn't. What kind of stupid question is that, anyway, Harv? You shoot the bastard if he shows up, that's what you do. I swear, sometimes I think you must be a half-wit."

"There ain't no call for you to say such to me," said Harvey resentfully.

"Just keep your eyes peeled and your rifle handy. I'll be back before you know it."

Chandler fitted foot to stirrup and mounted up. Harvey handed him his rifle and watched him ride south along the creek toward Gilder Gulch.

Less than an hour later, Gordon Hawkes found a spot on a high hillside above the bend in the creek from where he could look down and see the place where his son had staked a claim. Pretty Shield was with him; she confirmed that this was the right spot. There were two men working a sluice box at the gravel bar.

"Looks like they didn't waste much time moving in on a vacant claim," muttered Hawkes. "This man, Mitchell Doone—he said he and his brothers had a claim upstream?"

"Yes." Pretty Shield pointed. "Just above the bend, I think."

Hawkes headed along the hillside, leading his mustang through the trees, with Pretty trailing along behind. Before long they were in position to look down at a claim located north of the bend. Hawkes saw only one man, who was pouring buckets of water into the top of the sluice box.

"That must be one of the brothers," Pretty told Hawkes. "The man in the gold camp, the one who helped us, said there were two of them."

Hawkes nodded. Sitting on his heels and leaning against the trunk of an aspen tree, he watched the man below. He had a clear shot and at this range, a few hundred yards, he was certain to hit his mark. On the lower part of the hillside most of the timber had recently been cut down, used for shelters on the claims along the creek or hauled into the gold camp. This gave the mountain man a clear field of fire.

But he chose not to shoot. Instead, he wondered where the other brother was. And why weren't the Doones—the men who had the most to fear from his presence here—waiting in Gilder Gulch where it would be somewhat safer for them?

Pretty Shield was thinking along the same lines. "It could be a trap," she said. "Don't go down there."

He looked at her. "If they won't come to me I guess I have no choice but to go to them."

"What if I were to bring him to you?"

"You shouldn't even be here in the first place, Pretty. I don't want you to get hurt."

"I won't get hurt. I will go down there and he will see me, and he will come after me just like those men did before. Do you remember?"

"I remember. And you were lucky to get away from them."

"I run very fast. Luck had nothing to do with it. I will run and he will follow—and we will see if there is a trap set for you."

Hawkes shook his head. "I don't know. It sounds too risky to me."

Pretty reached out and gripped his arm. It was the first time she had dared touch him in a long time. "I have to do this now because I did not do enough before. And I do not want to lose you, too."

The mountain man grudgingly reconsidered. She was right—the one man down there might well be a Judas goat, staked out, so to speak, to lure him into ambush. And while Hawkes was not all that concerned about his own life, he wanted one thing more than anything else—to finish what he had set out to do and avenge his son's death. That meant he had to stay alive until the job was done. He had to win, no matter what the cost.

The man down there wasn't likely to be lured away from the claim by anything Hawkes could think to do. But he might very well go after an Indian woman. And if he could be lured away from the claim, that would spring the trap if indeed one existed.

"Okay," said Hawkes. "But I don't want you to

get too close. Let him see you and try to get him to come after you."

Relieved and grateful, Pretty Shield smiled. "Thank you," she said softly. She went to the mountain mustang and freed the Joslyn carbine from the saddle, taking the shot pouch that went with it.

"What do you think you're doing?" asked Hawkes.

"You have shown me how to use this. Now I will."

"Remember one thing, Pretty. He's mine."

"I know," she said, and started down the slope.

Harvey Doone looked up pretty often from his work—he felt like a sitting duck out in the open like this, and he didn't have much confidence in his brother's assurances that Hawkes would do his killing up close. So he happened to spot Pretty Shield the moment she emerged from the brush on the far side of the creek. Harvey recognized her right away. He had seen her with Cameron Hawkes, working their claim.

His first thought upon seeing her was that he had nothing to fear. She was a woman, after all, and Harvey Doone had a low opinion of women in general. Then she raised the Joslyn carbine and, cursing, Harvey dived behind the sluice box, hitting the ground just as the carbine spoke. The .54-caliber bullet splintered a timber above his head. Harvey cursed some more. Not only was she a woman with a gun, she was a woman who could shoot. And she had come here to shoot him because of what had happened to her man. And all the while, mused Harvey bitterly, he'd been worried about Gordon Hawkes.

Crawling a dozen feet to where his rifle was propped up against the sluice box, Harvey risked a quick look across the creek. She had been waiting for him to show himself—and fired a second time. This bullet slammed into the sluice box, too close to suit Harvey. Recovering from his initial shock, Harvey started getting mad. This was humiliating, being pinned down by a woman, and an Indian at that. He had never killed a woman before, but this was the first one who had tried to plug him.

Checking the rifle to make certain all was in order, Harvey stood up and brought the long gun to shoulder and drew a bead on—nothing.

She was gone.

No. There she was. Running away. He caught a glimpse of her through the brush.

Harvey took a shot, but he wasn't as good a marksman as his brother, especially when the target was on the move. And this particular target was moving fast. He had never seen anything with two legs run like that. His bullet kicked up dust a good ten feet behind her.

Judging that if he spent a precious thirty seconds reloading the rifle, she would have too great a lead and be impossible to catch, Harvey threw down the empty long gun and took off after her. He had his pistol and a knife and he figured that would be all he needed. Splashing across the creek, he lumbered uphill after her as fast as he could go. She was well ahead of him now, flying across the ground, leaping over some of the tree stumps that covered the lower flank of the rise. Grunting with exertion, Harvey tried to at least keep pace. He was stronger than she, but also more than a hundred pounds heavier, and he was not accustomed to running long distances.

Just as he was about to decide that he'd made a mistake in discarding the empty rifle, the woman stopped running and turned to look back at him. She was nearly to the tree line, and for an instant Harvey thought that maybe she was about to aim that carbine at him again. He hesitated, reaching for his pistol, but then she darted in among the trees and he resumed the chase.

Harvey lost sight of her a moment later, but continued churning up the hill until he had reached the crest. There he halted, his chest heaving, looking this way and that, wondering where the hell she had gone. There was no sign of her, and no sound to be heard except the soft sigh of a breeze in the tops of the trees.

"You."

Harvey whirled at the sound of the man's voice.

Though he had never before seen the buckskinclad man who stood before him, he knew it had to be Gordon Hawkes. Harvey's hand dropped to the butt of his pistol, but before he could yank the gun from his belt, Hawkes had swung his Plains rifle around and had him covered.

"Go ahead," sneered Harvey. "Better kill me now, you coward."

"What's your name?"

"Harvey Doone."

"You're the wrong one," said Hawkes. "Where is your brother?"

"You want my brother, you have to go through me."

"I can do that."

Hawkes tossed his long gun to Pretty Shield, who had reappeared from behind a tree, and while the Plains rifle was still in the air, Harvey pulled his pistol free. Hawkes, too, had a percussion pistol, and brought it into play. The two men fired simultaneously, so that the two gunshots sounded like one. They stood no more than thirty feet apart, and both men hit their mark. Struck high in the chest, below the clavicle, Harvey staggered backward and would have fallen had he not fetched up against a tree. With a bullet in his left leg, Hawkes somehow managed to stay on his feet. Hurling the empty pistol away, he drew the Bowie knife from its sheath and closed on Harvey. Snarling with the ferocity of a wounded grizzly, Harvey pushed off against the tree and lunged at the mountain man, brandishing his own knife. The men collided like a pair of rams. Steel rang against steel. Harvey was bigger and was coming down the slope, and his charge threw Hawkes back. The mountain man stumbled and fell, locked in combat with Doone. As he hit the ground, Hawkes arched his back and rolled, tossing Harvey over his head. Scrambling to his feet, he closed on his adversary again, but Harvey was quick—coming up on one knee, he lashed out with the knife, and Hawkes gasped as cold steel ripped his flesh, a long and deep lateral cut above the navel. An inch or two deeper and Hawkes would have been disemboweled. Instead, the mountain man was able to move in, and blocking Harvey's arm as Doone tried another slashing thrust, he plunged the Bowie knife into Harvey's chest, turning the blade sideways so that it passed neatly between the ribs. The point of the blade punctured Doone's heart. Harvey uttered a short, strangled sound and then died on his feet. His rigid body toppled backward.

Clutching at his midsection and no longer able to stand, Hawkes fell sideways. Pretty ran to him. She pressed her hands against the wound in his belly, trying to stanch the flow of blood. He grabbed one of her blood-slick hands with his own.

"Go get the horse," he said, his voice taut with pain. She began to rise but he held onto her hand and added, "Pretty, we've got to get away from here. You've got to keep me alive. My work is not done."

"I will keep you alive," she said, nearly in tears, for she feared that she would be unable to do what he asked.

Chapter Thirteen

When the soldiers came, nearly everyone in Gilder Gulch was out to observe their arrival. Such an event even drew many of the placer miners off their claims. The bluecoats had camped the night before at the Horseshoe Pass way station, and a gold seeker had pressed on through the mountain—at times a perilous passage in the dark—to get word to the inhabitants of the camp.

It took the soldiers most of the day to make that same passage, so it was late in the afternoon when they rode into town—two dozen of them, their horses trail-worn, their uniforms dusty, their sunburned faces gaunt and, in most cases, dark with beard stubble, the visors of their forage caps pulled low over watchful eyes. Their short blue fatigue jackets had yellow lapels and piping, while their gray trousers had black seat linings and were tucked into tall black boots adorned with jingling spurs. The entire contingent was equipped with .54-caliber Windsor percussion rifles of Mexican War vintage, and each man carried a heavy cavalry saber in an iron scabbard that was suspended from a white leather strap running from the left side to the right shoulder.

For the most part the Gilder Gulch men were quiet and subdued as they watched the soldiers ride down the street by twos, trailing a dozen pack mules which carried tents and provisions along behind them. Some were glad to see the bluecoats. Others were ambivalent. For their part, the soldiers weren't sure what to make of this decidedly lukewarm reception. They had been led to believe that they had been sent here to protect the gold camp and its occupants from a lawless element. Like all soldiers, they seemed supremely indifferent about the job at hand. The only thing that seemed sufficient to pique their interest was the calico queens, some of whom had strayed from Paradise Alley to witness their arrival.

Luther Harley joined Charles Devanor and Joe Duff in front of the tent saloon, where they stood with a small crowd of miners who had previously been inside partaking of Duff's bad whiskey. The officer at the head of the bluecoat column steered his horse toward the knot of men. Checking his mount, he swung out of the saddle, stiff from long hours on the trail, and handed the reins to a sergeant who remained mounted alongside a trooper who carried the stars and stripes. He had taken the flag out of its canvas casing and unfurled it prior to the contingent's entrance into the gold camp.

The officer was a young man—younger than many of the men under his command—tall and rangy, with a shock of yellow hair under his blue forage cap. His face was angular, his jaw strong, his eyes a muddy brown. Harley pegged him at once as the product of the military academy at West Point. He was confident, direct and businesslike, and he was comfortable with the authority of the rank he had earned and the orders that he carried.

"Good afternoon, gentlemen," he said, with a brisk nod. "I am Lieutenant Brandon Gunnison, Third United States Mounted Regiment."

Harley glanced at Devanor and Duff. Neither man seemed inclined to respond to the lieutenant's greeting. So the newspaperman stepped forward to extend a hand to Gunnison.

"Luther Harley, editor of the *Gilder Gulch Argus*, Lieutenant."

Gunnison pulled off a leather gauntlet and grasped the proffered hand. His grip, noted Harley, was firm.

"I believe that makes you the one who sent for us, then," said Gunnison.

Harley nodded. "That I did. We've been having a little trouble around here."

Gunnison surveyed the crowd behind Harley. "The commanding general of the western district of the territorial governor thought it was big enough trouble to warrant our coming here."

"Well," said Duff dryly, "Harvey sent that letter four weeks ago. Things have happened since then, and I'm not too sure we have much of a problem anymore, frankly."

"We've been pretty busy fighting Arapaho dog soldiers these past few months," said Gunnison. "There's been an uprising. A number of emigrant trains were attacked. Some men killed, a few women and children carried off."

"In other words, Joe," said Harley, "they got here as quickly as they could."

"In other words," said Gunnison. "Why do you say you don't have a problem any longer?"

Duff glanced at Harley. The saloonkeeper wasn't eager to tell the whole story. It was one that he wished had never happened. His situation here had been as perfect as he could have asked for—until Cameron Hawkes had thrown the corpse of Mitchell Doone into the mud at his feet. From that point on things had started turning sour. Chandler Doone had nearly killed him. Then Gordon Hawkes had frightened and humiliated him. And then nearly half the population of the gold camp—from Duff's point of view, half of his clientele—had left Gilder Gulch. The arrival of the soldiers was just another chapter in this story.

Harley detected Duff's reticence and stepped into the breach. "He means that since I sent the letter there has been only one more killing."

"Hawkes?" asked Gunnison.

"He killed Harvey Doone. There was evidence to indicate that Hawkes was severely wounded in the fight. Perhaps mortally wounded."

"But his body has not been found," Devanor hastened to add. "That's not to say Chandler Doone didn't try to find him."

"Well, I know you hope Hawkes is still alive," Duff told the gambler. "As far as you're concerned, he killed the wrong Doone."

With a shrug, the gambler deigned not to answer.

"Whether Hawkes is alive or dead," said Harley, "the fact remains that there has been no sign of him for several weeks."

"I see." Gunnison scanned the street. "Regardless,

my orders are to remain here until, in my opinion, order is restored."

"You don't seem to understand, Lieutenant," said Duff. "Order has been restored."

"Really? I just rode past your cemetery. A lot of men lie buried there—and I'll wager very few passed away peacefully in their sleep. The situation I was sent here to resolve did not start with this man Hawkes. However, that is an incident I intend to look into, believe me. Where is this man Chandler Doone?"

"We haven't seen much of him lately, ever since he buried his brother Harvey," said Duff.

"He spends a lot of his time up there," said Harley, gesturing at the mountains that enclosed the valley. "Looking for Hawkes. Says he won't rest until he finds him. Or his body."

"Who can blame him?" asked Duff. "He's lost both of his brothers. He lives for one thing—vengeance."

Gunnison turned to Harley. "I take it you have a printing press. I want some broadsides printed up. Until further notice there will be a curfew in this camp. And it will be strictly enforced. Anyone abroad after dark will be arrested and brought before me. He had better have a very good reason for being on the street."

"After dark!" Duff couldn't believe his ears. "That's . . . that's . . ." He was momentarily at a loss for words.

"That's the way it's going to be for now," said Gunnison firmly.

"So we will be under martial law," remarked Devanor.

"That's right. It's better than no law at all. Mr. Harley?"

The newspaperman nodded. "I can produce your broadsides for you, Lieutenant."

"Good. Now, if you will excuse me, gentlemen, I will see to my command. We will camp just north of town." Gunnison touched the visor of his cap and turned back to his horse. Taking the reins from the sergeant, he climbed into the saddle and rode up the street, followed by his troops.

"Curfew at dark," rasped Duff bitterly. "God damn you, Harley. That's what you were really after, isn't it? You wanted to put me out of business. Not just me—but all of us, the ones you call predators. That includes your friend here." The saloonkeeper gestured angrily at Devanor.

"You don't know what you're talking about" was Harley's brisk retort. "I sent for the Army to save this town—and save lives, too. Might even save your business, though to be honest I am not overly concerned about that."

"Save the town?" Duff laughed. "This isn't a town. It's a gold camp. These men work their claims, and they work 'em hard, during the day. Then they come here or go to Paradise Alley for a little recreation after the sun goes down. Now they can't do that. They can't get a drink and blow off a little steam or they'll get arrested. How long do you think they'll stay here under those conditions?"

"They'll stay, a good many of them, as long as there is gold to be found," replied the newspaperman. "And now they will be safe from vengeance seekers—and vigilantes."

Duff shook his head and looked at Devanor. "You might as well pack up and move on. There will be mighty slim pickings around here for the likes of you from now on."

"The soldiers won't stay forever," said Devanor.

"Well, if they stay very long I'll be packing it in, that's for sure. If Gunnison is bent on killing the goose that lays golden eggs, I'm moving on to find another goose."

Scowling, Duff pushed through the crowd of prospectors and entered his tent saloon.

"So you really want to save Gilder Gulch from itself," said Devanor, smiling with faint derision at Harley.

The newspaperman held up a hand. "I know what you're going to say. That it can't be saved. I happen to disagree. I kind of like it here."

The gambler shook his head. "I hate to be the one who has to tell you this, but you've just bought into another lost cause, Luther."

Lieutenant Gunnison approached his task of bringing law and order to Gilder Gulch with speed and ruthless efficiency. Bluecoat details became a constant presence in the gold camp, while others regularly patrolled the claims up and down the creek. All claims had to be recorded in order for ownership disputes and claim jumping to be curtailed. A stout log structure was built to serve as a jail, and Gunnison filled it up in no time with men who tried to slip past the details in an attempt to partake of a whiskey at Joe Duff's place or a woman in Paradise Alley. And still Gunnison found the time to investigate what he called "the Hawkes affair" in his official report.

When Chandler Doone reappeared in the valley after another fruitless week-long search for Gordon Hawkes, two soldiers promptly took him into custody and brought him before the lieutenant.

Gunnison was sitting on a camp stool behind a small wooden folding table in front of his tent in the cavalry bivouac when Doone was marched in at the point of bayonets. He noticed blood on Doone's chin from a busted lip, and the pair of troopers looked disheveled.

"I see he put up a fight," said Gunnison.

"Yes, sir, he did," replied one of the cavalrymen, and it was all he could do to refrain from slinging some well-chosen epithets at his prisoner in the lieutenant's presence.

"You got no call to arrest me," rasped Chandler Doone, glowering indignantly at Gunnison. "I ain't broken no law."

"I'll be the judge of that, Mr. Doone. I take it you've had no luck finding Gordon Hawkes. Do you still think he's alive?"

"Far as I'm concerned he is. Until I see his dead body I will not rest."

"There will be no more killing around here if I have anything to say about it."

Doone laughed—a short, sardonic bark. "That's what you say. We'll just wait and see."

"I could have you put in chains, and in that way make certain you can do no harm to anyone."

"You might as well stand me up in front of a firing squad right now, then. 'Cause as long as there's breath left in my body, I'm going to keep looking for Hawkes."

"Did you take the life of his son, Cameron?"

"I sure as hell did," said Doone proudly. "And don't even try to call that murder. It was a fair fight."

"Ten of you against one. You call that a fair fight?"

"He killed one of the men who rode with me. He had a gun, and he had a chance. Which is more than you can say for my brother, Mitchell. If you're looking for a murder, there's one for you. Cameron Hawkes murdered my brother on account of that damned Indian squaw of his. I had a right to do what I done."

"No, you didn't. Even if it was murder, that didn't give you the right."

"The hell you say. An eye for an eye. Says it right there in the Good Book."

"And if what Cameron Hawkes did was self-defense, then what you did in response was a criminal act."

"You charging me with a crime?" asked Doone, his eyes narrowed to slits.

"I'm sure you've committed more than a few. I've been talking to some of the men around here. There has been a good bit of robbery here, and sometimes murder to go along with it."

"I had nothing to do with any of that," sneered Doone. "And you can't prove that I did."

"This is not a court of law, mister. I don't have to prove anything in order to lock you up. And I think that is exactly what I need to do."

Chandler Doone snarled an oath and took a half step toward Gunnison. But he didn't get any farther than that, because one of the soldiers hit him in the back of the head with the stock of his Windsor rifle. Out cold, Doone crumpled and fell heavily at the lieutenant's feet. The soldier looked at his handiwork with considerable satisfaction.

"Put him in irons and throw him in the brig," said Gunnison.

"That'll be a real pleasure, Lieutenant," said the soldier.

"I think we might have to haul this one back to Camp Collins with us, sir," suggested the other trooper.

Gunnison was inclined to agree.

On the eighth day after the arrival of the soldiers, Devanor took Alice Diamond for a walk along the Gilder Gulch street. It was early in the afternoon and the sun was warm, a beautiful day for a stroll. Devanor only wished they were strolling down San Francisco's Market Street instead of this dusty, rutted expanse.

The gambler had been able to spend a lot more time with Alice of late, and he was glad of that, but this newfound leisure time stemmed from the fact that he was finding it increasingly difficult to scare up a decent poker game. As they walked past the tent saloon, he noticed that, as usual, there was very little activity there. One of the bluecoat details, consisting of three men, stood near Joe Duff's establishment, talking and smoking. When night fell, there would be an additional detail patrolling the street, just in case someone tried to violate the curfew. That was happening much less frequently now. Those reckless enough to have challenged Lieutenant Gunnison's order early on were currently whiling away their time in the new jail. It seemed everyone else had learned from the mistakes of those unfortunates.

"I think Duff was right," said Devanor, surveying the nearly empty street.

"What was he right about?"

"He predicted that the presence of the soldiers would put a stranglehold on this town. It has certainly been bad for business. Did you know that several of the women over in Paradise Alley left town yesterday? I expect more will follow shortly."

"What are you saying, Charles?"

"That this camp is dying."

"Surely not. So much gold has been found already. More prospectors are bound to come, and even those who've gone will probably return, now that the soldiers are here to protect them."

"Perhaps," said Devanor, obviously thinking her assumptions were dubious. "But for the present I will not be making much money."

"Well, you know there is more to life than making money."

He glanced at her and saw the saucy smile and the slightly raised eyebrow and knew what she was implying. "Why, Miss Diamond," he said, laughing and feigning astonishment, "have you no shame?"

"Not around you I don't."

"Keep talking like that and we will have to turn right around and go back to the hotel."

"Oh, I wouldn't complain, not in the least."

Devanor stopped and turned to face her, taking

both her hands in his own and gazing earnestly into her eyes.

"Alice, would you . . . would you marry me?"

She was stunned, and for the moment speechless.

"I realize that I don't have much to offer. Men in my profession—well, we tend to be drifters, quite often because we aren't wanted in any one place for too very long. And we take risks—financial as well as physical risks—to ply our trade. But for you, Alice, I would consider . . ."

She freed one of her hands and touched his lips with a finger. "Don't you dare change for me, Charles. I want you to stay just like you are."

"Umm, is that a yes? Are you accepting my proposal?"

There was, he thought, a trace of sadness in her smile. But he might have only been imagining it.

"Yes, I am accepting it!" she exclaimed, and threw her arms around his neck and kissed him exuberantly.

After a moment he pushed her gently away. "You're going to get us arrested if you keep that up," he said, chuckling.

Alice looked around at the soldiers who were loitering in front of Joe Duff's tent saloon. They were watching, and she laughed softly.

"Oh, they are just envious of you, Charles, that's all."

"Yes, any man who sees you on my arm will have a very good reason to dislike me. We'll go to San Francisco, and be married there."

"And live happily ever after?"

"But of course. I wouldn't have it any other way."

"And how many children will we have?"

"Alice!" He no longer had to feign astonishment.

She laughed at the expression on his face. "I think I want to have at least a dozen, since you're to be the father."

"A dozen! My God, Alice, we'll need a mansion to house them all."

"Naturally. But you were planning on buying me a mansion anyway, weren't you, Charles? A nice big house on a hill?"

"San Francisco has hills, by the way," he said.

"I know that's where you want to go," she replied, suddenly subdued. "When were you thinking of leaving?"

"The sooner the better, I say." Devanor sensed her uncertainty. "Look, Alice, it's safe now. No one has seen Hawkes for weeks. There is no danger anymore."

"You can't be sure of that. He might still be out there." She was gazing past him now, at the high gray peaks.

"No, I don't think so. If he was still here, he wouldn't have stopped. I'm not sure that Harvey Doone killed him, though some people think that's what happened. It may be that Hawkes was badly wounded—so badly that he had to give up and go home. But regardless of what did happen to him, you have nothing to fear, Alice. Unless . . ."

She looked at him, afraid of what he was going to say.

"Unless," continued Devanor, reluctantly, "you have some other reason for not wanting to go to San Francisco."

"What would that reason be?"

"I have no idea. I was hoping you would tell me."

"I have kept no secrets from you, Charles."

"We don't have to go to San Francisco, you know. We can go anywhere you like. But sooner or later we will have to go *somewhere*. Hell, even Joe Duff has been talking about pulling up stakes. He sees the writing on the wall, I think."

"Duff is leaving? When?"

Devanor shrugged. Her hand still in his, he continued walking down the street. "I'm not really sure. But I do know that he has been talking about moving his whole operation to some other camp—lock, stock and barrel. He says he may ride out with the soldiers when they go. By then he may not have any business left."

"Why would he want to wait until the soldier's leave?"

"He's made a lot of money here, Alice. God only knows how much. But he's got to take it with him and I suppose he thinks it will be safer if he rides with Lieutenant Gunnison and his men."

"But doesn't Duff have men of his own? What about your friend, Wiley Roe? And that half-breed. What is his name, anyway?"

"I don't think anyone knows what his name is. Yes, Duff has Wiley and the breed on his payroll. But he's not going to take any chances with all that money and gold dust he has."

They walked in silence a moment, and Devanor realized with some dismay that Alice had very deftly switched the subject, so that San Francisco and their departure from Gilder Gulch were no longer the topic of conversation. She was a clever one! Exceptionally bright. And he was glad of that—except, perhaps, in this one instance.

"How much do you think he has?" asked Alice.

"Duff? I really don't know. If I had to guess, I would say at least fifty thousand dollars, most of it in gold dust. But he could have raked in twice that amount."

"Then I don't fault him for wanting the soldiers as an escort. Charles—maybe we could leave with the soldiers, too."

"That could be a week or two away, Alice. Perhaps even longer. Do you really want to stay here that long?"

She smiled and curled her arm under his, pressing her body against him. "I know we can find something to do to keep us busy."

He laughed. "Oh, we're back to that, are we?"

Alice pretended to pout. "Well, if there is something else you'd rather do . . ."

"Okay. We'll leave when the soldiers leave. Deal?"

"It's a deal."

"Hawkes really had you spooked, didn't he?"

Alice stopped walking and tugged on his arm. "Come along, Charles," she said with a smile that was calculated to make his pulse quicken. "Let's get back to the hotel—and pretend we're on our honeymoon."

Devanor turned on his heel and headed back up the street with her. It was an offer he was powerless to refuse.

Chapter Fourteen

For the first time in a very long time Gordon Hawkes awoke in the morning feeling like he was going to live.

He lay abed in his old cabin, the one he had abandoned months ago, after the gold seekers had come to the valley. The rooms—there were three of them—were virtually empty but for the bed frames he and Cameron had built. When Cameron and Pretty had gone down to the gold camp, they'd left a few belongings, like the thin mattress upon which Hawkes now lay. As he had done every morning, Hawkes looked around the room, Cameron's room, and experienced that excruciatingly painful emptiness he knew so well and yet would never, he thought, get used to. Grace had slept in the bedroom, on the other side of the common room, the one Hawkes and his wife had occupied. And Pretty had slept on blankets in the common room; that Eliza permitted Pretty to live under the same room was remarkable enough, but she had told Cameron that he could not share his bed with the Indian woman unless they were married.

Hawkes didn't know for certain whether Cameron and Pretty "knew" each other in the biblical sense, but he thought it likely that they did. Cameron had fallen in love with her, almost in spite of himself. And Hawkes thought that Pretty, in her own way, had cared deeply for his son even though she had not loved him. But if they had done anything, it had been discreetly—mostly, suspected Hawkes, out of respect for Eliza's feelings.

Cameron and Pretty being together had been something Hawkes hadn't cared to dwell on while his son was alive. But lately he'd thought about it a lot. He was glad that Pretty had been there for Cam, that Cam had experienced that part of life with a woman as good and as loving and as passionate as Pretty. Hawkes knew she was all of these things, and more, from his own experience. Before, he had avoided the subject, and in that also avoided as much as it was humanly possible the complications of jealousy. For to acknowledge that he could be jealous of his own son for being with Pretty would force him to acknowledge his true feelings for Pretty. And those feelings were wrong. So very wrong.

Still, he was grateful to Pretty and he wanted to tell her so, to thank her for taking care of his son to the best of her ability. Yet he hadn't done it, and wasn't really sure how to go about it. Pretty was convinced that she had failed Cameron, and Hawkes too. Even the mention of Cam's name would cause her fresh anguish and worsen her burden of guilt. In time, Hawkes thought, they might be able to speak of such things. Now, though, the emotions ran too high and the situation was too complicated.

Lying there, Hawkes listened for any sound from the other room that might indicate that Pretty was up. Soft early morning light stole through the window. She usually rose with the dawn, and dawn had come and gone.

Moving cautiously, Hawkes threw the blanket aside and off the bed, planting his bare feet on the dusty puncheon floor. He was naked, his midsection and shoulder tightly dressed. There was very little pain, which both pleased and amazed him. For a while it had been touch and go. Being a man accustomed to depending on his physical ability, he had grown impatient with his weakened body. But now, finally, he could feel some of his strength returning.

Pretty had brought him here because she could think of no other place to go. The journey had taken one whole day and the better part of a night, with Hawkes clinging somehow to the saddle while she led the mountain mustang. She had come to some sort of understanding with the horse, which surprised Hawkes, as the mustang had never really tolerated anyone else but its master. Once or twice Hawkes had lost consciousness and slipped from the saddle, until finally she had tied his wrists to the saddle horn and one of his ankles to each of the stirrups.

Hawkes didn't remember arriving at the cabin, or much at all of the next week, because even though Pretty removed the bullet from his leg, the wound became badly infected. For a time he had been delirious with a fever, but a poultice that Pretty placed on the wound drew out the toxins and Hawkes slowly improved. He came to one day to find that the swelling had gone down substantially and that Pretty had sewn the knife wound together using a needle and ordinary thread which she had found in the cabin. He had no memory of her performing that task. The knife wound, too, began to heal.

His recuperation took time, for he had lost a lot of blood and was as weak as a baby. The locations of his injuries, coupled with their severity, made the slightest movement on his part a painful experience. Nonetheless, Hawkes worried about staying too long in the cabin. He assumed that at the very least Chandler Doone would be out searching for him, and possibly the entire gold camp had been mobilized to do the same. If they looked hard and long enough, they would find the cabin. And if that happened, he was in no condition to put up much of a fight.

But Pretty Shield refused to even consider moving him. She would not take the chance, afraid that his condition would worsen on the trail. He had been as near death as she cared for him to go. And she could not bear the thought of losing him.

"If they come here I will kill them," she said when he tried to persuade her that there was danger involved in staying. She said this with such quiet ferocity that Hawkes had no doubt she would do anything she had to in order to protect him.

"They might cut our sign, and it would lead them straight here," he warned.

"I covered our trail. You do not need to worry. All you have to do is rest."

For a while that was all Hawkes *could* do. He had time to do a lot of thinking. Eliza was very much on his mind. She and Grace were alone, deep in the mountains, about three days' travel to the west. And they had been alone for a while now. In his grief and desire for vengeance upon learning of Cameron's death he had scarcely given a thought to what Eliza and his daughter must be going through. Eliza did not know for certain that her son was gone, though she had feared the worst, based on what Pretty Shield had told them. The task of giving her the news was one Hawkes dreaded fearfully. Not knowing what had become of her son—or, for that matter, her husband—had to be sheer torture for her. And knowing what she had to be going through created a dilemma for Hawkes. *I should go back and tell her and stay with her as she tries to cope with her son's death,* he told himself. There was just one problem with that.

Chandler Doone was still alive.

He knew what Eliza would say about that. She would tell him that vengeance was the exclusive province of the Almighty, and that Chandler would pay a terrible price exacted upon him in the afterlife. She might even go so far as to remind her husband that he had a daughter who needed him, too. She would not tell him that she needed him herself. With Eliza it was never about her own needs. But he knew she did need him—alive and well.

So if he went home to tell her about Cam, he would not be able to leave again, at least not in order to return to this valley and finish the job he had started. And even if he could, what guarantee did he have that Chandler Doone would still be here when he got back?

Nor could he send Pretty home with the news. This was not something he could delegate to someone else to do. Pretty could tell Eliza that her husband was still alive, but that would be a small comfort, for Eliza would know he was still on a quest for vengeance and might not stay alive for long. Then there was the problem of persuading Pretty to leave him. Hawkes seriously doubted that he could accomplish that.

Day by day the mountain man's condition improved. Slowly he regained his strength. Each morning Pretty ventured out to hunt or fish, and always came back with something—a rabbit or a few trout. When finally he could stand after being bedridden for so long, she made a crude but sturdy crutch for him. In a few more days he was able to dispense with the crutch. He pushed himself from that point on, trying to speed up the healing process—pushed too hard, in Pretty's opinion. But trying to get him to take it slow and easy was a futile endeavor. He knew she had an ulterior motive and one day confronted her about it.

"I know you're hoping I won't go back to the gold camp," he said. "You're trying to delay that from happening. Maybe you think I'll change my mind. I'll be honest, I've thought about quitting. But I just can't do it, Pretty. For some reason I just can't."

"Cameron would not want you to do this."

"I know," said Hawkes sadly. "He would want me to go home, to take care of his mother and his sister. I don't know—maybe I'm no better than Chandler Doone, because I'm doing exactly what he would do."

"I will not try to stop you. I know I cannot, anyway. All I can do is try to help, try to keep you alive, so you can go back to your family one day."

"You're not coming back with me when I do finally go home, are you, Pretty?"

She shook her head, unable to meet his gaze. "I had an excuse to stay, when your son was in love with me."

Hawkes nodded. He understood completely. Eliza had tolerated Pretty's presence for Cameron's sake. It was possible that Eliza would let her stay even now—there seemed to be no limit to her tolerance—perhaps because she knew how much Pretty meant to her husband. That would be just like Eliza, always willing to sacrifice herself for the sake of others.

But Pretty Shield was not going to force Eliza to make that sacrifice any more than she would place Hawkes in such a position. She knew that it was not in Hawkes's nature to send her away. She also knew that her presence was a constant torment for him. So she would be the one to sacrifice herself this time, by leaving.

With a soulful sigh, Hawkes realized that what Pretty intended to do was best for all concerned—and that he would not try to talk her out of going.

"Well," he said wistfully, "I'll miss you, Pretty."

She looked at him, then, hoping for something more from him, even though she realized that it was wrong to hope for such things.

But there was nothing more forthcoming. Hawkes simply walked away.

For several more days he tried to strengthen himself, striking out on foot and climbing steep slopes until exhaustion overcame him. Finally he declared himself ready to go. He still limped slightly, but his wounds were nearly healed. And he could stomach no further delay. The sooner he finished the task at hand, the sooner he could go home to Eliza and Grace.

Pretty Shield did nothing to try to stop him. She was resigned to the fact that Hawkes would not leave this job half-done. And for his part, Hawkes made no attempt to prevent Pretty from coming with him. They were in this together, and he was willing to accept that now.

Nearly six weeks after arriving at the abandoned cabin, Hawkes and Pretty rode away on the mountain mustang, heading down the valley toward Gilder Gulch. Summer was over, and the aspen, cottonwood and willow were shedding their foliage. The leaves fell like a golden shower in the woodlands. Pretty rested her eyes on the swaths of gold, interspersed with russet and orange, of the changing trees on the forested flanks of the mountains. She had always loved to watch the magic wrought upon the earth by the changing of the seasons. But now she saw autumn in a new and bittersweet light, as the beginning of an end, the dying that was a prerequisite for the rebirth of spring. It seemed to her to be an appropriate setting, for this journey with Gordon Hawkes would be her last.

Returning to his quarters after a late dinner, Luther Harley passed by one of Lieutenant Gunnison's details. The soldiers were heading in the opposite direction, moving up the street while he headed down it. By now the newspaperman had become acquainted with most of the soldiers in Gunnison's command, and generally he liked them. To a man they were veterans of skirmishes with hostile Indians, but only the sergeant, a man named Burleson, was old enough to have served in the late unpleasantness between the United States and the Republic of Mexico, which he had done with distinction. Harley had learned that the studied indifference of the soldiers to their mission and their continual grousing about army life was in most cases just a pretense. As a whole they were proud of the uniform they wore.

Harley surmised that the lieutenant was in no small measure responsible for this attitude among his men. It seemed that Gunnison was a soldier's soldier. Tough but fair-minded, he drove his men hard, yet drove himself harder. He was universally admired and respected; these men would follow their lieutenant straight into the fires of hell if he so ordered them. That was remarkable in the sense that traditionally West Pointers were viewed with disdain—mixed, Harley thought, with some measure of class envy—by the men in the rank and file.

The soldiers liked Harley, too. His genuine interest in them, stemming from an insatiable inquisitiveness about the human experience, had engendered a good rapport. So it was not unusual that the detail paused to talk to him.

"Looks to be another quiet night," Harley told them. "It seems to me that you boys won't have a whole lot to do."

"Well, I say it's a shame the lieutenant has put Paradise Alley off limits to us," said one of the troopers, grinning like a schoolboy. "If he hadn't, and it got *too* quiet, we could go there and for sure stir up a little excitement."

The soldiers laughed, and Harley chuckled right along with them. "Lieutenant Gunnison is just trying to look out for you," said the newspaperman. "Keep you from straying off the straight and narrow. And it's out of respect for his efforts in that regard that I cannot offer you a drink from my whiskey flask." Checking his pockets, Harley smiled ruefully. "Which I don't have with me anyway."

"If you did have it, we'd have had to arrest you, Mr. Harley," said one of the soldiers. "And confiscate the whiskey."

They laughed again, for all knew what he meant by "confiscate."

"I certainly don't want to see the inside of that jail," said Harley. "It's a little too crowded, for one thing."

"Oh, we're letting most of the prisoners go free tomorrow. The lieutenant's orders. Guess he figures they've learned their lesson."

"What about Chandler Doone? Is he going to be released as well?"

"From what I've heard," replied the soldier, "we're going to be hauling him back to Camp Collins. The lieutenant thinks he's responsible for some killings in these parts."

"Possibly he is," said Harley. "But I don't know how you could begin to go about proving that."

The soldier shrugged. He didn't care about that— it wasn't his job. "I don't know about that. All I know is rumor has it we'll be moving out soon. Least that's what the sergeant says. Seems those Arapaho dog soldiers are up to their old tricks again and we have to teach them another lesson."

Parting company with the troopers, Harley mulled it all over. It was good news, he supposed, for men like Joe Duff and Charles Devanor. The curfew and the presence of the soldiers had ruined their business. But was it good news for the town as a whole? Harley figured that Lieutenant Gunnison was probably right about Chandler Doone, and if Doone was dragged off in shackles, the gold camp became that much safer. It all depended, decided the newspaperman, on what had become of Gordon Hawkes. Harley had a hunch that Gilder Gulch had seen the last of the mountain man. Either Hawkes had called off his quest for vengeance or he had died of wounds he'd received during his fight with Harvey Doone. Harley shook his head. So many needless deaths— Mitchell and Harvey Doone, Cameron Hawkes, Josey Crane, Joe Harris and maybe even Gordon Hawkes, as well. After spending his adult years on the wild frontier, where life was often very cheap, Harley wondered why he wasn't inured to death.

He went from contemplating the tragedy of the deaths of others to the imminence of his own demise when he walked through his door into a pitch-black room—and felt an arm fasten around his neck, followed by the unmistakable pinprick of a knife's point right below his jaw.

Kicking the door shut, Hawkes tightened his grip on Harley until he was sure the newspaperman could make nothing but strangling noises.

"Raise the alarm," said the mountain man, "and it will be the last thing you ever do. Now, are you going to be quiet if I let you go?"

Harley nodded, clawing ineffectually at the mountain man's arm. Then, abruptly, the arm was gone, and he could breathe again. Wheezing, Harley stumbled away and fetched up hard against his hand press.

"Pretty, light the lamp," said Hawkes.

A moment later the room was filled with lamplight, and Harley was staring at a buckskin-clad apparition before him. The buckskins Gordon Hawkes wore were stained with dried blood. The sandy beard on his gaunt cheeks begged for a trimming. His eyes seemed to lie deeper in their sockets. His clothes hung loosely on a frame that had noticeably thinned since Harley had seen the man last. Indeed, it looked almost as though Hawkes had come back from the dead.

"Are you insane?" breathed Harley. "You must be, to have come back here."

"What are the soldiers doing here?"

"I sent for them. They've come to restore some order and sanity to this godforsaken place. For the love of God, Hawkes—go home!"

"I haven't finished yet."

"You'll never get Chandler Doone now. The soldiers have taken him into custody."

"What did they do that for?"

"They think he's responsible for several murders."

"But not my son's?"

Harley shook his head.

"Then that's not good enough."

"So now you plan to take on the United States Army." Harley shook his head. "You are a madman. And you've got to be stopped. I'm sorry about your

217

son, and I understand why you want to avenge him, but this—this is going too far."

Hawkes bristled. His anger barely contained, he took a menacing step closer to the newspaperman. "You *don't* understand. You couldn't. And nothing will stand in my way."

Harley glanced at Pretty Shield. "Can't you make him see reason? I know you love him. Anybody can see that. And if you truly do love him, you would try to talk him out of this. He'll only get himself killed. And others will die, too, I'm sure. And all for what? It won't bring his son back. It won't erase the pain."

Pretty just shook her head and said nothing.

"I have the names of some of the men who rode with Doone," said Hawkes. "Jeffers. Radcliffe. Beechum. Mellock. Are they still around?"

Tight-lipped, Harley stared at Hawkes for a moment, then went to his desk and jerked open a drawer and reached for the whiskey flask that lay within. He froze when he heard the sound of a gun's hammer being cocked.

"I'm not the killer in this room, Hawkes," Harley said coldly, and held up the whiskey flask.

Hawkes lowered the pistol and eased the hammer down.

Harley took a long swig from the flask, gasped at the whiskey's fire and wiped his chin with a sleeve.

"Beechum and Radcliffe are gone," he said, "along with about half of the rest of the gold hunters who were here. I think Tom Jeffers is still around, though he keeps to his claim, and I haven't seen him in town recently. As for John Mellock—well, he couldn't go anywhere if he wanted to. He's the one who was seriously wounded in the fight with your son. They couldn't get the bullet out of his shoulder. He's in constant pain." Harley searched for even a glimmer of compassion in the mountain man's features—and saw nothing but stone-cold fury. "I suppose you'll be happy to put him out of his misery, won't you?"

"And the half-breed," said Hawkes. "Is he still here?"

"Oh yes. He still works for Joe Duff."

"The man who runs the saloon?"

Harley nodded. "You shouldn't have any trouble with Mellock," he said sourly. "And probably not much with Jeffers, either. He is just a placer miner, after all. And a pretty unlucky one at that. But the half-breed—he will give you a good run for your money, I expect. So who will you do away with first, Hawkes? How about John Mellock? Start with the invalid and work your way down the list."

"Where are the soldiers holding Chandler Doone?"

"They built a jailhouse near their encampment at the other end of town. That's where Doone is being kept. Right where he belongs, if you ask me—behind bars. Frankly, I think that's where you belong, too. Why don't you surrender yourself to Lieutenant Gunnison? Then they might throw you in with Doone. You two mad dogs can tear each other's throat out, and this will finally be over. But you had better hurry. The soldiers will be leaving any day now, or at least that's what I hear. And they intend to take Doone with them when they go."

"Where do I find Tom Jeffers?"

Harley shook his head adamantly. "You know,

killing Jeffers will make you as bad as Chandler Doone. Worse, because you know better. I don't think Doone does. Your soul will burn in hell."

"I'll worry about my soul. You worry about yours."

"Oh, so you'll kill me if I don't tell you, is that it? But you will have to do that anyway, won't you? Because if you don't I will raise the alarm as soon as you walk out that door."

"That's okay," said Hawkes. "I'll find them myself. Pretty."

She blew out the lamp, plunging the room into darkness.

Harley stood very still, barely breathing, straining to see and hear. But he heard and saw nothing. Minutes passed. Were the mountain man and the Indian woman gone? He simply couldn't tell. Steeling himself, he lighted the wick on the lamp and quickly surveyed the room. The door was slightly ajar. Hawkes and Pretty were gone.

Moving to the door, Harley opened it slowly and cautiously peered out into the night. There was no sign of the mountain man. A part of Harley wanted to bolt the door and huddle in a corner and drink himself into blissful oblivion. But the newspaperman ignored that cowardly instinct for self-preservation and ventured out, hastening up the street in search of the detail he had been visiting with only moments before. It was his duty to spread the unwelcome news that Gordon Hawkes was back—and still looking for blood.

Chapter Fifteen

When Lieutenant Gunnison heard from Luther Harley that Gordon Hawkes was back, he didn't doubt the newspaperman for a moment. It was manifestly clear to him that Harley was deeply concerned, as well as very apprehensive. No less importantly, he was obviously stone-cold sober. He knew Harley liked strong spirits, and while he had no evidence to indicate that liquor impaired the man's judgment, it was good to know that it wasn't a factor in this case. So Gunnison did not hesitate, summoning Sergeant Burleson to his tent before darting back inside to finish dressing, as Harley's arrival at this late hour had caught him sleeping. In fact, Gunnison had just finished writing in his journal and turned in; he'd managed to doze off only minutes before. But he was accustomed to going long periods with little or no sleep. One never got enough sleep on the campaign trail against hostile Indians, and Gunnison had been campaigning ever since he'd shipped out of West Point. He figured his four years at the military academy had prepared him well for this aspect of field command; many were the nights that he had burned the midnight oil preparing for the next day's classes, drills or examinations.

By the time he was back in uniform and emerging from his tent a second time, Sergeant Burleson was on the scene.

"Sergeant, Mr. Harley here is going to tell you where you can find two citizens by the names of Tom Jeffers and John Mellock. I want you to send a couple of men to both locations."

"Yes, sir. Begging the lieutenant's pardon, but why do we want these two men?"

"Gordon Hawkes is back."

Burleson cocked an eyebrow. "Well, I'll be damned. I kind of figured him for dead."

After informing Burleson as to where Jeffers and Mellock could be found, Harley said, "Hawkes is a man who won't die easy. And, Lieutenant, while by no means do I presume to tell you how to conduct your business, but . . ."

"But you're going to do that, just the same," said Gunnison dryly.

"I don't think two men are enough for the task at hand."

"Mr. Harley, every one of the men in this command has seen action. They are as tough and as capable as they come."

"I'm sure that's true, Lieutenant. But you haven't met Gordon Hawkes."

"No, not yet. But I fully intend to. Sergeant, carry out your orders—and make it quick."

"Yes, sir!" Burleson snapped off a salute and whirled, bellowing names as he strode between the orderly rows of tents.

"You are welcome to stay in camp, sir," Gunnison

told Harley. "Should Hawkes find out somehow that you came here . . ."

"That's the thing," said Harley. "He knew I would. I told him I would. I thought for a moment he might kill me."

"And why didn't he?"

Harley shrugged. He'd had time to reconsider his condemnation of Hawkes as someone who was no better than Chandler Doone. "Because, in my opinion, Lieutenant, Hawkes is not a cold-blooded killer, at least not by nature. You might say that this extraordinary tragedy has turned him into something that in fact runs counter to his nature."

"That may be so," said Gunnison. "But my job is to stop him. And that is precisely what I will do, one way or another. If he puts up a fight, my men are not going to withhold their fire just because Hawkes is grief-stricken over the loss of his son."

"Of course not," sighed Harley. "I appreciate your offer, Lieutenant, but I'm going back home. I'm fairly certain Hawkes will do me no harm."

"What if you're wrong?"

Harley smiled faintly. "Well, it wouldn't be the first time. But it would be the last."

When the two soldiers arrived at Tom Jeffers's claim located south of town, they stepped down off their horses and approached the cabin with all due caution, their Windsor rifles held at the ready. One stayed back while the other went to the door and knocked. No sound came from within. The soldier knocked again and glanced at his companion, who shrugged, then continued to scan the darkness. All he could hear was the murmur of the nearby creek and the soughing of the wind in the trees on the slopes above. Far off in the distance, a coyote yapped a lament to the stars.

"Maybe he isn't here," said the soldier at the door.

"Oh, I'm here all right," came a voice from the dark.

Both soldiers whirled to see the barrel of a shotgun jutting out from behind a corner of the cabin.

"Seeing as how this is my claim, here is right where I am supposed to be. But you two—you're not supposed to be here. And that can be right unhealthy."

"Is that you, Jeffers?"

"Who wants to know?"

"Lieutenant Gunnison sent us."

"What for? Why would he do that? What am I supposed to have done? I didn't break his damned curfew, I can tell you that right now."

"It isn't what you've done, but what you might do," said the cavalryman. "Which is die."

"What are you talking about?"

"Gordon Hawkes. He's back. Luther Harley saw him tonight, in town."

Tom Jeffers stepped out from behind the corner of the cabin. He had pulled his trousers on over faded yellow long johns, and he was barefoot. Peering at the soldiers, he lowered the shotgun and took a long, ragged breath.

"Is that so," he said. "I guess Harley was sober."

"Hawkes is here. And he's after you. He asked Harley where you lived."

Jeffers surveyed the night. "Well," he said at last, "I can't say that I blame him."

"So you've seen no sign of him?"

"I'm still breathing, ain't I? What do you think?"

"I think you had better come with us."

"And what will you do with me? Lock me up in that damned jail of yours to keep me safe? No thanks!"

"You work this claim on your own?" asked the soldier.

"Used to have me a partner. But he lit out a few weeks back. Before you boys even got here. He figured being my partner wasn't very healthy, after everything that had happened. So yeah, I work it by myself now. And that's one reason why I ain't going to let you take me off to your camp just so you can watch over me. I stay off this claim even one day, I might come back here to find some stranger has moved in. Then I'd have to kill him, or he'd do for me." Jeffers shook his head. "Thanks, but no thanks."

"You recorded your claim, didn't you?"

"Yeah, I did. A lot of good that will do."

"If a claim jumper tried to move in on you, we would move him right back out."

"Maybe you would. Then again, maybe you wouldn't. I ain't going to count on it. I'll stay put right here and take care of my own claim. And my own neck. Now you boys run along back to your lieutenant. Oh, and sorry for pointing this scattergun at you. I've got a little trapdoor in the back wall of the cabin. Somebody comes knocking in the middle of the night, I just crawl out the back and slip around here and get the drop on them. Just like I did with you boys."

The soldiers exchanged uncertain glances. Their orders had been to find this man, inform him of the danger posed by Gordon Hawkes and offer him protection. Sergeant Burleson hadn't said anything about what to do if Jeffers refused the offer. It hadn't occurred to the sergeant, or to the soldiers, that he might do that.

"Well," said one soldier to the other, "maybe we should just stay here and look after things. Or one of us can stay and the other report back to the lieutenant."

Jeffers bristled at the notion that he needed to be looked after. "If you stay, it won't be in my cabin."

"Why the hell not?" asked one of the soldiers, exasperated by Jeffers's attitude.

"Because he's got gold in there, that's why," said the other. "And he doesn't trust us."

"I don't trust anybody. Nothing personal. You might be as honest as Jesus Christ himself, but I know what gold can do to somebody."

"That's good," said the first soldier in disgust. "We come here to save your hide and you call us thieves. Jeffers, I hope the lieutenant tells us to come back and drag you back to camp by your ears. Come on," he said to his companion. "Let's get out of here."

The soldiers mounted up and rode away.

Jeffers went back inside the cabin, using the trapdoor. He made sure the front door and the wooden shutters on both windows were secured. Then, with a lantern turned down low, he sat in a dark corner with the shotgun across his knees—and waited.

The minutes crawled by. Jeffers was tired; he had worked hard all day taking gold out of the creek. According to his calculations, the claim was nearly played out; he had harvested a couple thousand dollars in dust out of it and was in a hurry to finish. Even before receiving the unpleasant news that Gordon Hawkes was back, he had decided to leave Gilder Gulch soon. What had happened here—and, more to the point, the role he had played in those dark events—troubled him deeply, and he figured the only thing that would help was a change of scenery. Had it turned out that Hawkes was dead and Chandler Doone was hauled away by the Army and peace was restored to the valley, it would have made no difference to Jeffers in the long run. He would still have wanted to get the hell away from this place. Now, with the return of the mountain man, he was just in a bigger hurry.

He dozed off eventually—then his eyes snapped wide open, and when he saw the mountain man standing there in front of him he thought for an instant that he was having a bad dream. Hawkes was pointing a pistol at him. Jeffers remembered the shotgun in his lap—only the weapon wasn't in his lap anymore! Panicking, the gold seeker scrambled to his feet, and froze when he heard the double click of the hammer on the mountain man's rifle as it was cocked.

"How did you get in here?" asked Jeffers, his voice raspy with fear.

"The trapdoor."

"But how did you . . .?"

"How did I know it was there? I saw you use it just a little while ago."

Jeffers stared at him, slowly comprehending. "You followed those soldiers here."

"Sure I did. I wouldn't have known where to find you, otherwise. They led me right to you."

"Christ," muttered Jeffers. How ironic, he thought, that the soldiers who had been sent to save his life had in fact signed his death warrant.

"You must be Jeffers," said Hawkes. "You were there when my son was killed. So you know why I'm here now."

Resignation overcame the prospector, a bitter flood. His shoulders sagged. "Yeah, I know," he said.

When the soldiers dispatched to the claim belonging to Tom Jeffers got back to the encampment, they were met by Lieutenant Gunnison.

"Where is Jeffers?" asked Gunnison. "What happened?"

"We told him about Hawkes, Lieutenant. But he wouldn't come back with us. And he didn't want us to stay, either. Said he thought we might steal his gold."

Gunnison shook his head. "Gold. It makes fools of men. You two get back there and bring Jeffers in and I don't care if he wants to come back with you or not. You understand me?"

"We just weren't sure what to do, Lieutenant. We . . ."

Gunnison made a curt gesture of dismissal. "Never mind. Now you know. Do it."

The two soldiers sheepishly turned their horses around and started back for the Jeffers claim.

"I know you're going to kill me," said Jeffers, "and I just want you to know I don't hold it against you."

Hawkes stared at him, wondering if the prospector was sincere, or playing some kind of game designed to prevent him from doing what he had come here to do.

"If I was in your place," continued Jeffers, "I'd be doing the same thing, I reckon. And what we did— well, that was just flat-out wrong. I knew it was even before I . . . before I saw your son fall."

"Then why? Why did you do it?"

Jeffers shrugged. "Been asking myself that same question ever since. Not sure I'll ever really know. It didn't have anything to do with your son, or whether he did kill Mitchell Doone in cold blood or self-defense. Of course, I'm just speaking for myself. I don't know about the others. It was right after the big flood, you know, that did a lot of damage. It pretty much wiped me out. Had to start all over."

Hawkes nodded. Pretty Shield had told him about the flood that had come on the night Mitchell Doone had appeared with murder on his mind.

"I guess I was mad," continued Jeffers. "Mad at the world. And I was afraid, too. I admit it. Afraid of Chandler Doone. He didn't ask us to come along, but once I was in I was afraid of what he might do if I backed out." The prospector managed to look Hawkes in the eye. That wasn't an easy thing to do, to look squarely in the eyes of the man who was about to kill you. "I ain't trying to make excuses. Doubt that would do any good anyway."

"Then what *are* you trying to do?"

"Just explaining why I don't fault you for what *you're* about to do."

Hawkes lowered the pistol.

He didn't know why, but he couldn't pull the trigger.

Jeffers stared in disbelief. What was the mountain man doing? Was Hawkes toying with him? If so, that was cruelty beyond even Chandler Doone's capacity.

"You have a choice," said Hawkes flatly. "Get out now and stay alive."

Jeffers nodded. "I'll go. I was planning to leave anyway."

"I mean now. Tonight. And don't come back to these mountains. If I ever see you again, I'll kill you."

"Why are you doing this? Why are you letting me go? You killed Josey Crane."

Hawkes nodded. "And that's why. Because killing him didn't help. And killing you won't either."

"For what it's worth, Hawkes, I'm sorry for what happened to your son."

"It's not worth anything to me," snapped Hawkes.

They both heard and recognized the sound at the same time—horses at the gallop, coming closer.

"Must be the soldiers coming back," said Jeffers. "You'd better get out of here."

A shot rang out even as Hawkes turned toward the trapdoor.

"Damn it," he said. He knew it was Pretty who had fired that shot.

Whirling, he went to the cabin door and threw it open.

The two cavalrymen had turned their horses in the direction from whence the shot had come, a slope east of the cabin where once a stand of birch trees had stood, now a field of ax-shattered stumps. That was where Hawkes had left Pretty, and he knew it was she who had fired that shot— he recognized the distinctive report of the Joslyn needle gun he had placed in her keeping. Knowing that he was in the cabin and seeing the soldiers arrive, she had fired both to warn him and to draw the attention of the cavalrymen. Both men were drawing their rifles from saddle boots, and Hawkes had no doubt that they would shoot Pretty without regard for the fact that she was a woman. Without hesitation, Hawkes raised his pistol and fired.

A shrill whinny presaged by seconds the thrashing collapse of one of the soldier's mounts. The other trooper turned and spotted Hawkes framed in the cabin doorway, silhouetted against the lantern light from within. He snapped off a shot with his Windsor, but the mountain man was already on the move. He dashed off around the corner of the cabin. Still mounted, the soldier whipped his horse around, spurred the animal into a leaping gallop and gave chase. Meanwhile the other bluecoat, stunned from the fall, picked himself up and, swaying slightly, stared at his dying horse.

Hawkes had left his Plains rifle behind the cabin. He snatched it up on the run and headed for the creek, looking over his shoulder as the cavalryman thundered around the cabin. The man had put his empty rifle back in its boot and was brandishing his heavy saber, its blade catching a glimmer of moonlight. Running hard, Hawkes splashed across the shallow creek, sensing that the mounted soldier was closing fast. At the last possible moment he dived sideways just as the saber cleaved the space he had occupied only a heartbeat earlier. Stumbling, Hawkes sprawled in the creek, submerging the Plains rifle as he caught himself. The cavalryman checked his horse sharply and turned it around. Realizing his long gun would not fire with its powder wet, Hawkes grabbed the barrel with both hands, preparing to use the weapon as a club to deflect the next stroke of the saber.

Then Hawkes heard the unmistakable bark of the needle gun again, and the trooper toppled sideways out of his saddle. The mountain man turned to see Pretty near the cabin. The other cavalryman saw her, too, and was swinging his rifle around to take aim at her.

Shouting a warning to Pretty, Hawkes lunged at the cavalryman and swung the Plains rifle, knocking the man down before he could fire. As the trooper tried to get up, Hawkes hit him again. The stock of the Plains rifle connected with the base of his skull and he sprawled unconscious, facedown in the creek. Hawkes grabbed him by the back of his fatigue jacket and dragged him to the creek bank. Pretty Shield met him there.

"Watch him," said Hawkes curtly. "If he comes to, knock him out again. But try not to kill him."

Wading back out into the creek, he found the other soldier and brought him to the bank. Pretty's bullet had hit him high in the left arm. Bleeding and half-drowned, he was cussing a blue streak.

"Damn it, Pretty," said Hawkes. "You nearly got yourself killed. I told you to stay up on that hill." He looked at the two soldiers lying at their feet. "Well, at least they're still alive."

"No thanks to you, Hawkes," said the wounded cavalryman.

Hawkes relieved both men of their pistols and tossed the weapons into the creek. Then he took Pretty by the arm and led her a short distance away, out of the soldier's hearing range.

"Pretty," he said, "I'm going to take those two men back to their camp and turn myself in."

She stared at him in speechless astonishment.

"The one I want is Chandler Doone," he said. "And he's in the custody of those soldiers. That newspaperman was right when he said I should surrender to the lieutenant. It's the only way I can get close to Doone."

"They will take you away," she said. "And what if they find out about the murder charges against you?"

"Then I reckon I'll hang. But I have to take that chance."

"Gordon, please . . ."

"No, it's the only way now. You had better go, Pretty. There's nothing more you can do for me here."

"What about Eliza? What about your daughter?"

Hawkes grimly shook his head. "I just can't let Chandler Doone live after what he's done. The rest of them—Jeffers and the others—that's one thing, but

Doone, no." Reading the look on Pretty's face, Hawkes added, "I know you don't understand."

"No, I do not understand. And I do not want to leave you."

"You have to, this time."

"But where will I go?"

"I've been thinking about that." Reaching under his buckskin tunic, Hawkes took out a beaded white wampum belt and offered it to her. "Come on, take it."

Because she knew what it was, she hesitated, but at his insistence she took the belt from his hand.

"As long as you have that, you can live in peace among my brothers, the Absaroke. It's up to you, of course, but in my opinion the Mountain Crow are your best bet. If you need help, you can ask it of Little Thunder and He Smiles Twice. They are good friends of mine and honorable men."

She gazed at him, wondering what to do, wondering if she would ever see him again. Never before had she felt so lost, so alone, so unsure of herself. Why, why did it have to be this way? Why did he have to pursue this deadly crusade? She knew that she would never understand. If only it could end differently. If only Hawkes would give up his quest for revenge and go home to Eliza—then Pretty thought it would be much easier for her to leave him forever, as she knew she must, because in that case at least she would be assured that he was safe and well. But this—this was almost intolerable, because it was reminiscent of her last moments with Cameron.

"Now, go," said Hawkes brusquely. "Take my horse. He seems to like you well enough."

Pretty looked away so that he would not see the tears she could scarcely restrain.

"Pretty."

"Yes," she said, still looking down.

"Thanks for everything," said Hawkes, struggling to find the right words, the ones that would perfectly express what was in his heart. At such times the right words usually eluded him—he was frustrated by his incompetence in this regard. "Thanks for taking care of my son. And for taking care of me. I will always . . ."

Now she looked up into his eyes, lips parted breathlessly as she waited, hoping, longing, for the word.

"I will always think about you," said Hawkes.

"I will always *love* you," she said, her chin lifted in defiance against the Fates that tormented her.

In anguish, he turned away. "Go on," he said brusquely. "Go, now, please."

She turned away and he went back to where the soldiers lay, retrieving the one's horse and bidding the wounded trooper to get into the saddle, helping him comply. Only then did Hawkes risk looking back toward the spot where Pretty had stood. She'd disappeared into the night. It was almost more than he could do just to stand up straight and breathe normally, so severe was the pain of parting from her.

He managed to get the unconscious soldier up onto the horse, draping him over the saddle in front of the wounded man.

"Hold on to your friend," said Hawkes. "I'm taking you back to your lieutenant."

"Why in the hell would you do that?" asked the

soldier, thinking that the mountain man had to be lying, but unable to figure out why he would bother lying.

Hawkes didn't answer. He gathered up the reins in one hand and, with the Plains rifle in the other, started in the direction of the gold camp.

Chapter Sixteen

When Lieutenant Gunnison was informed that a man who said his name was Gordon Hawkes had brought two of his men in, one of them unconscious and the other one wounded, he wondered if it was some kind of ruse. Just to be on the safe side, he ordered out all the men in camp. With several details on patrol that night, this only amounted to ten men, but they all grabbed their weapons, boiled out of the tents in various stages of undress and headed for the sentry post on the southern perimeter of the camp.

He got his first look at Gordon Hawkes by lantern light—and knew right away that this had to be the man who'd been causing so much trouble in these parts lately. He looked plenty tough. It wasn't just the old bloodstains on his buckskins. And it wasn't just the fierce and fearless look in his eyes. There was something about the mountain man that made every one of the soldiers present wary.

Sergeant Burleson was there, holding a pistol on Hawkes. The sentry had called the sergeant up when the mountain man had arrived, and Burleson had watched over things while the sentry ran to Gunnison's tent to inform the lieutenant. Burleson had ordered Hawkes to shed his weapons, and now the sergeant turned the rifle, pistol and Bowie knife over to a soldier. Gunnison ordered two other soldiers to take care of the men Hawkes had brought up. Then he turned his attention to Hawkes.

"Are you responsible for that?" he asked, with a gesture at the pair Hawkes had dealt with earlier.

"You could say that."

"What about Tom Jeffers? Is he dead?"

"Nope."

"Why not? That's what you're here for, isn't it?"

"I'm here for the man who shot my son."

Gunnison nodded. "I see now. And you know I have him, don't you?"

Hawkes smiled coldly. "I was counting on that."

"Where is Private Smith's horse?"

"Private Smith?"

"The man whose skull you apparently tried to crack open."

"Oh. We weren't formally introduced. He'll live. But I had to kill his horse."

"Had to?"

"A man on a horse has a big advantage over a man afoot. I had to try to even the odds."

Gunnison glanced at Burleson. "A two-man guard for Mr. Hawkes, Sergeant, and bring him to my tent."

"Yes, sir."

"The rest of you stand down," said Gunnison and, turning briskly on his heel, he headed back into the encampment.

Burleson selected two men, who flanked Hawkes with bayonets affixed to their Windsor rifles. The sergeant led the way to Gunnison's tent. The rest of the soldiers were slow to disperse. They had heard a lot about Gordon Hawkes since coming to the gold camp. The prospectors had spun some pretty wild tales about the mountain man. It was said that for sport, when boredom overcame him, he battled grizzlies with his bare hands. And that he had been raised by a wolf pack after having been abandoned by his fur trapper father and his Indian squaw. One rumor had it that Hawkes had come west with several other adventurers, and when the party faced starvation in the heart of a particularly brutal mountain winter, Hawkes had murdered and eaten his companions just to stay alive. Another story was that the mountain man had wiped out an entire Indian village just for something to do, still another that he had done the same to a wagon train of emigrants bound for Oregon. Hawkes, it was said, was such an amazing marksman that he could shoot at a bird on the wing at three hundred yards and clip its tail feathers.

Not that the soldiers were inclined to put much credence in such tall tales. But they did know that Hawkes had taken on an entire gold camp single-handedly, and struck fear into the hearts of two hundred or more who were not the fainthearted type.

When Burleson reached the lieutenant's tent with his prisoner, Gunnison was pacing like a caged lion, back and forth, back and forth, hands clasped behind his back, his brow furrowed. Hawkes, the sergeant and the two guards waited while Gunnison paced for another minute before halting abruptly to peer grimly at the mountain man.

"The Moslems have an interesting tradition," he said. "If a loved one is murdered, you may buy the right to have vengeance on the murderer, on condition that you pay a sufficient fee to the bey or khalif or whoever is in charge of things. Then you have purchased your right to retribution and your freedom from consequences. Unless, of course, the person you kill is the loved one of someone else who can afford to pay the price."

"That's real interesting," said Hawkes dryly. "Now, I know you're not suggesting I pay you to let me settle my differences with Chandler Doone."

"Certainly not. You won't get close to Doone as long as he is in my custody. Surely you didn't think I would just throw you in that jail with him."

"Why not? This is between him and me."

"Not anymore it isn't. I'm curious, Hawkes. Clearly you're no fool. But it was foolish of you in the extreme to come here tonight. You would have done better to pick a likely spot along the trail and wait until we took Doone out and killed him with a rifle shot."

Hawkes shook his head. "No. He's going to be looking me right in the eye when I take his life."

"You don't seem to understand. You're not going to get that chance."

"I might. That's why I'm here."

Gunnison shook his head and sat on a camp stool behind a folding desk that stood beneath a tarp erected in front of his tent. "I am taking Chandler Doone to Camp Collins."

"What for?"

"Because I believe him to be a thief and a murderer."

"He's a murderer, surely."

"He was wrong to take the law into his own hands where your son was concerned, yes. Whether that was murder or not isn't for me to decide. But I strongly suspect that he has killed others in cold blood, right here in the gold camp. At the very least he is a troublemaker, and I intend to remove·him from this valley. And that goes for you, too, Hawkes. I'm going to take you to Camp Collins, too. There, I'll let my commanding officer and territorial authorities decide what's to be done with the two of you."

Hawkes nodded. *And what if they find out about the murder charges against you?* Pretty had asked.

All along he had known that that was a risk—one he had to take. A planter in Louisiana and a lawyer in Missouri had been killed in cold blood, and in both cases he had been wrongfully accused of the crime. The first had occurred twenty-five years ago; in the other case only a dozen years had passed. He had no idea if, after all that time, the law was still looking for him. But the chance that the law *was* still looking had been enough to keep him in exile in the mountains.

At the present time, though, it wasn't really a consideration.

Because he had no intention of going to Camp Collins.

"I'll be honest with you, Hawkes," said Gunnison. "After talking to the gambler Devanor and a few others, I don't doubt that Mitchell Doone visited your son's claim that night with murder on his mind. But even if that's so, it doesn't give you the right to come here and play judge, jury and executioner. Harvey Doone, for instance—as far as I can tell he wasn't involved at all in your son's death. But you killed him anyway."

"That was a fair fight."

"Yes, perhaps. And Chandler Doone says he killed your son in a fair fight, too."

"And when he and I meet, that'll be a fair fight, too," said Hawkes.

Gunnison shook his head. "There has been too much killing already. It stops here and now. Sergeant."

"Yes, sir," said Burleson.

"I'm placing you in charge of the prisoner. Put him in irons, under guard, but I don't want him anywhere near Doone, understand?"

"Yes, sir!"

"We'll start for Camp Collins day after tomorrow. I think now that we have Mr. Hawkes here, and Mr. Doone, this valley will be a much safer place."

When Devanor arrived at Joe Duff's tent saloon, it was still morning, and he didn't expect there to be much going on. So he was surprised to find about two dozen prospectors gathered there. Everyone seemed to be talking at once. The crowd was electrified with excitement. The gambler got the attention of the nearest man by grabbing his arm.

"What's going on? Did somebody start a war?"

"The soldiers captured Hawkes."

"They didn't capture him," corrected a second man. "He gave himself up."

"He was out at the Jeffers claim when the soldiers found him," said the first. "Guess he was aiming to do away with Tom, since Tom was one of the men who rode with Chandler Doone."

"That's not how it happened," said the second.

"How do you know? You weren't there," snapped the first man, perturbed.

"Yeah, well, neither were you, you knobhead."

"You better have a care calling me names, you son of a bitch."

Devanor shook his head and went to the bar, where Joe Duff was talking to Wiley Roe, The Banker and a bartender. The saloonkeeper stopped talking as the gambler drew near.

"Wiley," said Devanor, "there are two men over there in need of some attention from you."

Wiley looked just in time to see one of the quarreling placer miners give the other one a hard shove.

"Throw them out," Duff told Wiley. "I guess you heard the news, Dev."

Devanor laughed. "A couple of versions of it, yes. Is it true that Hawkes gave himself up to the soldiers?"

Duff nodded. "That seems to be the case."

"I guess he thought that was the only way he could get to Chandler Doone."

"Yeah, which means he's none too smart," sneered Duff. "Gunnison is hauling them both off to Camp Collins, and I say good riddance. They're leaving tomorrow morning. I'm going with them."

"You sure you want to leave now? It looks like Gilder Gulch might survive, after all."

"You think so? To tell you the truth, I think this town is jinxed, that's what I think. I've decided to leave this saloon open." Duff gestured at the bartender. "Frank here will look after things while I'm gone. And The Banker will be sticking around, too. Me, I'm going to take my profits to St. Louis, and come back in the spring. Then we'll see how things are here."

Devanor nodded. "Sounds reasonable enough."

"What about you?"

"I'm leaving, too."

The gambler walked out of the tent saloon and made his way back to the hotel. When he got to his room, he found Alice sitting on the edge of the bed in her silk wrapper, gazing out the window.

"I've often wondered how you stand it," said Devanor, "being cooped up in this room hour after hour, with nothing to do."

She smiled at him. "I do a lot of thinking. Mostly about you and me."

"Well, the next window you stare out of will at least offer a view. Pack your things, Alice. We're going to San Francisco."

"What? When?"

"Now. Today!"

"But . . . but I thought we were waiting for the soldiers."

"They're pulling out tomorrow. But we don't have to wait. Gordon Hawkes turned himself in to Lieutenant Gunnison. So, you see, there's no more danger. We can leave here at once. In a couple of weeks we'll be in San Francisco. Then we can get married—

and start working on those children. How many did you say we were going to have again?" He grinned.

"But . . . this is so sudden . . ."

"It's a good time to go. Winter is on its way, Alice. We can be sure to get over the Sierras before the first heavy snow."

"Whether we leave one day sooner won't make any difference in that regard, surely."

Devanor pulled his valise out from under the bed. He stood there, holding it, his exuberance ebbing fast. It suddenly occurred to him that Alice wasn't telling him everything. Of that he was suddenly and completely convinced.

"What's going on, Alice?" he said softly. "Why don't you want to leave Gilder Gulch? Something is holding you here. Tell me what it is."

"Don't be silly, Charles. Why should I want to stay here?"

"I have no idea. I was hoping you could tell me."

"I don't know what you're talking about, darling. You're imagining things."

"I don't think so."

She stood up and went to the window, her back to him.

"There is something here that I want," she said.

"Here? What? What could you possibly want here?"

She hesitated, then turned to face him. "Joe Duff's gold."

Devanor stared at her a moment, trying to digest this totally unexpected news. A cold chill ran down his spine. He didn't want to believe what he had just heard. Didn't want to because if it was true then it meant that what he thought he'd had with Alice was just an illusion. No, worse than an illusion. A lie.

"You want Duff's gold," he said flatly. "You mean you want to steal it."

"Yes, Charles, I want to steal it. I'm going to steal it. I doubt that he will just give it to me."

"So that's what this is all about. That's why you moved in here with me. To be closer to the gold. I guess you knew The Banker had a room right down the hall, and that he kept Duff's strongbox with him at all times."

"I know more than that. They keep a lot of the gold dust and the money in a second strongbox—hidden under the floor in that room."

Devanor was astonished. "How did you find that out?"

"It doesn't matter. You're wrong, though. That's not why I moved in here with you. I had no thought of Duff's gold when I did that. The idea came to me later. I kept seeing The Banker with that strongbox, either going to the saloon or coming back here. And I started thinking about what was in it. A lot of money, Charles. More money than I guess I've ever seen. More than you could make in years. And I want it."

Devanor nodded. "Now I see why you never wanted to leave. It had nothing to do with Hawkes, did it? It never did."

"You don't like Duff. You've told me so yourself more than once. He's not your friend. What would you care if someone stole all his money?"

"I wouldn't care. That's not what I care about."

"Then . . . why are you so angry? I want it for the both of us. Then we really could have that big house on the hill." Alice came to him, resting her hands on his chest, looking up at him with a sweet smile and soft eyes. "Think about it, Charles. We could be rich. We could live in high style. We would never want for anything ever again."

"I never wanted for anything," he said. "Well, that's not exactly true. I did want one thing. Funny, I thought I'd found it, too."

She knew what he meant by that, and shook her head. "No. Don't do that. I want you. And I want the gold, too. Why can't I have both?"

"Because while I may belong to you, Alice, heart and soul, that gold does not."

She stepped away from him, a quizzical look on her face. "I don't understand you. I really don't. Why this righteous indignation? You're not a lawman. You're not a preacher. You're a gambler, Charles. What you do is almost like stealing. Those miners don't stand a chance against you in a poker game."

"And just how were you proposing to take that gold, Alice? What about the breed and Wiley? Duff hired them to keep people like you from doing exactly what you're talking about. This is not a game. They would kill you. And your being a woman wouldn't stop them."

"That's why I need your help, Charles. I can't do it alone. Together, though, we can do it. I'm betting Wiley wouldn't kill you. In fact, if you talked to him, he might even help us."

"Wiley may be a bone breaker, but he's an honest man. Yes, he likes me, and I like him. But he'll be loyal to Joe Duff because Joe pays him. Wiley may be a little simpleminded, but he's got integrity. And

I wouldn't try to use him, or undermine that integrity. Not a chance. Forget it."

"Then you won't help me," she said coldly.

"Alice, I want you to forget this crazy scheme. It's too dangerous. I don't want anything to happen to you. I want you to come away with me. Right now. We'll go to San Francisco and make our dreams come true. We don't need Duff's gold to do that. I know I don't. All I need is you."

For a moment she said nothing, staring at him, and Devanor thought that perhaps he had succeeded, that he had made her see reason.

"If you really loved me," she said, at last, "you would help me."

Devanor shook his head in despair. Where moments before his thoughts had been filled with grand and joyous expectations of the life he and Alice would have together, now his future looked as bleak, if not bleaker, than it had when he had first arrived in Gilder Gulch. Bitterly he realized that he should have known that his dreams had only been illusions.

"Well," he said, forcing a smile, "as they say, lucky at cards, unlucky at love."

"Then you won't help me."

"No, I will not. Not because it's wrong, but because it is too dangerous—for you."

"And you think, hope, that if you don't help me I will give up on the idea," she said angrily. "Well, I won't! If you don't help me, someone else will."

Devanor just nodded—and left the room without another word.

He walked for a long time, aimlessly, paying no attention to his surroundings, moving in a fog of misery that obscured the whole world. Now and then he would be confronted by an obstacle—a building, the creek, a steep slope, a group of prospectors walking along the street—which would force him to emerge from gloomy introspection to look about and get his bearings. Several times he came to the conclusion that the best thing to do would be to go back and get his belongings and then buy a horse and leave the gold camp. Leave now and not look back. Forget Alice, forget his dreams and mark it down to experience. In his life he had suffered many setbacks, endured many disappointments. This was just one more, after all, and as he had overcome those in the past, so he could overcome this one. He had arrived at the gold camp alone, self-reliant, strong of will, needing no one, or at least halfway believing that to be the case. Why couldn't he leave in the same condition? It wasn't as though he had no experience in such matters. He had loved before, and lost.

The problem in this case was that he hadn't loved, not quite like this, before. And it didn't have to end this way. He could still have his future with Alice. All he had to do was help her steal Duff's gold. Yes, it was dangerous, but he wasn't concerned for his own safety. It was Alice that he worried about. But Alice was going to go through with her scheme, regardless of whether he helped. And he didn't doubt that for a moment.

What he couldn't shake—what he had to learn to live with if it turned out to be true—was the suspicion that she had been using him, had been playing him along from the start. That everything she had done was not out of love for him but because she had been scheming to steal the gold from Joe Duff. She had claimed that she wanted the gold for them both, but Devanor doubted that was really the case. *If she wanted the gold, she should have moved in with Duff instead,* he mused. *Of course, Duff was no fool. At least not as big a fool as I am.* Duff hadn't been the one to hang around her shack in Paradise Alley like a lovesick boy. Duff hadn't been the one who'd enticed her away from the life she had been leading. And Duff hadn't been the one who had fallen in love with her. Joe Duff wasn't like that. He was in love with only one thing. Profit. Riches. And he would have seen right through Alice Diamond.

But every time Devanor reached the point of leaving, of putting it all behind him, he faltered. Because he told himself he could be wrong about Alice. Maybe she really did want to be with him. And if there was the smallest chance of that being true, how could he leave? So she did not love him enough to forget her dangerous scheme. But maybe she did love him, some.

I'm in a losing game, he thought bitterly, *but I just can't fold my hand.* Like a greenhorn poker player, he couldn't bring himself to cut his losses. He had to stay in, play the game out, even though the odds were stacked against him, because there was still that slim possibility that he could salvage the future.

Faced with yet another obstacle, he looked up and found himself back at the hotel.

When he entered the room, Alice was standing at the window.

"I was hoping you would come back," she said with a tentative smile.

"I was hoping I wouldn't," he replied.

Chapter Seventeen

As they had when the soldiers arrived, the denizens of Gilder Gulch came out in force to see them depart. The sun had not yet risen above the line of peaks to the east, and the autumn morning more than hinted at the coming of winter, so that the exhalations of man and beast vapored in front of their faces, and men huddled shivering in their coats with collars pulled up and hat brims or cap visors pulled down low to shield their eyes from cutting gusts of wind.

Lieutenant Gunnison had agreed to let Joe Duff accompany him to Camp Collins. He had done likewise where Charles Devanor and Alice Diamond were concerned. Duff would be joined by the half-breed whose name nobody knew and the goliath named Wiley Roe. Gunnison could guess why they were coming along—to guard the pair of iron strongboxes that were strapped to the back of Duff's pack mule. Adding the two prisoners, Gordon Hawkes and Chandler Doone, that made seven civilians with the column. This did not bother Gunnison overmuch. Unlike many of his fellow soldiers, he did not hold civilians in contempt. And he had made it clear to both Duff and Devanor that he was in command;

they would do what he told them to do when he told them to do it, as long as they rode with his troops. If they balked at an order or failed to obey one or made any trouble for him, they would be on their own.

All of the civilians save for the prisoners rode horses. Devanor had paid top dollar for two mounts for himself and Alice, while Duff had acquired three for himself, the breed and Wiley Roe. In addition, Gunnison had needed a horse to replace the one Hawkes had shot; he had provided the previous owner with a chit redeemable at any Army post for money in payment or another horse. Doone and Hawkes rode mules, and Gunnison had made sure they did not ride too near one another. Both men wore iron shackles on their wrists, and each was assigned a pair of guards. When they dismounted, their feet would be shackled as well. Gunnison was not going to take any chances with either one of them.

As the column trailed Gunnison down the Gilder Gulch street, Luther Harley came forward to say his good-byes to Devanor. The troopers and their prisoners were first in line, followed by the contingent's pack mules; Duff's party came next, with Devanor and Alice bringing up the rear. Spotting the newspaperman, Devanor checked his horse and extended a hand. Alice stopped her horse, too.

"Well, Charles," said Harley, seizing the proffered hand, "I never did get your story."

"It's not really one that's worth telling, Luther."

"You should let me be the judge of that."

"Maybe I will, if we meet again." Devanor scanned the gold camp one last time. "So now it's all yours.

Maybe you can make something of this place, after all. If anyone can do that, it would be you."

"As I recall, you never thought Gilder Gulch would last."

"I'm still not sure it will. Those things that last are usually built on a better foundation than greed. But I hope I'm wrong."

"At least now we have a chance, with those two men out of the picture." Harley gestured at the cavalry column, and Devanor knew he meant Gordon Hawkes and Chandler Doone. "Well, I wish the two of you every happiness, Charles, and the best of luck."

"Thanks, Luther. But as I keep having to remind you, luck has nothing to do with it."

Harley laughed. "That's right. Come back and see me sometime."

"I doubt I'll be back this way. Good-bye."

"Take care, Charles."

The gambler goaded his horse into motion, and he and Alice rode on in the wake of the column.

Gunnison called a halt around midday. They had passed over the high saddle from where one could take a last look back at the gold camp nestled in the valley far below, and then had begun a gradual descent toward the canyon passage, where a creek twisted and tumbled down a fairly steep decline in miles of white water. Beyond the canyon the creek would become more sedate as it led them into a valley where it would eventually converge with an unnamed river. From the point of that convergence— which Gunnison intended to reach by nightfall and make camp there— they would be able to see Horseshoe Pass to the east.

The cavalrymen dismounted and loosened saddle cinches to let their horses blow after the long climb from the gold camp. A couple of fires were built, and coffeepots were balanced on rim stones. While they waited eagerly for the contents of these coffeepots to boil, the soldiers sat or squatted around the fires and made small talk. A major topic of conversation was the problem the United States Army was currently having with the Arapaho dog soldiers. Gunnison couldn't help but overhear, though he sat on a lichen-covered rock some distance apart from the enlisted men, scanning the surrounding high slopes with a pair of field glasses. He heard not a single reference to the fact that the Arapahos—formerly peaceable where whites were concerned, being nothing more than an occasional curiosity—had suddenly become hostile after waves of emigrants had begun traversing their homeland, killing the game and bringing diseases that swept like wildfire through their villages. As far as the soldiers were concerned, the Arapahos were just obnoxious obstacles to the progress of Americans as they pursued their manifest destiny. Gunnison saw things in a slightly different light. He could sympathize with the Indians. Had the shoe been on the other foot, he would have defended his homeland against foreign encroachment. But he was wise enough to keep his sympathies to himself. Such sentiments would bring the suspicion and scrutiny of his superiors down upon him. And even while he could sympathize with the dog soldier and admire him for his courage and resourcefulness and audacity, Gunnison would fight him fiercely, holding nothing back, because that was his duty. And he always did his duty.

In a similar fashion he felt sorry for the mountain man, Gordon Hawkes. He had sensed that Hawkes hated the gold camp and its inhabitants, not only because of the fate that had befallen his son, but also because of what Gilder Gulch and the gold seekers represented. In a word, progress. And progress was a threat to Hawkes and all like him. Westward expansion marked the end of a way of life that Hawkes had pursued, usually with the intent of leaving civilization far behind. Gunnison felt sorry for the man, yes. But that didn't change anything. The mountain man could expect no favors from him.

Putting the field glasses away, Gunnison stood up and walked over to where the prisoners were being held. He checked to see that the leg shackles had been placed on Doone and Hawkes once they'd dismounted, and that the two men were being kept well apart. In both cases he was satisfied.

One of Doone's guards approached him.

"Lieutenant, Doone says he needs to talk to Joe Duff. I told him I had to check with you about that."

"Talk to Duff about what?"

"He says it's about some money he owes Duff."

"Are the two of them friends?"

"That's not what I've heard, sir. In fact, I hear that Doone almost killed Duff once."

"Okay. But Duff must be unarmed and must keep his distance from the prisoner. I want nothing to be passed between them."

"Yes, sir."

"I'll tell Duff myself." Gunnison moved on along the

line, to the place where Duff was supervising Wiley Roe, who checked the ropes holding the strongboxes in place on the frame that was strapped to the mule's back. The half-breed, a sawed-off shotgun cradled in his arm, stood nearby keeping a watchful eye on everything and everyone—including the lieutenant.

"Chandler Doone wants to talk to you, Mr. Duff," said Gunnison.

The saloonkeeper appeared surprised. "Talk to me? What for?"

"I'm told it's in regard to some money he owes you."

"He doesn't . . ." Duff stopped abruptly, blinked, and then smiled. "Oh yes, I remember now."

"But you'll leave your pistol with me," said Gunnison, holding out a hand, palm turned up.

Duff looked at the lieutenant's hand, hesitated, then shrugged and handed over his pistol. "Sure. You're the boss." He turned to the breed. "Keep an eye on things until I get back."

"Good idea," said Gunnison. "I want to remind you, Mr. Duff, that although I'm allowing you to ride with us as far as Camp Collins, I accept no responsibility for those strongboxes or their contents—and neither will the United States Army. Their safekeeping is entirely up to you."

"Yeah, I know," replied Duff. "And Wiley and the breed will make sure they stay safe."

Gunnison nodded. "Fair enough." He walked on to where Charles Devanor was building a small fire. Alice sat on a rock nearby, her shoulders hunched under the gambler's dusty black frock coat.

"Are you doing all right, miss?" asked Gunnison.

"Yes, thank you. Just a little chilled."

"It is pretty cold. If the two of you would like some hot coffee, you are welcome to some of ours." Gunnison gestured toward the soldiers' fires.

"Thank you," said Devanor. "We might take you up on that."

"And if you are hungry, I can offer you some hard-tack and jerky."

"Thank you so much, Lieutenant," said Alice.

"May I ask, how far do you two intend to travel with us?"

Alice and Devanor exchanged glances. "I expect no further than the way station on the other side of Horseshoe Pass," replied Devanor. "From there we will ride south. Strike the Overland stage route and travel it to California."

"South, you say? Keep in mind that the Arapahos are stirring up trouble in that part of the country."

"There's trouble everywhere you look these days, Lieutenant. Doesn't matter which way you travel."

"You have a point there, Mr. Devanor. Well, I'll have one of my men bring you that coffee. Oh, and we'll be moving on shortly."

Devanor nodded. As Gunnison moved away, the gambler looked at Alice. She was watching Wiley and the breed—and the strongboxes lashed to the mule. Devanor lit the kindling, and when he was sure the fledgling fire would withstand the occasional strong gusts of cold wind sweeping down from the high slopes, he walked over and sat on the rock beside her. He didn't put his arm around her; instead, he clasped his hands together between his knees and stared at the struggling flames.

"When are we going to do it, Charles?" she whispered.

He sighed audibly. "Well, we don't have much time. I suppose it has to be tonight."

"And how will we do it?"

"*We* aren't. I am. You're going to stay out of it entirely, Alice."

"Then how are *you* going to do it?"

Devanor looked up and across at the breed and Wiley Roe—and shook his head. "I really don't have a clue. Maybe I should challenge Duff to one hand of five-card draw. The stakes—his loot, and you."

"That's not funny, Charles."

"What would you do to get your hands on that gold, Alice? How far, I wonder, would you go?"

Her cheeks darkened with anger. "I ought to slap you."

"Yes, you probably should. But that's risky—I might come to my senses and walk away."

"But you won't do that, will you?"

"No. God help me, I can't."

"What are you going to do, really? You must have some idea."

"Well, I have to kill the half-breed. And Duff, too. Maybe even Wiley, though I hope not. Because if I don't they'll come after us. And they wont' stop until they catch us. Especially Duff. That gold in those strongboxes—that was his big strike. He's got his whole future staked on that gold. He'll stop at nothing to hold on to it, or to get it back."

"Can you do that? Can you kill those men?"

"Yes."

"Have you ever killed a man before, Charles?"

He looked at her, and saw nothing to indicate that the prospect of men losing their lives for the gold she coveted bothered her in the least. She was asking him if he could take another man's life as mildly as if she was asking if he could saddle a horse.

"Yes," he said coldly. "I've killed a couple of men. One over a card game. That was self-defense. He thought I was cheating. He drew his pistol first, and I had no choice."

"And the other?"

Devanor smiled bitterly. "The other was the very next night. You see, some acquaintances of the man I shot came looking for me. They were a rough lot, intent on avenging their friend. I barely got out of the hotel alive. My friend, Andrew Roberts, gave me his pistol because all I carried at the time was my pocket derringer. Those men chased me through the streets. I turned down a dark alley, hoping to give them the slip. Then I heard a noise behind me. I turned, saw the shape of a man in the darkness. I thought it was one of those men. I fired . . . and killed an innocent old drunk."

"Oh my God," breathed Alice.

The gambler nodded. "Then I heard the men who were after me, they were running to the sound of the gunshot. I ran, stumbled and fell over the body of the man I had just killed. I dropped Andrew's pistol. I didn't have time to look for it, so I just got up and ran away, and managed to elude the ones who were chasing me."

"So that's why you knew your friend was innocent when the vigilantes hanged him."

"Yes. They found his pistol next to the body, assumed he fired the shot. But I was the one. I should have told the truth, should have turned myself in to the vigilance committee. But I left San Francisco that night because I didn't want to die at the hands of the vigilantes or those other men. Even though I knew they would find that pistol and might learn the identity of the man to whom it belonged."

"But why didn't your friend tell the truth? Why didn't he say he had given you the pistol, to save himself?"

"Perhaps he tried to. I don't know. Maybe he tried and no one would listen. Mobs don't listen, Alice. And they don't care about the truth. So now you know. I was a coward. I ran away to save my own hide, and a friend died for a crime that I committed."

"Why didn't you tell me this before, Charles?"

"Because I was afraid of what you might think of me."

"And you're no longer afraid of that? You no longer care what I think?"

He shook his head. "It doesn't really matter at this point."

Alice looked away. "Because you don't think I really love you. Perhaps you think that as soon as we have the gold I will leave you anyway."

"All I know," said Devanor grimly, "is that I love you. And I don't want to see you hurt. That's the only reason I'm here."

For a moment she was quiet. At last she said, "And when we have the gold, where do we go? Will the soldiers come after us?"

"That's likely. Not for the gold. I understand that the lieutenant has told Duff that the gold is his problem, not the Army's. But they will because of the killing. Unless I give them something else to chase after."

"What would that be?"

"Gordon Hawkes," said Devanor.

When Joe Duff approached the spot where Chandler Doone was sitting with his back to a tree, flanked by a pair of rifle-toting soldiers, one of the latter came forward to intercept him.

"Are you carrying any weapons, sir?"

"I gave my pistol to the lieutenant. That's all I carry."

The soldier nodded. "The lieutenant said you are not to get too close to the prisoner, sir. We will not allow anything but words to pass between the two of you. I hope that's understood."

"I understand."

The soldier rejoined his comrade and Duff stepped closer to Doone. About ten feet away he stopped and glanced at the soldier he had spoken to, who nodded. The saloonkeeper sat on his heels, elbows resting on his knees, and peered at Doone. The man looked the worse for wear after spending nearly a fortnight in the jail. He was dirty and unshaven. He wore shackles on his wrists and ankles, and the heavy iron had rubbed his flesh raw.

Doone turned his head and glowered at his two guards. "I want to talk privately. So why don't you boys walk on over yonder. You can still keep an eye on me from there."

The soldiers exchanged glances. Then one shrugged and led the way. They walked off twenty paces before stopping to turn and watch Doone and Duff.

"So what game are you playing, Chandler?" asked the saloonkeeper. He was a little perturbed, wanting nothing more to do with Doone or any other aspect of this deadly business of vengeance-seeking that had cost him so dearly, not only in lost profits but on two occasions in damaged pride—the first when Doone had come within a hair's breadth of killing him, and the second when Hawkes had appeared in his tent that morning, scaring ten years off his life. The tone of his voice was now curt and condescending; he would never have spoken to Doone in such a manner had the latter not been wearing iron. But his fear of Doone manifested itself in this way. He was like the child who prodded a caged lion with a stick—something he would not dream of doing if the cage wasn't there.

"You don't owe me money," continued Duff. "I would have remembered."

"No, but I could owe you some," said Doone with a crooked smile.

"What the hell are you talking about?"

"You know why they've got me in these things?" asked Doone, lifting his arms and rattling the chain that connected the iron shackles on his wrists.

"Sure I do. The lieutenant thinks you've murdered some prospectors and robbed a good many more."

Doone nodded. "That's right. The lieutenant, he's a smart son of a bitch, I'll give him that."

"So you're saying it's true. Are you the reason we found a dead man in an alley every other week or so? And all those others with their pockets empty and their skulls cracked?"

"Well, I'm not sure I can take the credit for all of them," said Doone. "But I did more than my fair share of the work. And I've got a lot of gold dust stashed away in a safe place. Want to know how much?"

Duff shrugged, feigning indifference. "Sure, why not?"

"I calculate between five and ten thousand dollars' worth. And that's just the gold dust, mind you. Throw in some hard money and timepieces and the like and you've got maybe another thousand."

Duff let out a low whistle. "That's a good bit. Was it just you, or did Harvey and Mitchell lend a hand?"

"Mitch helped out sometimes. He had a taste and a talent for that kind of work. But not Harvey. He stuck with the claim. I don't think we took more than a thousand dollars' worth of gold out of that claim, though, all told. Course, that's not how I expected to make my fortune in Gilder Gulch, anyway." Doone grinned.

"Right. Well, I'm real glad you've got yourself a fortune now. Though I don't see you getting a chance to spend it anytime soon."

"I don't care about that anymore. All I care about is *him*."

Duff looked in the direction Doone was looking—and saw Gordon Hawkes. The mountain man was sitting on a rock a hundred feet away, with his pair of guards hovering nearby. Hawkes was drinking coffee out of an army-issue tin cup. He wasn't paying any attention to them, Duff noticed, or to anyone else for that matter. He seemed more interested in the mountains.

"I don't follow you," said Duff.

"He killed my brother Harvey. Now that means Mr. Gordon Hawkes and me, we are due a reckoning."

"Christ," said Duff. "When does it all end?"

"It ends when he's dead—or I am."

"You're not going to get your chance at him," predicted Duff. "Lieutenant Gunnison isn't about to let you two have at each other. Though I for one wouldn't mind seeing it, to tell you the truth."

"Maybe you'll get to see it. All you have to do is set me free."

"What?" Duff was incredulous. "Have you gone loco?"

"Set . . . me . . . free," rasped Doone, spacing out the words as though he were speaking to a backward child.

"You're crazy, Chandler. Why would I do a thing like that?"

"Because if you do, all the loot I've got stashed is yours."

Duff glanced nervously at Doone's two guards, making sure they were out of earshot. Then he turned his attention back to Doone—and shook his head.

"Chandler, you seen those strongboxes of mine? I've got about sixty-five thousand dollars' worth of gold and hard money in those boxes. I don't need your loot."

"Sure you do. I bet there's room in those strongboxes for another ten thousand dollars. See, I know you, Duff. You're a greedy bastard if ever there was one. You never have enough."

Duff couldn't deny to himself that he was tempted. Ten thousand dollars would just about make up for the profits he figured he had lost because of the arrival of Gordon Hawkes and the imposition of Lieutenant Gunnison's curfew.

"Maybe I am greedy," he allowed. "But I'm not a lunatic."

"Nothing crazy about this deal. You wait until the camp is asleep tonight. Then you take care of my two guards. One of 'em has the key to these shackles. You let me loose, then you go back to your bedroll and let me worry about the rest. No one will ever know it was you."

Duff shook his head. He was a man well aware of his own limitations, and he knew that what Doone was asking him to do was beyond him.

"Okay, if you can't do it," said Doone, "then get the half-breed to do it for you. I know he can, and he will. He told me once that he only killed for money. So what you do is, you pay him a thousand dollars and he'll do all the dirty work. And you still come out about nine thousand dollars ahead."

Duff thought it over. "How do I know you're not lying? How do I know you really do have that much loot?"

"I've got it and you know damn well that I do. I robbed at least thirty men, and I made sure the ones I robbed had pockets full of gold and such."

Duff glanced again at the two guards. The prospect of their deaths did not bother him all that much. He had nothing against them personally, of course, but money was money. And he thought Doone was probably right about the half-breed. After all, the breed had been a manhunter once. And a damned good one, too, by all accounts. Or a bad one, depending on your point of view; it was said he never did bring them back alive. The breed was the kind of man who would do anything, as long as the price was right. And it occurred to Duff that if anything went wrong, he could blame it all on the breed, say it was all his idea and that he, Duff, knew nothing about it. That would work because in that scenario the breed would be dead anyway, killed by the soldiers for attempting to help Chandler Doone escape.

"So where is this loot of yours hidden?" he asked Doone.

"Near my claim. But I'll have to show you right where it is or else you'd never find it."

Duff was thinking fast now. He could send the strongboxes on to Camp Collins in the care of Wiley Roe and the breed. But then he had a better idea—better because he didn't really care to let those boxes out of his sight. He could tell Gunnison that he had decided to go back to Gilder Gulch, and worry about getting his profits into a bank's vault some other time.

"So what do you say?" asked Doone.

"I'll think about it."

Doone shook his head. "Not good enough. I need to know."

Duff stood up. "You'll know. If you're still wearing those shackles tomorrow, you'll know."

He turned and walked away.

Chapter Eighteen

The column moved on, passing without mishap through the canyon, along the oftentimes perilous trail that clung to a steep and rocky incline a hundred feet and sometimes more above the rolled waters of the tumbling creek. By mid-afternoon they were out of the canyon and soon entering a broad green valley, always following the trail, well established now by the passage of many gold seekers bound for—and some leaving—Gilder Gulch. The trail adhered faithfully to the creek, and the creek led them to a river, and it was here, at the confluence of the two waterways, that Gunnison called a halt for the night. The sun had long since slipped behind the high peaks to the west, and the sky was darkening as shadows filled the valley. To the east they could clearly see Horseshoe Pass; beyond it lay the high plains.

Again campfires were lit. Horses and pack mules were placed on picket lines, though Duff kept his mounts apart from those of the soldiers, as did Devanor and Alice. They camped on a low, grassy bluff overlooking the joining of creek and river, and the nearest stand of timber was a quarter of a mile to the north, so for their fires they used deadwood that had been deposited along the creek and river banks by past flooding. Duff and his men built their own fire some distance apart from the camp of the soldiers, and Devanor did likewise. The gambler took particular interest in Lieutenant Gunnison's disposition of his prisoners. The ankle irons of both Hawkes and Doone were lashed by means of short lengths of rope to their saddles. They could not run while wearing the shackles, and to walk at all would mean dragging the saddles along behind them, as the ropes were too short to permit carrying them. There were always two guards assigned to each man. Devanor was watching with interest when a pair of soldiers relieved the two watching over Hawkes; he took note of which man claimed possession of the keys that unlocked the shackles.

Gunnison had plates of food sent over, beans and biscuits. Alice didn't feel like eating but Devanor insisted that she try. He could tell she was nervous, and told her that there was no way to be certain when their next chance to eat might come. After eating, he settled back against his saddle, stretched out on a blanket and smoked one of his Mexican cheroots, watching the camps of Gunnison's command and Duff's party. He noticed that Duff's horses remained saddled, and that the strongboxes were still on the pack mule. He wondered why that was. It was almost as if Duff thought he might have to leave in a big hurry. But whatever the reason, it made what Devanor had to do somewhat easier. Those strongboxes, he knew, would be almost too heavy for one man to handle—unless that one man was a goliath like Wiley Roe—so it was a stroke of good fortune, decided the gambler, that tonight they were still on the back of that mule.

Alice lay in her blankets beside him, tossing restlessly, and after a while he said, "You really should try to get some sleep."

"Sleep? You must be making a joke. How could I possibly sleep tonight, of all nights?"

"It's likely to be a very long wait. You might as well sleep. I'll wake you when it's time."

It had been a long and strenuous ride, particularly for one unaccustomed to traveling by horseback, and eventually exhaustion overcame Alice, and she did sleep, though fitfully. Devanor didn't. He applied to this wait the patience he had learned at the poker table. He waited—and watched. Watched the fires die down. Watched those soldiers not on guard duty go to sleep in their blankets. Gunnison had not bothered setting out sentries, leaving to the four assigned to guard the prisoners the task of keeping an eye on the camp and the picket line as well.

As the camp grew quiet, Devanor continued to wait. He watched the moon rise over the pass to the east and slowly move across the star-spangled sky. When it had begun its descent and drew near the white-capped peaks, he checked his keywinder timepiece. It was two in the morning. He reached out to touch Alice's shoulder. She awoke with a start and he put a finger to his lips, then bent down to whisper to her.

"I'm going now. When the commotion starts, get up and saddle the horses. If I'm not back by the time you're done, wait for me."

She nodded and, as he began to rise, touched his arm.

"Do be careful, Charles. I know you doubt me, but I do care for you."

The gambler did not reply, but moved away, walking into the soldiers' camp.

As he drew near the spot where the two guards watching over Hawkes were standing, they turned, having heard him, their rifles at the ready. With the moon behind him, Devanor's features were completely cloaked in darkness, and they could not see his face at all. One ordered him to identify himself.

"Charles Devanor. Relax, gentlemen." Brandishing a cheroot as he drew closer, he added, "I was wondering if one of you might have a match."

The soldiers relaxed. Devanor glanced at Hawkes. The mountain man lay on his side on a blanket not far from the edge of the low bluff. He didn't move, and Devanor assumed he was sleeping.

"I think I might have some," said one of the guards. He handed his rifle to his colleague and searched his pockets.

"I'm a pretty fair hand at poker myself," said the other soldier, grinning at Devanor.

"Are you?" said the gambler. "I would like to sit down to a game with you, then. But I doubt your lieutenant would approve."

"No, he sure wouldn't. You're right about that. Not while we're on the trail. Maybe you should come to Camp Collins. I'm betting I could beat you."

Devanor smiled. "I'd be willing to give you the chance—except that I don't think I would be very welcome in Camp Collins."

"Why not?"

"Because of this." Devanor raised his hand—and the soldiers found themselves staring down the twin barrels of the gambler's derringer.

Both guards froze—the one with a rifle held carelessly in either hand, the other with both hands shoved into pockets as he searched for a match.

"Keep your hands in those pockets," Devanor advised the latter. "And you—toss those rifles over the edge."

The soldier with the rifles hesitated, so Devanor stepped closer, until the barrels of his pocket pistol were mere inches away from the man's face.

"Do you think I'm bluffing?" asked the gambler.

The soldier tossed the rifles over the rim of the bluff. "You're in a lot of trouble now, mister," he said angrily.

"Oh, you don't know the half of it. Now, hand over the key to those shackles."

The soldier glanced at his comrade, who nodded—and then reluctantly produced the key.

"Good," said Devanor. "Now, I want you both to turn around and sit down with your backs to me, with your hands resting on top of your head."

The soldiers complied. Devanor relieved them of their pistols, sticking one of the guns under his belt, and grasping the other by the barrel, he murmured, "I am truly sorry to have to do this, gentlemen."

"What are you—" One of the soldiers turned his head.

Devanor hit him with the butt of the pistol and the man slumped sideways, out cold. The other soldier opened his mouth to call out even as he tried to scramble away, but Devanor struck him, too, and he fell unconscious.

Throwing a quick look around, the gambler was relieved to see that the camp still slept.

Except for Hawkes—who was sitting up now, watching him intently.

"What are you doing?" asked the mountain man.

"What does it look like I'm doing? I'm trying to help you."

"Why would you want to do that?"

Devanor smiled ruefully. "You don't want to know. And you probably wouldn't believe it even if I told you why. I'm not sure I believe it myself."

"You're the gambler. The one who tried to help my son."

Devanor nodded. "That's right. But I didn't do enough to help him. And I cannot do much to help you, either—except to set you free." He unlocked the shackles on the mountain man's wrists, and then the set on his ankles, which also freed him from the burden of the saddle.

"I think you'd better get going," said Devanor.

"I'm here for Chandler Doone and—"

There was a sudden commotion on the other side of the camp—the braying of a mule, the whinny of horses and then the drumbeat of shod hooves.

"The picket line," said Hawkes.

Men were leaping up out of their blankets—some not more than fifty feet away—but they were all looking in the opposite direction, toward the noise. Realizing they had a few precious seconds before they were discovered, Hawkes reached out and grabbed Devanor by the front of his shirt and rolled over the edge of the bluff, taking the gambler along with him. It was only twenty-five feet to the bottom, and they landed in mud at the edge of the creek. Hawkes felt a familiar shape beneath him. Groping about in the mud, he located one of the Windsor rifles belonging to the guards. He pulled it free from the clinging muck, detached the bayonet and tossed the rifle away.

Devanor handed him one of the pistols he had appropriated. "Take this," said the gambler. "You've only got the one shot, but I trust you'll make it count. Now, if you'll excuse me, I have a little unfinished business to attend to."

"As do I," said Hawkes grimly.

Devanor hesitated, then stuck out his hand. "Good luck to you."

Hawkes took the hand and shook it once. "Thank you for trying to help my son. And, whatever your reasons, for helping me."

Pistol in one hand, bayonet stuck beneath his broad leather belt, Hawkes moved away then, heading downstream toward the river. Devanor guessed that the mountain man intended to circle around to the other side of the camp, where Chandler Doone was being held. But the gambler had other things to worry about. He heard shouts from above, and knew that the escape had finally been discovered. He headed quickly upstream, looking for a likely spot at which he could ascend to the top of the bluff. He found what he was looking for a hundred feet farther on, and scrambled up the steep slope, pausing near the top to peer over the grassy rim. A mule passed close by on the run, braying and kicking, with a cursing soldier in pursuit. Horses and mules and men were running hither and yon; it was obvious to Devanor that someone had cut the picket line. But who? And why? Whoever had done the deed, and whatever the reason, they had made his job a little easier.

Climbing up over the rim of the bluff, Devanor got his bearings and started walking toward the spot where he thought Duff's camp lay. He could make very little out—all was darkness and confusion—but then he saw the familiar bulk of the pack mule laden with the strongboxes, and standing nearby, the equally immense shape of Wiley Roe. As he drew closer, Devanor saw Duff standing near Wiley, his back turned to the gambler. Duff was looking in the direction of the soldiers' camp. What worried Devanor was that he couldn't see the half-breed. As far as he was concerned, the breed was the most dangerous one of the three, and he didn't like it that the shotgun-toting manhunter was unaccounted for. But there was no turning back now. Devanor kept walking. At the last minute Wiley turned his massive head and looked at Devanor. He was holding the three saddle horses—his and the breed's and Duff's; Duff was gripping the pack mule's lead rope. A smile of recognition began to play at the corners of Wiley's mouth when he saw Devanor. But the smile died as Devanor walked right up behind Duff and planted the barrels of his derringer against the back of the saloonkeeper's skull.

"Don't do anything foolish, Joe," said Devanor calmly. "I don't want to blow your brains out, but I will if I have to."

"What the hell?" Duff's body tensed and he started

to turn his head, but Devanor pressed the derringer's barrels harder against his head and the saloonkeeper stopped moving. "Devanor! What are you doing?" he rasped.

"I'll take that mule, Joe."

"The hell you say."

"Mr. Devanor?" Wiley Roe looked perplexed.

"God damn it, Wiley," hissed Duff. "Do something, you idiot!"

"No, don't do anything, Wiley. Please." Devanor had the pistol he had taken from one of Hawkes's guards in his other hand; now he swung it in Wiley Roe's direction, making sure the big man saw it. "If you try anything I'll have to shoot you. And God knows I don't want to do that."

"Wiley, what am I paying you for!" yelled Duff. "The son of a bitch is trying to rob me, you stupid bastard."

"Joe, are you really ready to die for that gold?" asked Devanor. "Because you're mighty close. If Wiley makes a move I'm going to let loose with both barrels of this pocket pistol, and you'll be learning angel music before you hit the ground. So if I were you I'd tell him to stay right where he is."

Wiley was watching Duff now; he could see the saloonkeeper's face while Devanor could not. With a sinking feeling in the pit of his stomach, the gambler realized that Wiley was waiting for Duff to make the call, and if Duff wanted him to, he would move, regardless of the fact that Devanor had a gun turned on him, too. This came as no surprise to the gambler. Wiley wasn't all that bright, but he knew what loyalty was all about, and while there were many concepts he could not grasp, he understood that he was Duff's hired man and that he was supposed to do what Duff told him to. If Duff wanted him to jump off a cliff, Wiley Roe would have to do it. And it didn't matter that Wiley liked Devanor. Trying to walk a fine line between loyalty on the one hand and friendship on the other was beyond Wiley's capacity. At Duff's signal he would attack his friend and, if necessary, kill him; he would feel badly about it afterward, but would not hesitate an instant in doing it.

Devanor had only one hole card, and that was Duff's desire to stay alive. The gambler just wasn't sure that card was good enough to win the game, because Duff's whole life was in those strongboxes.

"Don't try anything, Wiley," said Duff bitterly. "He's not bluffing."

"Let go of the horses, Wiley," said Devanor.

Still Wiley was looking to Duff for direction, and only when the saloonkeeper nodded did the big man let the reins slip from his hand. All the commotion had the horses stirred up, and once freed they quickly trotted off into the darkness.

"Now give me that mule, Joe," said Devanor. "Nice and easy. I'm pretty nervous right now, so don't startle me."

"You should be nervous," said Duff coldly. "Because I'm going to find you. I'm going to track you down. And you will not die quickly, I promise you that, you son of a bitch."

"Right." Devanor knew that this was the only reason Duff was surrendering those strongboxes to him—because the saloonkeeper believed he had a good chance of getting them back. And the gambler had to admit that Duff was right about that. "Hand over the rope."

Duff gave him the lead rope.

Devanor began to step away, walking backward slowly, giving the rope a hard tug and thanking his lucky stars that the mule compliantly came along. Had the animal balked it would have put him in a bad spot.

The derringer no longer pressed against his skull, Duff slowly turned to face the gambler.

"I'll see you soon, Dev," he said, his face a study in hate and resentment.

Gunfire erupted on the other side of the soldiers' camp. Duff and Wiley looked in that direction, but Devanor didn't. He figured the shooting had something to do with Hawkes or Doone, or maybe both, and none of that was his concern anymore. He kept backstepping, until the darkness had enveloped Duff and Wiley, and only then did he turn, pulling the mule along behind him and making for the place where he hoped Alice and the horses were waiting.

They were right where he expected them to be. Alice was holding on to the reins of the horses, and Devanor was glad to see that both mounts were saddled. The shooting behind him had become very sporadic. Devanor took charge of one of the horses, lashing the mule's lead rope to the saddle horn.

"Hurry up," he told her. "Duff will be along."

"You didn't kill him?"

"Not yet." He mounted up and she did likewise. Glancing her way, Devanor saw that her face was alive with a fierce joy as she gazed at the strongboxes.

"You did it, Charles. You did it! We're rich!"

"That was the easy part, getting it. Keeping it will be something else entirely. Come on."

"Where are we going?" she asked, but he didn't answer, turning his horse sharply and kicking it into a canter, the pack mule obediently trailing along behind, and she wondered why he was heading back the way they had come, back toward Gilder Gulch, instead of toward Horseshoe Pass, but since he had the gold she had no choice but to follow.

It was dawn before the half-breed came back with the saddle horses, which had strayed a good distance during the night. Wiley Roe was sitting on his heels next to a fire, warming himself, for the morning was bitterly cold. Duff paced restlessly on the other side of the fire until he saw the breed coming with the three mounts, then he went out to meet him.

"Any sign of Doone?" asked the saloonkeeper.

The inscrutable breed merely shook his head.

Duff cursed. "That lying bastard. Tell me again what happened."

"I did what you paid me to do," replied the breed, with no emotion whatsoever in his voice. "I cut the soldiers' horses loose. When I got to Doone, there was only one guard. I think the other one had gone after the horses. I killed the guard with my knife, took the key from his body and set Doone free. Then there was more shooting, and when I looked that way, Doone started running, and that was the last I saw of him."

"Why didn't you try to stop him?"

"You didn't pay me to do that. You paid me to set him free."

Duff cursed some more as they returned to the fire. "To hell with Doone. I'll deal with him later. We've got to get those strongboxes back."

He was about to mount up when he spotted Lieutenant Gunnison coming toward him, and he felt like indulging in a little more swearing. Instead, he tried to construct an amiable expression with which to greet the West Pointer.

"I see you found your horses," said Gunnison. "We're still missing some of ours."

"You lost both of your prisoners, too, I hear."

"And you lost your gold. Bad night all around."

"Well, I trust you'll find Hawkes and Doone. Me, I'm going to get my gold back." Duff fit boot into stirrup.

"Hold on," said Gunnison. "Are you sure you didn't have anything to do with what happened last night?"

"I already told you, Lieutenant. Why would I want to help either one of those men escape? I'm telling you, it was Devanor. He did it to create a diversion—and then he stole my gold."

"One man did all that, eh? Cut Hawkes and Doone loose. Scattered the horses. Killed one of my men. And had the time to relieve you of your strongboxes."

"That's the way I see it," said Duff, looking Gunnison straight in the eye only because he felt like he had to. It was obvious that the lieutenant had grave doubts about him and his role in the events of last night, and Duff was afraid Gunnison might decide to detain him.

At last, Gunnison said, "I think that there is more

to this than meets the eye. But for now, I'll wish you luck in retrieving your strongboxes."

"Luck to you, Lieutenant, in recapturing your prisoners."

As Gunnison walked away, Duff nodded to Wiley Roe and the half-breed. All three men swung into their saddles. They rode over to where Devanor's campfire from the night before was located. There were so many tracks from the melee that had occurred only a few hours earlier that Duff wasn't sure if the breed could tell him what he wanted to know. But the manhunter was not perturbed by the profusion of sign, and in a matter of minutes was able to inform Duff that Devanor and the woman, with pack mule in tow, had headed north.

"North?" asked Duff. "You mean back towards the gold camp? That doesn't make any sense. Why would they go back there?" He had expected that the gambler and his prostitute accomplice had made a beeline for Horseshoe Pass.

The breed shrugged. "The tracks, they do not lie."

"And you're absolutely sure about this?"

The tall man turned his shoulder, not bothering to answer.

They rode north, and for a while Duff expected the trail to veer off to the east at any moment, east toward the pass, the way out of the mountains. But it never did, and eventually he reconciled himself to the fact that Devanor was indeed returning to Gilder Gulch. He couldn't figure out why, but he tried to look on the bright side. Chandler Doone might have been telling the truth about his cache of stolen loot, and if so, Duff suspected that Doone was going to return to the gold camp, too, if only to collect his stash. With any luck, mused the saloonkeeper, he would get his own gold back and have a shot at taking Doone's, too. One thing was certain: He was not about to leave the mountains empty-handed.

Chapter Nineteen

That morning, lying concealed in the tall grass only a few hundred yards away from the soldiers' camp, Gordon Hawkes watched the goings on and decided that Chandler Doone had indeed made good his escape.

There was no sign of Doone in the camp. Hawkes saw Joe Duff and his men depart, and that left only bluecoats on the scene, many of whom were ranging far and wide across the valley to retrieve the scattered horses and mules—and keeping an eye out for the missing prisoners in the meantime.

After parting company with Devanor several hours earlier, Hawkes had circled around to the river side of the bluff, for he had seen that Doone was being held on the far side of the camp from him. But before he could reach his destination, he had seen a soldier topple over the low bluff just ahead of him, and then spotted another man on the rim, who he was pretty certain, even in the darkness, was the breed manhunter. Reaching the fallen soldier, Hawkes had found him dead, his throat torn open. An instant later there had been some shooting, and Hawkes had vanished into the night, sensing at that point that entering the camp in search of Doone would be at best foolhardy, and probably suicidal.

But he had not strayed far, waiting for dawn so that he could see whether Doone was still in the camp. Now that he was sure Doone was gone, the question remained—where? Who had cut the soldiers' horses loose last night? Why had the half-breed killed that soldier? Hawkes could come up with only one answer that made any sense. The breed had helped Doone escape. That meant Joe Duff was a party to it, because the manhunter worked for the saloonkeeper.

Hawkes took note of the fact that Devanor and his woman were nowhere to be seen. He also noticed that Duff's pack mule, the one that had been carrying the strongboxes, was also missing. Had the mule run off? Or was there a connection between the gambler's absence and the mule's?

Slowly but surely, Gunnison's command was retrieving their mounts and pack animals. Working on the assumption that being mounted would facilitate his finding Doone, and help him get away from the soldiers, Hawkes kept his eyes open for an opportunity to grab a horse. That opportunity finally presented itself when a single cavalryman rode out of camp in the mountain man's direction, presumably on orders to locate the handful of mules and horses that were still missing. Hawkes judged that the trooper would pass within fifty feet of his hiding place. Making up his mind to act, knowing how unlikely it was that he would be afforded another shot at a horse, the mountain man crawled through the tall grass on a path that would intercept the rider's course.

As the horseman drew near, Hawkes grabbed a handful of grass, pulling it up by the roots, then broke cover to run the last few yards. The unsuspecting soldier had an instant to gape at him, and then Hawkes had closed the gap, striking the horse across the eyes with the grass. The animal snorted in fear and reared. Clutching the bridle strap with one hand, Hawkes took hold of the left stirrup and threw it, unseating the trooper, who somersaulted over the back of the horse. As the animal came down and began to run, Hawkes grasped the pommel and vaulted into the vacated saddle, hammering his heels against the horse's flanks to goad it into a stretched-out gallop. He bent low in the saddle, the horse's mane whipping into his face as he heard the soldier he had just victimized begin to shout.

Chancing a look back, he saw the trooper brandishing a pistol—his Windsor rifle was still in its saddle boot, the stock banging against Hawkes's leg. Turning the horse eastward, presenting the mount's right side to the soldier, the mountain man slipped down onto the left side, clinging to the saddle and using the horse as a shield, Indian-fashion. Cursing, the soldier held his fire now that he had no target, and in a matter of seconds Hawkes was out of pistol range.

Pulling himself back up into the saddle, Hawkes looked toward the camp and saw that a half dozen riders were coming out to give chase. He had a lead of about five hundred yards, which he managed to maintain until he reached the edge of some trees.

There he abruptly checked his horse, drawing the Windsor rifle from its boot. Dismounting, he led the mount into the trees and tethered it. He retrieved a shot pouch from the saddle and returned to the tree line. The soldiers were a couple of hundred yards away now, and charging hard. Hawkes brought stock to shoulder and drew careful aim. He fired—and the horse of one of the troopers went down, its rider flying over its head. Reloading swiftly, Hawkes aimed and fired again. This time he brought down Sergeant Burleson's mount at a range of about a hundred yards. Reloading a third time, Hawkes grimly shook his head, feeling a twinge of remorse at killing the horses. But he had no choice; he didn't want to shoot one of the soldiers if he could avoid it. And in the present circumstances, horses were worth their weight in gold. So he wasn't surprised when the four remaining riders checked their mounts, or when Burleson picked himself up off the ground, barking orders that had the soldiers dismounting, rifles in hand—all save one, who took charge of the others' horses and led them out of rifle range.

Burleson and his men began shooting into the trees, kneeling in the grass to present smaller targets, and advancing slowly. Hawkes admired their courage. And their marksmanship wasn't bad, either. A couple of bullets struck the tree behind which he stood. The mountain man fired once more, over their heads, before dashing deeper into the woods in a running crouch, using the trees for cover as he was chased by hot lead. Arriving at his horse, he leaped into the saddle and rode away. Burleson quickly lost sight of him. The sergeant shouted at the man holding the horses to come up. But before he could resume the chase, a bugler in the distant camp sounded recall. The detail returned, four in the saddle and two trudging along afoot.

"Sorry, Lieutenant," Burleson told a stone-faced Gunnison. "He outfoxed me. Soon as he'd gotten us out of our saddles he was back in his and making for the tall timber."

Gunnison nodded. "A sound strategy. And he certainly is hell on our horses. Now we're down to twelve mounts and four mules, Sergeant."

"Yes, sir," said Burleson sheepishly. He experienced an almost overpowering urge at that moment to get his hands around the mountain man's throat, so that he could strangle the life out of the man who had humiliated him in front of his lieutenant and made him look like a greenhorn—he, who had fought the Arapaho and the Ute and the Pawnee and Santa Anna's vaunted cuirassiers!

"Well," said Gunnison, "I have a lot of questions about what has happened here. But one thing is certain. Hawkes is going after Chandler Doone."

"So we go after Hawkes," said Burleson, relishing the thought.

"No, not us. I'm taking ten men, with horses, in pursuit of Hawkes. You will remain here with the rest and try to find the missing stock."

Burleson was keenly disappointed, but he knew better than to complain.

When they reached the canyon passage late in the morning, Devanor called a halt, much to Alice Diamond's surprise. She was tired and saddle sore and

286

needed a rest, but she thought stopping for even a moment was foolhardy. And when the gambler proceeded to untie the strongboxes that were lashed to the frame on the mule's back, she stared at him in astonishment.

"Charles! What are you doing?"

Devanor stepped back quickly as one of the strongboxes hit the ground. He went around to the other side of the mule to tamper with the rope, and a moment later the second box fell.

"Charles!" Alice dismounted and ran up to him, clutching his arm. "We must not stop here! Someone might be coming along right behind us. And whoever it is—whether it's Duff or the lieutenant or Gordon Hawkes—I do not want to be here when they arrive!"

"You can bet that someone is coming," he said, "and it will be Joe Duff."

"You said you were going to kill him."

"I said I was going to have to. Him and the breed and maybe even Wiley Roe."

"You should have done it last night, then," she said, chiding him.

He looked at her coldly. "Gunshots might have drawn the attention of the soldiers. And besides, I never saw the manhunter."

"You didn't? But . . . but where was he?"

"If I had to guess, I'd say he was busy helping Chandler Doone get away."

"What? But why? Why would he do that?"

"Alice, let's talk about it later . . . assuming we're alive later. Hurry and bring me your valise."

"My valise? Why do you want—"

"Alice!"

Turning, she went back to her horse and untied her bag from the saddle. While she worked, she chanced to look behind her and down at the angry, foaming waters of the creek as it rushed through the rocks one hundred feet below. The trail here was quite narrow, as it was during much of the canyon passage. Alice experienced a sudden attack of vertigo. Panicking, she clung to the saddle and squeezed her eyes shut, her pulse hammering in her ears.

"Alice, hurry up!"

She freed the valise from the saddle straps and made her way back to Devanor, still shaking. The gambler was too preoccupied to take note of her condition. He had freed his own case from the saddle of his horse. Taking her bag, he set it along with his on the ground near the strongboxes. Then he produced the pocket derringer and shot off the locks on both of the boxes. Throwing them open, he glanced up at Alice, who stood behind him, staring at the sacks of gold dust and hard money that looked, he thought, like piles of headless brown rats inside the containers. She was gazing at the sacks with a kind of rapture he had, sadly, never seen in her eyes when she looked at him. But then whether she loved him at all, or not, was no longer the issue, if it ever had been. That wasn't why he was here, doing this, risking everything. He was here because *he* loved *her*.

Dumping out the contents of his valise, Devanor began to transfer the sacks from one of the strongboxes into his now empty bag. She watched him, unable to comprehend why he was going to all this trouble.

"Help me," he said, and the brisk urgency in his voice galvanized her into action. She knelt down to empty her valise, and then proceeded to fill it with sacks from the second strongbox.

When all the sacks had been removed from the strongbox, Devanor placed his belongings from the valise into the box, shut the lid and put the bullet-bent lock back into place. Then he helped Alice finish with the second strongbox, and placed her things inside it. Standing, he glanced down the trail from whence they had come. Instinct warned him that they had precious little time. He figured Duff had made better time than they had; the pack mule had slowed them down. Reloading the derringer, he took Alice by the arm and pulled her to one side before whacking his horse on the rump with his hat. Startled, the animal galloped up the trail, followed by the pack mule.

"Charles, what are you doing?" gasped Alice.

He sent her horse on its way in the same manner, then turned to her—and smiled. "We won't be needing them any longer."

"I believe you've lost your mind," she said angrily. "Now how do you propose that we get away from Duff?"

"I am not proposing that we do. I came back this way, my dear, because right here is where I want to deal with Duff. They will be along shortly, and when they see those strongboxes they will stop. And you and I—well, we will be up there."

He pointed at the steep, rock-strewn slope above the trail.

Alice looked up, and then down at the valises. "And how are we going to carry *those* up *there?*"

"We don't have to."

Using both hands to get a good grip on the handles of his valise, Devanor carried it, straining under the burden, over behind a large rock a dozen paces along the trail from where the strongboxes lay. He went back to get the second valise and placed it behind the same rock. Piling smaller rocks around and on top of the bags, he soon had them effectively concealed.

"So you are going to ambush and kill them," said Alice.

"That's the idea. I doubt I'll have much choice. You don't have any objections, do you?"

"And what if they kill you instead?"

"Then you might consider trying to cut some kind of deal with Joe Duff."

She slapped him as hard as she could.

Devanor just smiled slyly. "Sorry. I was out of line. I'll try my best, of course, not to get killed. And then, when it's over, we'll use their horses to be on our way. Now, come on, we need to get up into those rocks and off this trail."

He started climbing. It was rough going, and often loose shale gave way underfoot, but he held her fast by the wrist and kept her from falling. She lost a shoe but he would not let her retrieve it, and they kept on. Alice dared not look down. Heart in throat, she realized that if she did fall she would probably careen all the way to the bottom, and she shuddered at the thought of her broken, bleeding body being washed away by the roaring waters of the creek so far below.

At long last he stopped—she was beginning to think he never would—and settled down among some big rocks perched sixty or seventy feet above the trail, directly above the spot where the strongboxes lay. She collapsed beside him, gasping for breath. Her dress was torn and she had scraped a knee and an elbow and was distressed to see that she was bleeding. Devanor checked his weapons—the derringer and the percussion pistol he had taken from one of Hawkes's guards last night.

"I wonder if Hawkes got away," he said aloud.

"I'm sure I don't care," she said.

"I do. I would like to think that he did. And that he will find Chandler Doone and have his reckoning."

She didn't say anything. Hawkes, Doone and all of that was a matter for which she had nothing but the utmost indifference. Laying her head back, she closed her eyes and tried to rest. But she was afraid, unable to relax because she was wedged against a rock, the only thing that prevented her from plunging to her death.

"This is a stupid idea," she said fiercely.

"One stupid idea begets another," he replied.

"Oh, and you think having all that gold to spend is a stupid idea? If that's the way you think then perhaps I *should* take it all."

"I assumed you would, all along."

"Then why are you helping me?" she cried, exasperated.

He glanced at her, and shook his head. "You wouldn't understand."

They fell silent. Saddened, Devanor decided that it was just as well—what else was there to say?

An hour passed. All Alice could think about was how far they could have traveled in that time, and she just got angrier. They had thrown away the lead they'd had on Joe Duff. And what if Duff wasn't coming at all? Then what would they do? Walk the rest of the way to Gilder Gulch? Devanor had been a fool to run off their horses. Men always thought they knew better. It was simply infuriating.

"I am *not* going to sit up here all day, Charles," she said.

"Quiet. I think I hear something."

She listened, and a moment later heard it, too— the sound of horses. Then she saw them, appearing around a bend in the trail, coming single file with Duff in the lead, followed by Wiley Roe, and the half-breed bringing up the rear. When he saw the strongboxes, Duff checked his horse sharply and took a long look around.

"See?" whispered Alice. "He's no fool. He thinks it's a trap."

"Shut up, Alice."

Duff dismounted. Wiley and the manhunter did likewise. The saloonkeeper glanced at the latter. "What do you think?"

The breed shrugged, busy scanning the slope above the trail.

"Maybe the rope broke and those boxes fell off the mule," said Wiley. He could see the rope lying across the trail near the strongboxes.

"Maybe," said Duff. Those boxes were too heavy for one man to get them back onto a mule and strap them down if they had somehow fallen. One ordinary man, anyway—he had seen Wiley Roe lift them both at once. Or was it possible that Devanor had had second thoughts, had abandoned the strongboxes in the hope that Duff would call off the chase once he had his gold back?

Or could it be an ambush?

"Wiley."

"Yeah, Boss."

"Go see if those boxes are empty."

Wiley Roe was simpleminded but he wasn't an idiot. He knew the danger, and he hesitated.

"Go on," rasped Duff impatiently. "Don't worry, we'll keep you covered."

Wiley made a face. He didn't see any alternative to doing what Duff told him to do. Duff was his employer, paid him a decent wage, and as far as Wiley was concerned that meant he had to do whatever the saloonkeeper said. Besides, Duff was smarter than he was, so he had to know what was best.

The big man walked up the trail toward the strongboxes.

Above the trail, concealed among the rocks, Devanor began to have some doubts about the success of his plan. He had entertained the hope that Duff would be so overjoyed to see the strongboxes that he might, at least momentarily, throw caution to the wind. Clearly, though, he had underestimated the saloonkeeper. Now Duff and the breed were just beyond effective pistol range from his position. He had thought that he might be able to bring down the manhunter—the most dangerous of the three—with a shot from the pistol he had taken from one of Hawkes's guards; then he would close in and deal with Duff using his derringer. As for Wiley—well, Wiley Roe had always been the joker in the deck. The big question would have been—what would Wiley do once Duff was dead?

Reaching the strongboxes, Wiley got down on one knee and lifted the lid to one of them.

"Is the gold there?" called Duff, too impatient to wait for Wiley to say something.

"No, sir," replied the big man. "Just clothes."

Duff swore under his breath. Devanor had transferred the gold to his saddlebags, or perhaps the valises he and the woman had been carrying, and left the strongboxes behind.

"Come on," he said to the half-breed. Leading his horse, Duff proceeded along the trail. The breed followed, but was careful to walk on the right side of his horse, gripping the reins up close to the bit chain. In this way he was partially shielded from anyone who might be lurking up on that rocky slope.

Seeing this, Devanor grimaced. He didn't have a clean shot at the breed. Wiley was not a target. Not yet anyway. That left Joe Duff.

"Why don't you shoot?" whispered Alice, agitated.

Duff was almost to the spot where Wiley stood beside the strongboxes when he glanced up the slope to his left and chanced to see Alice's shoe, the one she had lost during the climb.

"It's a trap!" he shouted, suddenly crouching and clawing at the pistol in his belt.

Devanor rose up from behind the rock, drew a

bead and fired. The bullet struck Joe Duff in the belly, making a distinct slapping sound. The saloonkeeper jackknifed, the pistol in his hand discharging and the shot plowing a furrow in the trail at his feet. Staggering backward, Duff stepped off the edge of the trail, tottered for an instant, and then with a howl of rage mixed with pain and horror, disappeared into the chasm below.

The breed was quicker than lightning. He fired both barrels of the scattergun. The booming report reverberated off the canyon walls. Devanor had waited a fraction of a second too long to see if he had accounted for Duff; some of the buckshot hit him, and as he instinctively twisted away, his foot slipped on loose shale and he fell, leaving a smear of blood on the rock behind which he had been hiding. Tumbling helplessly, he heard Alice cry out an instant before his head struck a rock, and he blacked out.

Tossing away the empty shotgun, the breed drew a pistol from his belt and looked up at Alice, who was now standing in plain view. He gazed at her impassively, then raised the pistol—to take careful aim at Devanor's motionless form, sprawled facedown halfway between where Alice stood and the trail.

"No!" she shouted. "Please! You don't have to kill him."

"I reckon I do."

Out of the corner of his eye, the breed saw Wiley Roe lunging at him. He wasn't sure why the big man was attacking him—and he didn't care. Whirling, he fired at point-blank range. He had plenty of experience in killing people, and he knew that the only way to stop a man Wiley's size was with a head shot. Wiley Roe landed at his feet. The manhunter wedged a booted foot under the goliath's shoulder and flipped him over, noting with satisfaction the blue-black hole right above the bridge of the nose.

Shoving the pistol under his belt, the breed looked up at Alice. "Where is the gold?"

"I have it. It's hidden. You can take half, just like we agreed."

The breed laughed. It was a harsh sound. "We agreed? I thought you and me were going to steal the gold together. I thought that's what we agreed on."

Drawing his knife, he started up the slope toward Devanor. Alice began to make her way down from the rocks, hoping to intercept him, but fearful of moving too quickly. Small stones were clattering down on either side of her.

"I didn't know he would help me," she said. "We were going to cut you in, I swear it."

"You lie," said the breed. "I told you about the other strongbox, the one kept in The Banker's room. I told you I would help you, but it wasn't just the gold that I wanted."

"I know. I know what you wanted. Leave him. Let's go now, and you can have the gold . . . and me."

"I'm going to make sure he's dead first. I'm going to cut his throat," said the breed, as he reached the spot where Devanor lay.

More small rocks were plummeting around Alice, making a staccato chatter, and then a louder sound caused her to turn and look up the slope. She gasped, staring with disbelieving eyes at a large boulder, bigger than a horse, tilting slowly, moving, then suddenly breaking free . . .

The breed bent down to turn Devanor over. As he did he looked in surprise first at the gambler's eyes, which were open and focused on him, then at the derringer in Devanor's hand.

As he thrust the knife into the gambler's belly, the breed felt Devanor clutch his arm and pull him closer and plant the barrels of the pocket pistol against his chest. He felt an instant of searing pain as the gambler pulled the triggers, discharging both barrels of the derringer—and then the manhunter's world went black.

Devanor heard Alice scream, caught a glimpse of her as she hurled herself down the slope, arms flailing as she tried in vain to keep her footing, and then he rolled away, throwing up an arm to shield his head as an avalanche of rocks reached him. He felt the slope beneath him shift, and then he blacked out again.

Alice could not keep her balance. She fell, sprawling, screaming, trying to get back on her feet, but the boulder struck her and the debris of the rock slide swept her over the trail, to deposit her broken, bleeding body into the angry waters of the creek below.

When Devanor came to, he realized almost immediately that it was because someone was going through the pockets of his frock coat. Since he was dying, the gambler felt deeply offended, and groped weakly to clutch at the arm of the human vulture that was preying on him.

This sudden and completely unexpected movement on Devanor's part startled Chandler Doone, who jumped back.

"Damn!" he shouted—then laughed, quick to recover from his shock. "I thought you were dead!"

"Not quite yet. So keep your hands off me."

Doone looked about him, paying particular attention to the barricade of rocks and debris that covered the trail.

"What happened here?" he asked.

"I-I can't feel my legs," said Devanor.

"Probably just as well. There are some pretty big rocks on top of 'em. Reckon they're crushed. And you've been shot. Knifed, too. You're a lot tougher than I gave you credit for, Devanor. But I can't say I'm sorry to see you dead. Well, almost dead anyway."

"My one regret," said Devanor, managing a sardonic smile, "is that I'm going to precede you to hell."

Doone chuckled. "Yeah, and by a good many years."

"I doubt that."

Doone glanced nervously down the trail, thinking about Hawkes, knowing that the mountain man was the reason for Devanor's last remark.

"I seen a couple of horses without riders headed down the trail," he said. "Recognized Joe Duff's horse, and the breed's, too. Where are them two?"

"They're dead. Wiley is too."

Doone grunted. "And the woman?"

Devanor drew a long and ragged breath. He had not seen Alice die, and hoped against all reason that she had somehow escaped the rock slide. But if by some miracle she had escaped, he didn't want Doone looking for her.

"She's dead."

"Well, well. What a bloody business," said Doone cheerfully. "Would like to stay and palaver with you in your last moments, Devanor, but I got to be moving along."

"I wish you would."

Doone nodded. "Dying ain't something you want to do in front of people. I guess maybe it's because you never know for sure how well you're going to do it. So long, gambler."

Leaving the cavalry horse he had purloined the night before, since there was no way to get past the rocks and debris except on foot, Chandler Doone clambered over the obstacle and continued on up the trail in the direction of Gilder Gulch.

Devanor wasn't sure—and didn't care—how long he lay there waiting to die, but eventually he began to drift off, only to struggle wearily back to consciousness when he heard a horse coming. He lifted his head to see Gordon Hawkes riding up the trail.

Spotting Devanor, Hawkes dismounted, drew his pistol and took a careful look around before approaching the place where the broken man lay.

"Doone passed by here," said Devanor. "I'm not sure how long ago. But he left his horse."

Hawkes nodded. "Yeah, I see that."

"Duff, Wiley, the breed—all dead. But Alice . . . Hawkes, do you see any sign of her?"

Detecting the anxiety in the gambler's voice,

Hawkes laid a hand on his shoulder. "Rest easy. I'll have a look around."

It didn't take him long to find her. He could see her from the edge of the trail, her body wedged between some rocks in the rushing water below, her skin so white that it looked as though she were made of marble, like an exquisite statuette that had slipped from a careless hand and now lay shattered beyond repair. He wondered if he should tell Devanor what he had found. Or should he spare the man that agony, at least.

"Did you find her?" asked Devanor, when the mountain man returned.

"No, I didn't."

Devanor looked him in the eye and said, "You're a poor liar, Hawkes. Too bad I never got you into a poker game. I would have won the buckskin off your back."

"I'll try to move the rocks off your legs."

"Don't. No point in trying." Devanor knew he was fading fast. "The gold—the gold from Joe Duff's strongboxes . . . in two valises hidden . . . hidden just up the trail, behind a rock."

Hawkes sat cross-legged near Devanor, close enough so that he could lay a hand on the dying man's shoulder.

"Will you do me . . . one favor?" asked Devanor, his voice so weak that Hawkes had to strain to hear his words.

"Yes, I will," said the mountain man.

"If you can . . . I'd like to be buried next to her."

"I'll see to it."

"I suppose everyone's luck runs out, doesn't it?"

Hawkes didn't say anything. He sat there and kept his hand on Devanor's shoulder—kept it there until he felt the last breath leave the gambler's body.

Rising, he took the Windsor rifle and shot pouch from the saddle of the cavalry horse that had brought him this far. He climbed over the rocks and debris and, after a quick search, found the valises that Devanor had hidden. He opened them, and took out the sacks one by one, emptying out the gold dust and the hard money, letting all of it fall over the edge into the creek below. The gold fell like a sparkling mist, captured by the waters and swept away. Not all of it was carried downstream, though—the pale body of Alice Diamond soon sparkled in the rapids.

When he was done, when all the gold was gone, Hawkes turned toward Gilder Gulch. He would come back to fulfill Devanor's last request. But first he had a reckoning to see through.

Chapter Twenty

When Chandler Doone arrived at his claim, he was relieved to find that no one had attempted to take it over in his absence. He had been gone for several weeks—ever since Lieutenant Gunnison had thrown him in jail. Doone could only conclude that his reputation had kept the claim-jumpers at bay. It didn't occur to him that with the departure of so many other gold seekers from the valley, far more productive claims had become available, and that the presence of the soldiers had discouraged many would-be claim-jumpers from moving in where they did not belong.

Doone immediately rolled the log out of the way and began digging for his cache. It was still there—sacks of gold dust and hard money and a few gold watches, all wrapped up in a burlap sack. He unwrapped the loot and sat there and grinned at it, gazing for a spell at the product of his bloody labors. There was enough here to keep him in whiskey and women for a long time. And when this ran out—well, he would just find another hunting ground and start busting heads and cutting throats until his pockets were full again.

His grin faded into a scowl as he thought about

Mitchell and Harvey. Chandler Doone had never in his life loved anyone, but he did miss his brothers' company, and he knew he had some unfinished business to take care of before he could leave this valley. It was a question of pride, really. That unfinished business went by the name of Gordon Hawkes. Doone had avenged his brother Mitchell's death and he was obliged to do likewise for Harvey. Besides, he had enough to worry about without leaving the mountain man alive. Although he had never met Hawkes, had only seen him from a distance when they had both been Gunnison's prisoners, he felt like he knew what kind of man Hawkes was. And if he was right, the mountain man would never give up trying to find him. *So I'm going to make it easy for him*, decided Doone. He was sure that Hawkes had escaped the soldiers just like he had. That meant he could also be assured that the mountain man was hot on his trail. And that suited Doone just fine.

Gathering up his loot in the burlap sack, Doone took one last look around the claim. There, in the trees across the river, was where Harvey had died. A sudden surge of anger made Doone turn on the sluice box and kick it. He kept attacking it until the wood shattered, until the frame cracked and gave way and the whole box collapsed. Only then did he head south along the creek in the direction of Gilder Gulch. This route took him past the claim that Cameron Hawkes had once worked, and where Mitchell had been killed. That put Doone in even a darker mood. Two gold seekers were working this claim; they had moved in shortly after the death of Cameron Hawkes. They were taking a good bit of gold out of the gravel bar located there, by all accounts. Both men were busy working a sluice box as Chandler Doone walked up. One of them reached for a rifle as Doone invaded the claim, striding right past the stone pile marker like he didn't even see it. When he saw the man go for his rifle, Doone grinned and held up a hand.

"Hold on now, friend," he said. "I didn't come to make trouble."

"You're Chandler Doone, ain't you?" asked the man with the rifle, squinting suspiciously.

"That's right. I'm heading out, but I need a few things first."

"I thought the soldiers done took you away."

"I guess not, 'cause here I am."

"I don't know what it is you need," said the other man, "but we got nothing to spare."

Reaching the sluice box, Doone looked about the claim and nodded at a horse tied up over near a lean-to.

"Well, I need me a horse, for one thing. And a rifle or a pistol. And I need some more gold dust."

The two men stared at him. Then the one with the rifle, backing up a little to put more distance between himself and Doone, swung his weapon around. But he wasn't quick enough. Doone grabbed the rifle barrel before the man could line up a shot. He gave the barrel a hard tug, wrenching the man off balance, and head-butted him. As the prospector reeled, Doone snatched the gun, then swung the stock at the man's head, connecting like a club. Out cold, the prospector crumpled at Doone's feet. The other man gave a shout and turned to lunge for his own rifle.

He didn't quite make it; Doone shot him in the back. Finding a shot pouch, Doone reloaded the rifle, and while he was doing that he noticed that the first man, facedown in the dirt, was starting to come to. Setting the rifle aside, Doone seized a handy pickax and buried the steel head in the man's back, snapping his spinal cord.

Doone searched the lean-to and found two large pouches filled with gold dust, and a smaller one containing some fair-sized nuggets. Saddling the horse, he put all his loot in a canvas warbag and tied it to the saddle before mounting up and riding toward Gilder Gulch. Now he had a rifle, a pistol and a hand ax, and he entertained the notion of robbing every claim along the creek between here and the gold camp, relieving all the placer miners of their gold. But he decided he really didn't have time for such sport. He didn't want to miss Gordon Hawkes, and he wanted a few drinks before the final reckoning with the mountain man took place.

Reaching Gilder Gulch, Doone made straight for Joe Duff's tent saloon. There were only a few customers at the bar, and one barkeep, the man named Frank, was dealing out the rotgut. The Banker sat behind his table with a new bodyguard, a man whose name was Tate. Duff had hired Tate to take over for Wiley Roe and the half-breed while they were gone. Rumor had it that the man had been a prizefighter in California, but had fled after beating a man to death with his fists in a quarrel over a woman of easy virtue.

When he reached the bar, Doone couldn't help but notice the way Frank and the other men were staring at him. He dropped the rifle and the warbag on the bar and looked at each one in turn.

"So what do you boys think you're staring at?" he asked, wearing a malicious grin. "Ain't you never seen a fugitive from justice before?"

Frank put a bottle of red-eye whiskey in front of Doone and judiciously backed away. Chandler Doone had never been one to trifle with, but Frank detected a mean glimmer in the man's eye that bode ill for anyone who crossed his path—and the bartender had no desire to be that anyone.

Taking a few swigs from the bottle, Doone closed his eyes and gasped, smacking his lips in delight and wiping his chin with a sleeve.

"Damn!" he roared. "This panther piss tastes good." He laughed at Frank. "I guess anything would after a few weeks with nothing but water to drink. Yeah, I know what you're thinking, and you're right. I got clean away from those soldier boys. Had to come back and collect a few things. Will be leaving out of here shortly, and I know you'll be sorry to see me go."

The other customers were edging toward the exit, and Doone let them go. He took another long swig, then slammed the bottle down and turned to gaze intently across the saloon at The Banker. There was another strongbox under the table, next to the man's feet, and Doone decided right then and there that he wanted what was in it.

As he crossed the saloon, Tate watched him warily, sensing trouble. The bodyguard carried a pistol but he didn't resort to it; he was a man accustomed to using his fists to deal with trouble. So he didn't stand a chance now—Doone walked right up to the table, smiling, and without warning brought up his pistol and fired it right into Tate's face.

"Jesus Christ!" shrieked Frank as Tate fell dead.

Doone tossed the empty pistol onto The Banker's table and watched the strange little man calmly remove his spectacles to wipe specks of Tate's blood off the lenses.

"Your employer, Mr. Joe Duff, is deceased," said Doone. "So it looks like you are out of a job."

The Banker put his see-betters back on, peered owlishly up at Doone and pursed his lips. "In that case," he said, "I may as well take my leave."

"You may as well. But leave that strongbox."

The Banker got up, straightened his vest with a tug here and another there—and walked out of the tent saloon.

Doone hefted the strongbox onto his shoulder and carried it back to the bar, where he transferred its contents to the warbag. When he was done, he took another drink from the bottle.

"Stand up, Frank."

Trembling like a leaf, the bartender reappeared— he had taken refuge on the floor behind the bar.

"Light me up a lantern, will you, Frank?"

"A lantern?"

"Are you hard of hearing? Do what I say or I'll blow your brains out, too. I don't like to kill dogs or bartenders, but don't rile me."

Frank produced a lantern. He lit it, left it on the bar in front of Doone and backed away. "Can I go now?"

"Yeah, you'd better."

Frank eased around the bar and made for the tent

flap, trying to keep an eye on Doone while at the same time negotiating through the tables and chairs that barred his path. He was afraid Doone might shoot him in the back. But Doone paid him no mind, and raised the whiskey bottle to his lips again. Frank saw his chance and bolted out of the saloon.

Doone took several more gulps from the bottle, then tossed it away, shouldered the warbag, picked up the rifle and, stepping away from the bar, used the rifle to strike the lantern, overturning it. The glass chimney shattered and the kerosene spewed, immediately igniting. A roaring flame leaped across the bar. In less than a minute the entire bar was ablaze, and Doone observed with satisfaction how the hungry flames leaped higher and higher, until the canvas roof of the tent saloon blackened, then began to burn. Smoke curled and eddied around him as he walked out into the street. As he turned around to watch, the entire roof of the saloon exploded into flames. Men shouted the alarm up and down the street. A gust of wind whipped up the fire, carrying burning remnants of canvas to adjacent structures. Then these, too, began to burn. Watching the black smoke plume into the sky, Doone chuckled, quite pleased with his handiwork.

"Doone!"

He whirled to confront Luther Harley, and the shocked expression on the newspaperman's face made him laugh.

"My God, Doone—what have you done?"

"What does it look like? I've sent a signal. Telling that son of a bitch Hawkes to come the hell on!"

Watching helplessly as the flames leaped like

demons from building to building along the east side of the street, Harley could only shake his head, horrified to the point of speechlessness.

"Don't you realize . . . this whole town will burn!"

"What do I care?"

"You sorry bastard!" cried Harley in a pure rage unlike anything he had ever experienced before—a rage so consuming that it blotted out his fear of Chandler Doone. "You've ruined everything! We had a chance to make something here and you've destroyed it!"

Doone kept laughing. He couldn't help himself; he found the concept of the gold camp ever amounting to anything the newspaperman might consider worthwhile to be ludicrous. As far as Doone was concerned, Gilder Gulch had served its purpose. Now it didn't need to exist anymore. He didn't want it to exist anymore, because this was where his brothers had been destroyed. That being the case, it seemed only right that the gold camp meet its destruction at his own hands.

Advancing on Harley, Doone was a little surprised that the newspaperman stood his ground. He prodded Harley in the paunch with the barrel of his rifle. "You'd better get out of my sight," warned Doone, "before I get a notion to make you pay for calling me a bastard."

"Go ahead!" shouted Harley. "I despise men like you, men who think they're strong, but who are weak. Men who think they're smart but do stupid things because they are cowards, afraid to do good because it's more difficult than doing evil, afraid to risk failure. You're weak, Doone. You don't have the guts to play by the rules so you break them instead."

Doone stopped laughing and prodded Harley again, this time much harder, so that the newspaperman doubled over in pain. Driving his knee into Harley's face, Doone watched with cruel pleasure as Harley fell, bright red blood spewing from a gashed lip.

"You ought to be a preacher!" said Doone, intending it as ridicule.

He happened to look up then—and saw Gordon Hawkes, walking up the middle of the street.

Doone's face brightened with malevolent joy.

Forgetting all about Luther Harley, he started after Hawkes.

The mountain man threw a quick look around. The inhabitants of Gilder Gulch were hastily clearing the street, gathering among the structures on the west side, while half of the buildings on the east side blazed in a roaring, wind-whipped conflagration that filled the sky with billowing black smoke. The fire was so intense, so large, that Hawkes could feel its searing heat. But he paid it no attention, focusing instead on Chandler Doone.

"Time for a reckoning, Hawkes!" cried Doone, and he raised his rifle to shoulder.

Hawkes had been waiting for that. He dived to one side, tucking a shoulder and executing a roll that brought him up on one knee just as Doone fired— and missed. Bringing up the Windsor rifle, Hawkes squeezed the trigger. The bullet staggered Doone, but couldn't knock him down. Throwing away his rifle in disgust, Doone brandished his pistol—only to remember that he had not reloaded it after shooting Tate. Cursing, Doone threw down the pistol, too. Resorting to the hatchet, he charged Hawkes, roaring like a lion.

Putting the Windsor down, Hawkes drew his pistol and stood, taking careful aim. It didn't deter Chandler Doone at all that he was running straight into the barrel of a gun, any more than it gave Hawkes pause that he was about to shoot a man whose only weapon was a hand ax. He fired, and saw the puff of dust coming off Doone's shirt at the point of impact. This time Doone went down. But, to the mountain man's surprise, he didn't stay down. Getting to his feet, Doone stood there a moment, shoulders hunched, head down, swaying slightly, glaring at Hawkes.

"You're gonna have to do better than that," he sneered. "I ain't as easy to kill as my brother. Better men than you have tried."

Hawkes tossed aside the empty pistol and drew from his belt the bayonet that he had brought out of the soldiers' camp. He wondered what it would take to stop Doone—and whether he could get the job done. The man had two bullets in his chest and was still on his feet, still dangerous. In spite of his doubts, Hawkes closed in. This was the man who had taken away his son, and in so doing had taken away a part of him, so that Hawkes knew he would never feel whole again.

Doone waited until Hawkes was only a few feet away before lunging, bringing the hatchet around in a slashing arc that the mountain man barely managed to elude. Quick as a cat, Doone brought a fist swinging in from the opposite direction that caught Hawkes on the shoulder and staggered him. Doone pressed his advantage, lashing out with the hatchet and missing again, but connecting once more with his fist, this time landing a solid blow to Hawkes's jaw. The mountain man went down, spitting blood. Closing in for the kill, Doone raised the hatchet high overhead and brought it down with all his might. But Hawkes scrambled up and, crouching, threw his body into Doone's legs, so that Doone tumbled over him, sprawling on the ground. Dropping to his knees, Hawkes used both hands to plunge the bayonet into Doone's heart.

With one last roar of defiant rage, Chandler Doone died.

Hawkes knelt there a moment, catching his breath, and noticed how the reflection of the fire behind him danced like the flames of hell in Doone's dark, sightless eyes.

When Luther Harley came up behind him leading Doone's horse, and put a hand on the mountain man's shoulder, Hawkes was startled.

"Is the madness finally over?" asked the newspaperman.

"Yes, it's over."

"Then you had better get out of here. I expect Lieutenant Gunnison will be along shortly, looking for you."

Hawkes got wearily to his feet. "I'd like nothing better than to go home," he said. "But I can't, not just yet. I promised to do something for someone."

"Who?"

"Devanor. It was a dying wish."

Harley paled. "Charles Devanor is dead?"

Hawkes nodded. "Yes. So is the woman named Alice. He wanted to be buried right next to her. I have to see to it."

"Please, allow me the honor of fulfilling that promise. Charles was a . . . well, I suppose you could say he was a friend of mine. I give you my solemn oath that his last request will be done. It's time for you to go home, Hawkes. And besides, you have an escort awaiting you."

"An escort?" Puzzled, Hawkes looked behind him as the newspaperman gestured.

Pretty Shield was standing there, holding the Joslyn carbine in both hands.

"Pretty! I thought you were—"

She tossed the needle gun to him, then looked down at the body of Chandler Doone. "I would have shot him if he had killed you."

"What are you doing here?"

"I never went away."

"Time enough for explanations later, I should think," said Harley. "The both of you must go, now." He handed Hawkes the reins to Doone's horse.

The mountain man swung into the saddle and extended a hand to Pretty, who smiled and allowed Hawkes to help her up behind him. She put her arms around him to hold on as, with a nod of thanks directed at Harley, the mountain man turned the horse and rode north out of the burning gold camp.

Paradise Alley and all the structures on the east side of the street were smoking ruins when Gunnison and his horse soldiers arrived. They were on foot, having been forced to leave their mounts on the trail in the canyon passage, which had been blocked by the rock slide. Gunnison halted the detail where the body of Chandler Doone lay, the bayonet jutting from his chest, his eyes staring sightlessly at the darkening sky. Some of the inhabitants of Gilder Gulch began to gather, including Luther Harley.

"What happened here?" asked Gunnison. "Where is Gordon Hawkes?"

Harley scanned the grim faces of the prospectors standing around him. "Hawkes?" he said. "We haven't seen him, Lieutenant."

"Oh, really." Gunnison pointed at Doone's corpse. "Then who is responsible for this?"

"Doone was on a rampage. Killed a man, set the town on fire," replied Harley. "Some citizens were forced to take matters into their own hands. It was entirely justified, believe me."

Gunnison pulled the bayonet out of the body. "Then I wonder where this came from."

Harley shrugged. It was plain to see that Gunnison did not believe a word of what he'd said. The lieutenant surveyed the crowd.

"Does anyone here want to tell me what *really* happened?"

There was no reply.

Gunnison nodded. "Well, then, I will have to report that Gordon Hawkes escaped into the mountains." He spared Harley one last look—the newspaperman thought he detected just the trace of a smile at the corner of the lieutenant's mouth—before leading his trail-weary troops back the way they had come.

As Harley and the prospectors watched the soldiers depart, one of the placer miners asked, "What do we do with Doone's loot, Luther?"

"You can split it up among yourselves, I guess. Or, we can use it to rebuild Gilder Gulch. Make a real town out of it, a town with a future, a place to be proud of. It's up to you."

"Well," drawled the gold seeker, "I don't know about the others, but I'd just as soon stay on."

"Me, too," said a second man.

"Count me in," said a third. "Besides, we still haven't found the mother lode." He grinned.

"Yes, you have," said Harley. "You just don't know it yet."

On the way home, Pretty Shield told Hawkes her story—how she had been unable to leave without knowing what would become of him. So she had stayed, and watched from afar as the bluecoats departed for Camp Collins, taking Hawkes away in shackles. She had not interfered during his escape from the soldiers or during his fight to the death with Chandler Doone. It had been very difficult for her to stand back and do nothing when she had seen that he was in such danger. But she had done it, and Hawkes knew why. For his sake. Killing Doone had been something he had to do to free himself from the demons that haunted him.

The journey took several days. They did not speak of the future—a topic neither wished to dwell upon, even though they knew it was one they could not avoid for very long. When at last they reached a spot high on a hillside from where they could look down at the cabin Hawkes had built for his family some months ago, Pretty Shield knew it was time to go. She watched him watching the smoke curling out of the cabin's chimney. It was late in the day, and they both knew that Eliza and Grace were inside preparing for supper.

Hawkes started eagerly down the slope, leading the horse. Belatedly, he realized that Pretty was not with him. He stopped, and gazed at her a moment, then went back to her and handed her the reins.

"Where will you go?" he asked.

She held up the Absaroke wampum belt he had given her, and this was all the answer he needed. Sensing that she did not want him to see her turn away, that she wanted to spare him that, Hawkes smiled and continued down the hill.

When he reached the cabin, he set aside his weapons, picked up an ax and went to work splitting some of the wood that was piled up against the side of the structure. The noise he made brought his wife and daughter through the doorway. Seeing him, Grace flew into his arms, laughing and crying with joy at the same time. Eliza set down the rifle she had carried out and smiled at her husband—a smile bright and warm with vast relief and unconditional love.

"You're just in time for supper," she said.

Carrying his daughter, Hawkes followed Eliza inside, and refrained from looking at the high hillside because he knew no one would be there.